THE ASOKA TRILOGY
BOOK III

———~———

According to the Sanskrit text Mudrarakshasa, four centuries before Christ, Chandragupta Maurya, Samrat of Bharatvarsha, after a great victory over Seleucus I the Greek, suddenly abdicated his throne, disappearing to Shravan Belgola in South India, having converted to Jainism. The bards have explained this abdication as the result of a series of sixteen dreams Chandragupta had. But what exactly did he see in those dreams?

Fifty years later, according to the fourteen Rock Edicts, his grandson Asoka, after a great victory in the Kalinga war, decided to give up warfare and convert to Buddhism. Bards ascribed this sudden change of heart in the war-mongering King, to what he saw on the battlefield of Kalinga. But what exactly did Asoka see?

In these pages lie the answers...

The narrative is tight, fabulously detailed, and gritty... You will not be able to put this book down. With a beyond-impressive 4.1 rating on Goodreads, Shreyas has definitely captured the imagination of readers. N*agpur Today*

Prince of Pataliputra is an excellent debut work, bringing the spirit of a thriller to the historical fiction genre. *Blog: The Corporate Slacker*

The conversations made me feel I was listening to the characters speaking. The storytelling skills are well polished and there isn't a dull moment in the book. *Blog: Vanya's Notebook*

With good storytelling skills, powerful characters and twists, Shreyas Bhave makes a great debut with his historical fiction. Garnished with conspiracies, clever strategies, subtle romance and bitter betrayals, the book is a fast-paced read. What appealed the most was the way Chandragupta's journey is shown in parallel to Asoka's journey. *Blog: Purba's Library*

Bringing alive the figures of Asoka, Chandragupta, Chanakya, Radhagupta from the pages of history and intermeshing them in a fiction is no easy feat but Shreyas Bhave achieves it without effort. *Isha Aggarwal Blog: rainingreviews*

The story starts with a prologue that is absolutely brilliant. it will make you turn the pages quickly. *Parikshit Shah, Goodreads*

Shreyas Bhave has absolute control over the facts and has wonderfully transformed them into a high paced, thrilling novel. I loved the way he has used parallel stories, which is unique. *Pooja Srivastava, Goodreads*

Book II definitely delivers on the promise of Book I. Highly recommended to all lovers of historical fiction. The author has researched well and this can be seen in the plot. *Pankaj Goyal Blog: the bibulous bibliobiuli*

Storm From Taxila is a mind-blowing, action-packed book, full of mysteries, twists and turns. You will be surprised by the eye-opening strategies used to win the war. The characters are combined strategically to deliver a saga which will always be in your mind. *Shafaque Eqbal, Amazon Review*

NEMESIS
OF
KALINGA

THE ASOKA TRILOGY
BOOK III

SHREYAS BHAVE

PLATINUM PRESS
PREMIUM FICTION

ISBN 978-93-52010-62-2
© Shreyas Bhave, 2019
Cover Design: Paramita Bhattacharjee
Layouts: Hitanshi Shah
Printing: Thomson Press (India) Ltd.

First published in 2019 by

PLATINUM PRESS

An imprint of LEADSTART PUBLISHING PVT LTD
Unit 25, Building A/1, Near Wadala RTO,
Wadala (E), Mumbai 400 037, INDIA
T + 91 96 9993 3000 **E** info@leadstartcorp.com
W www.leadstartcorp.com

Disclaimer This is a work of fiction. The opinions expressed in this book are exclusively those of the Author and do not pertain to be the views of the Publisher.

To Parul Singh

About the Author

SHREYAS BHAVE, an Electrical Engineer from VNIT Nagpur, is one of India's youngest experts on Railway Electrification. He also administers an entrepreneurial community at www. ourfirstmillion.org. Possessed of an abiding love of history from childhood, Shreyas was inspired to take on the challenge of writing a fictionalized account based on historical record, supplemented by rich folklore, which continues to surround the legendary figure of Asoka. Apart from writing, Shreyas enjoys song-writing and composing music, sketching and watercolour painting. He plays the guitar. He enjoys hiking up to the many hill forts of Maharashtra, replete with history and ghosts of the past.

Shreyas can be reached at: theasokatrilogy@gmail.com

Other books by Shreyas Bhave
Prince Of Patliputra
Storm From Taxila
Prisoner Of Yakutsk

Author Disclaimer: Though based on real events and individuals, this is a work of fiction and should not be taken as an accurate historical account. The author does not claim that all incidents and descriptions in the book are historically exact or documented; they should not be used as references by scholars and students. Some incidents have been taken from traditional folklore and cannot be proven. At no time has the author intended to hurt the religious sentiments of individuals or groups. References to religion or caste have been made solely in the context of the era and the characters involved.

Contents

AUTHOR'S NOTE

~

Much of what we know of Mauryan times stems from the works of novelists of that age rather than from the writings of historians. The ensuing result being that we are no longer sure what we read is fact or fiction, or a strange amalgamation of both.

Today, we have a plethora of books to draw information from about Mauryan times, be it Charles Allen's *The Search For India's Lost Emperor* to the Dutch author Wytze Keuning's non-fictional trilogy on Ashoka's life. Closer to home, we have had cinematic ventures from the Shah Rukh Khan starrer *Asoka* (2001), to the Colors produced series for the small screen, *Chakravartin Ashok Samrat*.

However, in the end, all writings and depictions tend to draw their information from the same limited set of documents. Surprisingly, many of these come from a small island that has been central to our epics since the days of the *Ramayana*. Thus, a Sri Lankan text, *Mahavamsa*, chronicles the history of the island from 543 BC, while also narrating events in the neighboring Indian peninsula. It is written in Pali, an important language in Buddhism of the era. *Dipavamsa* is another record from Sri Lanka, considered to be even older. The fact that Ashoka sent two of his own progeny to spread Buddhism in Sri Lanka, may have something to do with these writings.

The sources from India are surprisingly less historical. *Divyadana* is a set of Buddhist tales, thirty-eight in all, that tell of the rise of the sect from its very earliest days. One of the stories is called *Asokavadana*, literally 'Legend of Asoka'. The word 'legend' does perhaps support a certain historical scepticism about the authenticity of this text, but surprisingly, it is this document modern writers on Ashoka and Mauryan times usually draw from.

The most well-known facts about Ashoka is that he killed ninety-nine of his brothers; that he was an evil King (Chandasoka), before being transformed into a peaceful Buddhist; that he was changed by the bloodshed of the Kalinga war. All these notions stem directly from the *Asokavadana*, which its writers claimed to be legend.

The remaining sources are Ashoka's own rock edicts, which survive to this day, along with the chronicles of Greek historians who visited the subcontinent in those times, or later. The subcontinent then had many more Greeks than our right wing idealists would like to believe today, and there were Indo-Greek kingdoms and settlements as far as Varanasi.

What I found in all these texts was that they ran as legends should, full of metaphors and parables, telling of events too grandiose and vague to have happened in reality. For example, there is the story of how Radhagupta gifted an elephant to Ashoka, for him to ride to the palace where Bindusar was to appoint his successor. To me, this was a metaphor to underline the fact that the Minister called Radhagupta, played a pivotal role in Ashoka's rise to the throne. Nevertheless, I have used the elephant event in Book II. The *Asokavadana* is replete with such metaphors, which are poetic renditions of some other real events.

It was at this point that I realized how vague our knowledge about Ashoka is, and how little we know about one of

the most important figures of our national history, whose symbol flies proudly on our national flag. The Asoka trilogy is thus an attempt to establish how the events then actually unfolded, drawing on the mentioned ancient texts and their subtle legends.

Book III of this trilogy, *Nemesis of Kalinga*, describes at its core, two important conflicts of Indian history – one is the war between Chandragupta Maurya and Seleucus Nicator 1, while the other is the Mauryan invasion of Kalinga.

The Greco-Mauryan conflict of the 'fifty years ago' storyline, between Amatya Rakshasa and Arya Chanakya, is described vividly in ancient texts. It also forms the crux of the plot of *Mudrarakhshasa*, a play by Vishakhadatta. The writings mention that Chanakya defeated Rakshasa with a ploy using his signet ring. I have shown the same to be true in my book. The genius of the method he used can only be truly appreciated after reading about it.

In the parallel storyline, the Kalingan war is described as close as possible to how it must have run its course. It was a great historical event that had many important outcomes such as Ashoka's conversion, the assimilation of Bharatvarsha into a united country, and the golden period of Ashoka's rule during the later part of his life. The history of India, as well as Buddhism, could have been very different had the outcome of this crucial war been other than what it was.

The seafaring nature of the Kalingan people is referenced strongly in all the texts. It was common knowledge that seafarers from Kalinga sailed far and wide in the Bay of Bengal and the Indian Ocean, and their influence can be seen in lands as far as South-East Asia. While the name Kalinga has faded in the country of its origin, there is still a place carrying the name today in the Philippines.

Regarding Chandragupta's abdication, historians tell of the sixteen dreams he saw, that caused him to reflect and renounce the throne as penance. My sceptical modern mind refuses to accept that an Emperor would abdicate his position based on what he saw in his sleep. Thus, in this book, I have credited his abdication to his realization of Chanakya's hidden secret. However, Chandragupta's sixteen dreams find their way in the book as normal occurrences during his reign. Studious historians reading this book will find them scattered in the Chanakya chapters, not as the cause of Chandragupta's abdication, but as elements of a classic tale.

The conversion of Ashoka from war-mongering King to peace-loving monk on the battlefield of Kalinga, is a much related event in Indian history. Once again, I have interpreted it differently, unable to place any credibility on the fact that a bloody battlefield alone could cause such radical change in the mind of a man who was a lifelong soldier. Instead, I have shown personal loss as the driving factor that causes the subsequent change.

The relationship between Chandragupta and Chanakya in this trilogy is one of the most complex I have ever attempted. It is open to various interpretations. The tragic way in which it ends, however, is fictional. In ancient history, as that of the Mauryas, we have such few sources to ascertain facts, that the boundary between fact and fiction often merges and disappears.

Hardeo's speech to Kanakdatta before the Battle of Kalinga is an ode to the spread of Buddhism in the world. I believe that several passionate men like Hardeo played a significant part in the spread of this culture out of the subcontinent. Though their contributions may not have been documented, they cannot be denied.

The characters of Kanakdatta, Hardeo, Shiva, Devdatta, General Bheema, and Governor Navin, are purely imaginary. However, those of Asoka, Devi, Chanakya, Radhagupta Chandragupta, Malayketu, Rakshasa and Karuvaki, are completely historical. Events portrayed in the book, such as the Kalinga war and Malayketu's war in the 50 years ago storyline, are also historical. Both the Ancient Brahminical Order and the Merchant's Guild are imaginary, though legend does speak at length of the secret orders of those times, from Ashoka's council of nine, to Chanakya's twelve intelligent men.

My sincere endeavour in this Asoka trilogy has been to transport my readers into the hotbed of ambition, politics and conflict of Mauryan times; to fill your minds and race your hearts. With your support, I hope to bring to life a thousand more stories culled from the fascinating pages of Indian history.

THE MAURYAN EMPIRE: 322-232 BC

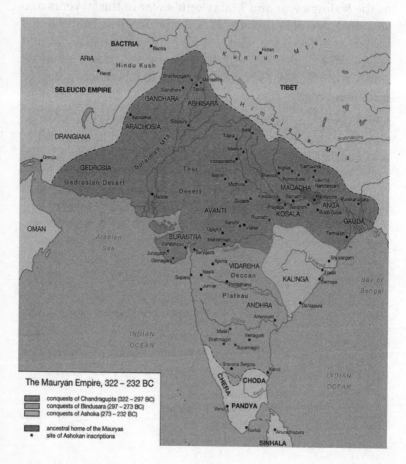

The Mauryan Empire, 322 – 232 BC

- conquests of Chandragupta (322 – 297 BC)
- conquests of Bindusara (297 – 273 BC)
- conquests of Ashoka (273 – 232 BC)

- ancestral home of the Mauryas
- • site of Ashokan inscriptions

In order of appearance; those relevant to events
50 years earlier, appear in italics

MAHARAJA SUSHEM: Governor of Taxila, son of Bindusar and grandson of Chandragupta. The common soldiers call him *Ardha-Yavana*, because of his Greek mother. In return, he calls them *Jadmuka* or 'stupid'. Despite the deep hatred of the army for him, not even the best Generals can deny his administrative prowess. Taxila has prospered exponentially under his rule. When he succeeds his father as *Samrat*, he is sure the whole subcontinent will follow him into greatness. Hence he initiates the holy *Ashwamedha Yadnya*.

HARIHARAN: Sushem's Minister and member of the Ancient Brahminical Order, he is characterized by his long white beard. Sushem treats him like filth, yet Hariharan follows his master unflinchingly. Is he just stupid or merely waiting for a moment to hit back?

TISSA/VITTASOKA: Sushem and Asoka's seven-year-old brother and Bindusar's youngest son. A sweet lad, everyone in Taxila adores him. He has been in Sushem's care since birth. Last in line to the throne, with 99 brothers before him, he is slated to be a small time Governor somewhere remote. Or does destiny have something else in store for him?

MAHARANI DIVIJA: Sushem's beautiful chief wife. A diva, who will become *Samardni*, she loves all things royal, except her husband.

RADHAGUPTA: Bindusar's Steward at Patliputra. His shaved head symbolizes intelligence, or so he tells everyone. His sharp eyes watch over the city. He makes his rounds, dressed in flowing saffron robes, collecting the *Samrat's* taxes. Is he really a loyalist or a conspirator?

KAUTILYA/CHANAKYA: *A legendary personality about whom a hundred stories have been told, he is seen as the Machiavellian mind that plotted to send Alexander back from India, to bring Chandragupta to power; who liberated the subcontinent from the evil Nandas. The only question that remains is: Did he really do all this?*

ASOKA: Son of Bindusar and leader of the expedition sent against the rebellious province of Avanti. Half-Buddhist by birth; Kshatriya of the highest degree by action; a trained soldier and horseman; a veteran of the bloody Southern Wars, will he be a soldier all his life or does destiny have a hand to play?

DEVI: Asoka's love interest. Beautiful and talented, she is an expert in poisons, an exquisite dancer and a woman of character, courage and passion. What more does a man need? But what does *she* need in a man?

PUSHYAMITRA: Asoka's Captain and an expert with both sword and bow. A new addition to the army, nobody knows his origins though he claims to come from the North. Will he protect Asoka, as is his duty, or turn against him?

CHANDRAGUPTA: *Chanakya's student and Samrat to be of the whole subcontinent, he is a resolute, calm and brave man. Will he succeed in upholding his principles and the name of his Guru?*

DILEEPA: *Also Chanakya's student and Chandragupta's friend. A quiet character, he prefers to work behind the scenes. Will he stay by Chandragupta's side?*

RAJA AMBHI: *Raja of Taxila 50 years before. Arrogant and proud, he is a typical royal. He has a treacherous nature. Will he survive the Greek invasion that is soon to come?*

RAJA PURU: *Raja of Paurava 50 years before. Tall as a tree and strong as a rock, he is a giant of a man and bows to no one, not even the Greeks. Will he survive the invasion from the West?*

ALEXANDER: *The legendary personality in his 20th year. He has come a long way from where he started. He has conquered the Persian Empire and stands at the door to the subcontinent. Soon, he will invade Bharat to fulfill his ambition of world domination. Will he succeed? Will he be allowed to succeed?*

CRATERUS: *Alexander's General and loyal follower; his master's favourite.*

COENUS: *Another of Alexander's Generals. A doubter and questioner, he is not the follower his master wants, but needs nevertheless.*

KANAKDATTA: A Buddhist weapons trader and Asoka's friend from the Southern Wars. People consider him the most dangerous man in Bharatvarsha. He has been everything from thief to soldier and is now the biggest weapons trader in the Indian subcontinent. But is he really Asoka's friend?

HARDEO: Powerful Buddhist Guild Master of Vidisha, he is a middle-aged man with a complex mind. What exactly motivates him? And will he be Asoka's friend or foe?

SHIVA: Son of Avarak, military leader of the rebels of Avanti, and also Asoka's friend from the Southern Wars, it is said he started the ongoing Avanti rebellion by killing the last Governor in his throne room. Will Shiva's hot head help him survive these tumultuous times or will he perish in the storm?

DHANANANDA: *Maharaja of Magadha 50 years before. Corpulent, evil and disrespectful, the list of his vices is long; but signal his end.*

RAKSHASA: *Prime Minister of Dhanananda 50 years before. Considered the only horse in a herd of donkeys by Chanakya, will he perish with his master or will his story take a different turn?*

AVARAK: *Leader of the Ancient Brahminical Order from 50 years before; now called Avarak, the One-Eyed. He is leader of the rebels of Avanti. What role did he play in the events of 50 years ago, and how did he lose an eye?*

GENERAL SUNGA: General of Patliputra, who led the army to the Southern Wars. A strict and unforgiving leader, he turned the conflicts into victory. Asoka served under him.

MAHARISHI DANDAYAN: *A sage from northwestern India, 50 years before.*

RAJA AJATSHATRU: Legendary founder of Patliputra and the Ancient Brahminical Order. A contemporary of the Buddha, and a prominent figure of the Haryanka dynasty.

DASHARATH: Chanakya's minion and a member of the Ancient Brahminical Order. A mysterious person, whose existence is not known by many, until now…

CUSKA: Asoka's Captain; he replaces Pushyamitra, the betrayer. Will he turn out better?

NIKUMBH & PRAJAPATI: Radhagupta's companions and members of the Order. But do they serve him or some other higher power?

RAJA JAIN: Erstwhile ruler of Junagarh and master of Uperkot, the greatest fort in the world.

MALAYKETU: *Son of Puru, sent by him to accompany Chandragupta in his expedition. Just as tall and strong as his father, he is also just as stubborn. Is it a good quality in troubled times?*

KARUVAKI: Lady Ambassador of Kalinga. Beautiful and capable, what is her role in Asoka's life?

PREFACE

The quill was long and sharp. It moved slowly over the yellowed parchment, leaving lines and shapes to seep into the texture of the fabric. The dark ink remained on the surface for a moment, like droplets of dark blood, before being sucked into the pores of the parchment as if by invisible leeches. My hand moved over the blank yellowness of the parchment, leaving marks that would last for generations to come.

The sand clock on the side table flowed with utter inevitability in the silence of the chamber; a gift from the Greek General Seleucus, that emptied once every six hours. I did not turn it, knowing my time was almost up. I kept writing as I waited for my opponent to finally come to me.

This was the endgame, the moment we had both been waiting for. For almost a year we had played this devious game of wits, one strike after the other, from the deep chasms of our minds. The only thing that remained was to see who would make the last move.

Crickets chirped in shrill chorus in the darkness outside my window, declaring the coming of night. The time of reckoning was approaching. *The devil is in the dark,* an old Sanskrit *subhashit* said. The though sent a sudden chill through my body and I felt something I had not for many a day – fear. I shook the feeling off. This was not the moment of my judgment. It did not matter whether I faced it like a coward, or with bravado. What mattered was how my opponent faced it.

I had already played my last move and now nothing was left to me but to wait. When the game had begun, he had been an aggressive opponent, always the one to strike first. He had been the one to break the rules first. I had waited. I had given him his chance. But now there was no other way. It had to end like this.

I kept writing. There was nothing else left to do. I poured my heart and mind onto the parchment before me. I had done all I could. The future was no longer in my hands. All that was left was to see what my opponent would do.

Would he come to assassinate me? A chill spread over my body once again. My work here was not yet done. The Aryas had not been unified. Chandragupta was not yet all-powerful. If my opponent decided to kill me, I had to put onto the parchment what needed to be done to strengthen the *Samrajya*. I wondered if he would heed what I wrote. Wondering was all that was left to me now.

Would he come and expose me? In exile, had he learnt the things I had done? I took a deep breath. *My secrets are my own*, I told myself. In any event, Dasharath stood outside my door, naked sabre in hand, ready to rush to my aid if anything untoward took place.

A wisp of air entered as the panels of the single window to my chamber opened with a creak. I had left them slightly ajar for a purpose. The single window on the western wall was the only way to reach me that night, and my opponent knew it, for it was his chamber I now inhabited.

The gust of air drew circles on the back of my neck, raising goosebumps. I heard the sound of soft boots landing on the wooden floor. *He had come.*

"I knew you would come," I said, not looking up, my hand continuing to move on the parchment like a honeybee upon a flower.

Prime Minister Rakshasa stared at my figure for a few moments. I felt his gaze burn a long line in the back of my neck. Then he folded his arms. I heard a soft sigh escape him as he said, "Let's do what needs to be done."

I did not answer. My hand moved over the parchment, scribbling like a madman, unstoppable and unyielding like a force of nature. *The moment of reckoning was upon us.*

"Arya," he said.

My hand stopped in mid-air. I felt the grasp of my fingers around the quill loosen and the slender feather fell from my hand onto the desk, its ink-laden tip making a blot on the yellow parchment. "Yes," I said, turning.

"Let's do what needs to be done," he repeated, looking me in the eye.

I looked down at his feet. He wore leather boots. *An assassin would prefer to be barefooted.* My eyes slowly moved up over his body. His long scabbard hung at his waist, the golden hilt of his sword shining in the yellow light from the lamps. *A murderer would prefer a dagger.* I looked up at his face, dreading what I would see. The lines there would tell me all I wanted to know. I took a deep breath and looked him in the eye.

I smiled. His eyes told me it was done. The game was over.

"Let's do what needs to be done," I agreed, smiling.

I had won.

262 BC

I was sitting in a chamber with a quill in my hand, vigorously scribbling on a piece of parchment. The stack of parchment grew beneath my hand. I scribbled frantically as I waited for my opponent to finally come and face me. When night fell, I knew I did not have to wait much longer.

He came as quickly as the wind, as eager to put an end to this game as I. "Arya," he said from behind me. "Let's do what needs to be done."

"I knew you would come," I said simply, not turning to look at his face. I knew what he was going to say; what he was going to do. I looked down at the vast stack of parchment before me and I smiled. I no longer cared. My work was done.

"Let's do what needs to be done," he repeated.

I nodded, finally looking up at him. His face wore the blank look I had expected. I smiled. It had been done. The game was over.

I had lost.

I
DEVDATTA:
ATTACK OF THE RED SERPENT

───────────∽───────────

263 BC KALINGA

The port was called Dantapura. It was the largest port he had ever seen, and he had seen his share in the course of his sea-faring life. The ocean breeze caressed his face, carrying a hint of salty water. It skipped playfully over his shaven head like an invisible nymph. The fragrance of the sea spread within him slowly; he could feel it from the tip of his nose to inside his chest. Devdatta breathed it in. From where he came, it was said that an experienced sailor could recognize an ocean from its smell, for they all looked the same. Now, standing where he was, staring at the vast expanse of water before him, Devdatta was not so sure.

The Eastern Sea loomed before him, spread to the horizon as far as the eye could see. The occasional wave crashed across the wooden ramparts of the Dantapura dock where he stood, causing it to shake. The water here was greener, thought to be deeper. The breeze was stronger, often temperamental, turning from friendly to treacherous. It was nothing like the Western Sea.

Devdatta closed his eyes as the sea breeze caressed his face. He felt like a changed man. How many years does it take to change a person, he wondered?

Three years ago, when he first came to these lands called Kalinga, all he had worried about was survival. It had meant adapting to the new surroundings. One by one, things had changed, and finally, so had he.

The first things to change were his ships. His ships had smaller sterns, suited to the fast Easterlies of the Kutch Sea. He had had to make the sterns bigger and the sail layered to face the powerful winds, replacing the single layer sail used in the West. What changed next was clothing. His sailors, used to the cold Western Sea, wore breeches of animal hide. Here, where warm winds blew, they wore a cotton lower garment wrapped around their waist, which the locals called *lungi*.

Devdatta stood on the steps that led down through the stockades. He had been walking these steps for months now, but they still felt foreign to him. He strode along the wooden boardwalk, the planks creaking under his weight. The ports of the West did not use so much wood. The docks there were lined with stone and mortar where the land reached out to meet the sea. Devdatta felt Dantapura somehow embodied the spirit of the people of Kalinga, for this land was filled with fishermen and sailors. Here, a boy learnt to row before he learnt his first letters.

But Devdatta was not a boy. He banished these musings as he caught sight of his ship, the one he called the *Kutch*, named after his homeland. It stood anchored across from the boardwalk, the pride of his fleet. It was the same ship that had brought to these coasts when he arrived here three years ago, the only ship he commanded, doing business in the lands and seas of the Mauryas. But he had come a long way since then, and now commanded a fleet of a dozen trade vessels. His sailors travelled as far as the islands which the locals called Java and Sumatra, bringing back rare goods.

Devdatta's hand moved over the golden threads that lined his doublet as he stepped down to the boardwalk. There had been a time when the only gold he ever saw was in the form of coins. Now, he wore gold on his person. He had come a long way.

"The Brahmin awaits you on deck," Anirbandha, Captain of the *Kutch*, said to him as he appeared at the wooden gangway. "It seems that when you went to call on him in the city, he was on his way here to see you, so you missed each other."

Devdatta nodded in acknowledgement. "It would appear we are both equally anxious then," he muttered, walking up the wooden steps onto the deck of his ship. The man he sought stood at the far end, looking out to sea. He wore a cotton shirt over a lungi lined with saffron thread. His head was shaven, except for a patch of hair along the centre, which he wore open.

"One of these days, you are going to have to tell me the secret of your open hair," Devdatta said, joining him.

The Brahmin turned towards him, smiling. "And one of these days you are going to tell me the secret of your immense wealth."

"My dear Vishnuvardhan," Devdatta said, hugging the man. "It's been a while."

"Indeed, my Lord," the Brahmin bowed. "I have been preparing for your return to Dantapura ever since you set sail against my wishes. I hurried to the docks as soon as I saw your symbol fluttering upon the horizon. But it seems you had already gone into the city."

Devdatta chuckled. "Business is business, my friend," he replied easily. "I wanted to go on one last trade voyage across the seas before politics kept me on land. And that meant visiting the Quartermaster and handing him the list of goods I had brought from my voyage."

"Yes, but this is not just politics," said the Brahmin seriously. "These are the famed Kalinga elections! You know what they say about that."

"Indeed, I do," Devdatta nodded. "That Kalingan candidates are more bloodthirsty than even Chandasoka."

Devdatta sighed. He found Kalinga a strange land. Here, they elected their Prime Minister through a voting process. Those who wished to be considered could declare themselves and give speeches to the people. The people of the villages, towns and cities then chose whom they wanted as their leader on the day the votes were cast. The man chosen was then hailed as their leader till his death. The last Prime Minister of Kalinga, Navin, had died two moons ago. Fresh elections were now afoot.

It was a strange way to choose a leader, thought Devdatta, but his advisor, Vishnuvardhan, had told him it was an ancient process called 'the holy way of the Mahajanpadas'. The only thing holy about it, however, was the name. The candidates were known to resort to violence to emerge victorious and the people viewed it like a pit fight. Hence the saying came to be, comparing the candidates to the new Mauryan Samrat, who was known to be as ruthless in his conquests as he was bloodthirsty.

"So what is it you have discovered?" Devdatta asked.

"I fear my news is both good and bad, my Lord."

"Tell me the good news first," said Devdatta. There was a saying amongst sailors that when the ship is sinking, sing only good songs.

"The other candidates in the election are weak." The Brahmin drew out a parchment from the leather pouch slung across his shoulder and handed it over. "You have no strong contender opposing you."

Devdatta read with interest. "Navin Kumar, son of the late Prime Minister..."

"A mere boy of eighteen; born and brought up inside the courtyards of a manor." The Brahmin shook his head. "The Kalingans will not accept a weak man. His late father was a famed pirate in his youth. The boy is nothing."

Devdatta nodded. "How unfortunate that the affairs of State kept Navin too busy to train his son. However, the boy no doubt has the support of Navin's old Council."

"I have a strategy for that," the Brahmin said. "We will discuss it later."

Devdatta scratched his chin. "General Bheem is the second candidate. Has the old boar got tired of leading the Kalinga army?"

"It appears the General has long nursed political aspirations. The only thing keeping him in check was Navin's powerful hold on the army."

"No one likes a rigid army man; least of all the free folk of Kalinga. However, his masculine image may charm the crowds." Devdatta's finger moved down the parchment.

"His masculine image may be an asset," the Brahmin agreed. "However, he advocates war against the Mauryas because of the blockade. The Kalingans do not want war."

Devdatta nodded. Five years ago, after the crowning of Mauryan Samrat Asoka, the markets of the sub-continent had been closed to Kalingans. It was part of the Mauryan Prime Minister's strategy to bring the upstart Kalingans to their knees. But Navin had been a shrewd man, an astute leader. The Kalingans were sailors, raised in families of fishermen. The food and goods had to be procured from the sea and beyond. It was in this transportation that Devdatta had accumulated his wealth. There were many seafarers here, but most were simple traders. They did not have experience of looting foreign coasts.

"Your speech will be welcomed by the people," the Brahmin said, nodding. "You are the third and final candidate. You speak of alliance with the Mauryas. We accept their authority and their taxes. Even in taxation a businessman can find opportunity for profit."

"So what is the bad news?" Devdatta asked, handing back the parchment.

The Brahmin turned away from the sea to face the port. "As soon as you step onto the platform today to declare yourself a candidate in the election, you are a dead man."

Devdatta felt his heart miss a beat. He knew the Kalinga elections were violent but he had not expected the violence to start before the election.

The Brahmin walked to the stern and Devdatta followed. The port of Dantapura lay before them. They could clearly see a high wooden platform in the empty space cleared in the dock markets. The crowd had already begun to gather; laughing and chattering amongst themselves as they waited for the speeches to begin. This was the day the candidates revealed themselves to the common folk. The campaigns would begin here, in Dantapura.

"Observe the buildings that line the docks," the Brahmin said, pointing. "Bowmen line the terraces. As soon as you start your speech, an archer will shoot."

"Who has ordered this?" Devdatta asked, narrowing his eyes in the sun. "Navin's men or the General's?"

"We do not know yet. The job has been assigned to a group of foreigners."

Devdatta's brows drew together. "But why?" he wondered. He had never done anything to hurt either of his opponents. He hardly knew them as their paths had never crossed. But that was about to change.

"They can see the outcome as clearly as we can." The Brahmin put the rolled parchment back in the satchel. "You are the one true candidate – a sailor by birth, a sea Captain by profession, you bring food and goods to the people, courageously running the blockade. You are a saviour. Unless they get you out of the way, neither of the others has a chance."

Devdatta cleared his dry throat. "How did you deduce all this?" he asked.

"A group of foreigners entered the city a week ago. They caused havoc in a local tavern and got into fistfights. I sent a few of my men to hobnob with them. Warriors have loose tongues after they have wine in their bellies. And if there are words said, I make sure I hear them."

"If you know who they are," Devdatta said, "why not seize them before I make my speech?"

The Brahmin shook his head. "And do it in a dark alley where no one will see? Why do you think they are choosing to murder you right there on the platform and not in your sleep? The people of Kalinga love a show, my Lord. If you can thwart an attempt on your life right in the middle of your speech, your popularity will soar."

"And what if they manage to kill me?" Devdatta asked dryly.

The Brahmin smiled. "There is a wooden table on the platform," he said, pointing. "If an arrow flies towards you, the table can be your shield. Meanwhile, your men, dressed as ordinary folk, will overpower the assassins. I have already briefed your Captain about this."

"My men are a hard lot, but they have never seen these assassins. What if they make a mistake?"

"They will not for I will be up there with them, with a sword in my hand."

Devdatta looked at the Brahmin, amused. "A Brahmin wielding a sword; now that will be a sight to see! Did they teach you sword fighting as well as theology in the University of Nalanda? You are a Brahmin, yet you do the work of a Kshatriya?"

The Brahmin shrugged. "What should stop me? I taught myself how to fight long ago."

Devdatta smiled. "Then I must say I will be delighted to watch you do that for me today."

A cheer from the crowd distracted their attention. It was almost time for the ceremony to begin.

"We must get going, my Lord," the Brahmin said.

"Yes, it is time." Devdatta placed a hand on the Brahmin's shoulder. "Promise me, my friend, that you will keep me alive today."

The Brahmin nodded. "And promise me you will give one hell of a speech after I do."

***

The Brahmin's vigilant eyes surveyed the cheering crowd as the names of the candidates were announced. Devdatta was to speak last. The Brahmin stood at the very back of the crowd, near the dock buildings. The mass of people had occupied the entire main street that passed through the docks. He noted the positions of Devdatta's five men, spread through the crowd, each at a vantage point.

From the corner of his eye he searched for possible assassins in the crowd. It was not long before he spotted them. They had changed into the local cotton garb and stood in the middle of the crowd, a group of five men. However, their leader still wore his distinctive hood. The Brahmin had first seen him in the tavern a few nights ago. His manner made it clear that he was the leader but the hood he habitually wore hid his face. The Brahmin wondered who the man was. But he knew he could not draw attention to himself.

As the first candidate, Navin's son, was announced, some in the crowd cheered while others hooted. The Brahmin watched a youngster climb up to the platform. There was barely any hair on his face. The Brahmin watched as one of the assassins cracked a joke and the others laughed. A chill went down his spine as his hand moved over the hidden blade at his side. He knew that each of the assasins carried a sword as well.

The youngster began his speech but the crowd began to heckle: *We can't hear you back here! Speak like a man!* Laughter rippled through the crowd. The youngster looked up, annoyed. He quickly finished his speech and then stood frozen, confused what to do next. A woman suddenly appeared at his side and placed a hand on his shoulder. In an instant the hostile crowd began to cheer. *Karuvaki... Karuvaki...*they chanted.

The Brahmin let out a long breath. It was Karuvaki, the Foreign Minister. It was common knowledge that she had been one of Navin's important advisors. A fisherwoman by birth, her rise had been legendary, and people cheered her name wherever she went. Now, she held the youngster's hand high in the air and called, "For Navin Kumar!" The crowd followed suit.

The Brahmin looked to his right. The assassins were nowhere to be seen. His heart missed a beat. Had they already moved up to the terraces? Then he caught sight of them. They had moved from their position in the centre of the crowd, towards the buildings. The Brahmin looked towards one of his men. The man was looking at him, waiting for the signal. The Brahmin nodded, watching the assassins make their way to the edge of the crowd.

There was another loud cheer as the name of the General was announced. Tall and muscular, he strode onto the platform. His moustache curled up onto his cheeks. "Men of Dantapura!" he began, his voice loud and confident.

Suddenly, there was a warning shout as a dagger was hurled from within the crowd. It missed General Bheem by five fingers but the General showed no signs of fear. The dagger was followed by a woman, who rushed onto the platform, carrying a sword. The crowd gasped as she raised it at the General screaming, "You killed my son!"

The General looked at her as he would a raging bull. "Yes!" he declared. "I have killed many sons. In the army, these things happen."

Enraged, the woman jumped towards the General, her sword raised. He caught the blade with his bare hands. Surprised, the woman paused and then twisted the hilt, trying to pull free. Blood began to flow from the General's hands. Suddenly, he let go and the woman staggered backwards, the sword falling onto the platform with a loud clang. The city guards rushed to take her into custody.

General Bheem raised his bloodied palms and showed them to the crowd. "This is how we must deal with the

Mauryas!" he shouted as blood dripped onto the ground. "And this is how I will deal with them if you say my name on election day!"

The crowd went hysterical, cheering and stamping their feet. Suddenly, the Brahmin felt a hand grasp his arm. It was one of Devdatta's men. He pointed towards the buildings. The assassins had disappeared.

"Quick, gather the others," the Brahmin instructed.

They made their way to an alleyway where a beggar sat, his back against a wall, a dirty cloth tied over his eyes.

"Which building?" the Brahmin asked urgently.

The beggar pointed to his right, quickly rising to his feet and pulling the cloth from his eyes. He was Anirbandha, Devdatta's personal bodyguard. "Those two," he said. "They divided into two buildings."

The men drew their blades and the Brahmin did the same.

"Let's make it quick," Anirbandha muttered, ordering the men with signs. "You take the western one and I'll take the eastern one," he muttered to the Brahmin.

The Brahmin nodded. Three of the men followed him. Anirbandha and another man went towards the other building. Suddenly, there was loud cheering. Devdatta must have been announced. They ran up the stairs silently. At the door to the terrace, one of the men took cover by the wall and peered out.

"What do you see?" the Brahmin asked.

The cheering ceased as they heard Devdatta's clear voice say, "My brothers of the sea..."

The Brahmin smiled. It was a good start. The common folk of Dantapura were mostly fishermen; he had raised the call of brotherhood with these men of the sea.

"Three men..." the man at the door whispered. "One readying the bow, two more standing guard."

The Brahmin looked out into the terrace. To their right, Anirbandha and his companion had climbed to the terrace of the next building. The Brahmin caught sight of the hooded man on the other terrace. Anirbandha signalled to him that the archer on their side was raising his bow.

"You take the guards. I'll take the archer," the Brahmin instructed.

The three men with him nodded.

Below them, the crowd cheered as Devdatta cried, "Kalinga does not need war!"

"Now!" the Brahmin said.

The men shot out onto the terrace like a sudden wind. The Brahmin raised his blade as he went straight for the archer. The blade dug deep into the archer's neck and the Brahmin pressed harder until he felt the sharp edge hit the bone. The archer let out a gasp but there was no one to hear him. The sound of swords falling to the ground told the Brahmin that the others had done their job. The archer in his grasp slumped to the ground and the wooden bow fell away from his hand. As the Brahmin looked down at his victim, he caught sight of a small vial lying beside the quiver of arrows. Quickly, he bent down and picked it up. It was filled with a clear, glistening liquid.

The Brahmin felt his heart beating hard against his ribs as he got to his feet. "Get to Devdatta!" he yelled at the men behind him. "Get to him fast!"

But the men were standing transfixed by what they saw on the other terrace. The hooded figure was watching them menacingly, bow in his hand, arrow pointed. The Brahmin caught sight of Anirbandha slumped against a wall, the soldier with him lying dead, a blade through his chest.

The hooded man gazed at the Brahmin. In that moment, the Brahmin felt time stand still.

"Together, we can being peace and make way for prosperity." Devdatta was finishing his speech.

Suddenly, the hooded man spun round and pointed his arrow at Devdatta. The Brahmin ran to the edge of the terrace, his eyes wide in alarm. "Look out!" he cried as the arrow flew from the assailant's bow, straight towards the man on the platform.

But Devdatta's eyes were on the terraces. In a swift motion, he grabbed the table and held it up in front of him. The arrow pierced the wood dead in the centre. Without the table, Devdatta would have been pierced through the heart. There were shrieks from the crowd as people began fleeing in all directions, fearing for their lives. The men with the Brahmin ran for the door and scrambled down the stairs.

The Brahmin remained where he was. He saw the hooded man had placed a second arrow in the bow and now stood ready to shoot. In one fluid motion, the Brahmin pulled the dagger from his waist and threw it with all the strength in his arms. The hooded man bent like a reed in the wind but the blade slashed across his hood, ripping the fabric, a hair's breadth from his face. The man's face was exposed. The Brahmin stared transfixed. The assassin returned his gaze with equal intensity, then he backed away towards the low parapet that circled the terrace, his bow pointing at the Brahmin's heart.

Devdatta's men rushed onto the terrace. The assassin kept moving, his eyes fixed on the Brahmin's face. In one swift move, he leapt over the parapet and disappeared into the alley below.

Two of the men helped Anirbandha struggle to his feet. He was badly injured. "Follow the man!" he said hoarsely.

Immediately, the men ran to the parapet and jumped down into the alley behind the assassin. The Brahmin blew out a long breath.

"Well it certainly went as planned," he heard someone say. He turned to find Devdatta gazing at the fallen bodies.

"Are you much wounded, Anirbandha?" Devdatta asked his Captain.

But the Brahmin quickly cut him off, saying, "We need to talk, my Lord."

"Why so fearful, Vishnuvardhan? Surely the danger has passed?"

"No, my Lord, the danger has just begun."

"What do you mean?"

The Brahmin bent and picked up the small vial still lying beside the fallen archer. "Look at this."

"Is it poison?" Devdatta asked. "To coat the arrows?"

"Not just any poison," the Brahmin replied. "It is called *Kalkoot*. It causes instant death."

"Did you discover who sent the attackers?"

"I no longer need to," The Brahmin said, walking towards the edge of the terrace. He could see the ships in the dock standing out like black shapes against the bright sky. "The recipe of *Kalkoot* is known only to a few. The assassins were sent by the Ancient Brahminical Order."

"How can you be so sure?"

"The man who escaped is a Brother of the Order. I know him."

Devdatta looked at the Brahmin, his brows lifted in surprise. "How do you know all this?"

The Brahmin sighed. "The time has come to tell you the truth. My name is not Vishnuvardhan and the story I told you of my past is untrue. I am not a graduate of Nalanda."

"Then who are you?"

"It is a long story and I hardly know where to begin. I come from the land of the Mauryas, just as you do. I was once a member of the Ancient Brahminical Order, until its leader sought to kill me. I escaped, vowing revenge. It is to remind myself of my vow that I wear my hair open."

"Who are you? What is your name?" Devdatta folded his arms across his chest.

The Brahmin's eyes were fixed on the far horizon where the water rippled in an endless stretch of sea. The time had come to reveal himself he knew.

"I am Radhagupta," he said.

2
ASOKA:
THE CORPULENT KING

PATLIPUTRA, 263 BC

In his dreams, all he saw was the waterfall. The same episode would come to him again and again, usually before he awoke to another day. Sometimes, he would see the same thing while dozing off during Council meetings or in the audience chamber. But each time, he would see it as clear as day.

There was no forgetting her face. Devi was beautiful. Her eyes blinked playfully when she looked at him, smiling at some joke he had told her. He felt the contours of her body as she pressed onto him, locked in an embrace. He could feel the cool lake breeze blowing, causing goosebumps to rise on his skin as they lay beside the water. He heard her laughter ring in his ears, her warm breath fall on his cheeks as her soft palms brushed against his own. He felt so happy. And then the dream would vanish as he awoke.

Today was no different. When Asoka opened his eyes, he saw the shapely form of a woman lying beside him. Cool breeze did indeed flow over them, and he could hear the sound of falling water, soothing on his ears. Had his dream come true?

It did not take more than a moment for Asoka to realize he was wrong. It was still early and the sun's rays had still not penetrated the dark veil of the sky. But Asoka knew where he was – lying on a large ornate divan, with the softest of cotton cushions under him. The woman beside him ws Asandhimitra, his wife, or was it Padmavati, a woman from the harem he had recently taken a fancy to? Extending his arm, he touched the woman's exposed, fair back. The woman moved instinctively at his touch, still asleep. He caressed her soft back from her shoulders down to her round, fleshy buttocks. It was indeed Asandhi. He could feel her slightly protruding mole below her waist. Padmavati had no moles.

Asandhi clutched at the muslin covers as Asoka withdrew his hand. Turned on his side, he propped himself up on one elbow. As he did so, he felt the liquid move in his belly. His head throbbed. His gaze fell upon the large bronze jug and goblets on the table beside the bed. A sour smell filled the chamber. Asoka sighed. It was the wine from last night. It was why he did not remember which of his wives or women he had spent the night with. *You used to be able to handle your wine well,* he told himself remorsefully as he sat up. Ignoring the uneasiness in his stomach, he bent forward and kissed his wife on the cheek. Even in her sleep, Asandhi smiled.

Asoka rose to his feet and looked around. They were in the Rang Bhawan, a place he had got accustomed to in the last year. It was located in the eastern part of the huge palace, down a flight of stairs down from his own chambers. The *bhawan* was beautiful. Though shrouded in ambient darkness just then, he knew it in every detail, having spent most of his nights there instead of in his own bed. The divans were placed around a central courtyard with a beautiful pool in the middle, where lotuses bloomed. Servants cleaned the water every day so the Samrat and his companions could step in to swim and bathe. It had been designed for a King to spend time with the ladies of his harem, or his wives, as it pleased him.

Asoka realized his throat was parched. Silently, in the darkness, he searched for water, careful not to disturb his sleeping wife. When he had drunk two goblets, he felt better. Beads of perspiration had formed on his forehead and his *angavastram* felt damp on his body. Asoka had a sudden desire to enter the cool water of the pool. He let his clothes fall to the ground and then descended the stone steps into the pool. As his feet touched the water, he felt a sudden chill run from the top of his head to his buttocks.

Seeing him enter the pool, two women suddenly emerged from the darkness, one carrying a lamp which caused shadows to play on the wall behind, and the other carrying a brass tray of aromatic oils and pastes. They were women from his harem, his concubines, but their main job was to look after him and tend to his daily routine. Two of the harem women remained on duty throughout the day and night, attending to whatever desires of the flesh or mind the Samrat demanded.

As Asoka lowered his body into the pool, one of the women quickly fell to her knees and placed her hands on his bare shoulders, massaging his taut muscles. The other set the tray on the ground beside the pool and began to undress silently. She would be the one to enter the pool with him and help him bathe. Asoka closed his eyes as he felt the soft hands massage his arms. He felt his body relax in the cool water. He heard the gentle splash as the second woman entered the pool. Soon he felt her soft bosom and taut nipples tease one side of his body.

Asoka kept his eyes closed, his head relaxed on a marble headrest, as the women worked with their hands upon him. He was too satiated with wine and sex to feel aroused even though they tried for some time, teasing him with soft touches and warm flesh. They covered his torso with rough powders and smooth pastes which filled the air with enticing aromas. Right there, standing in the pool, Asoka suddenly understood how his father Bindusar, had fathered a hundred children, a question he had often pondered during his days as a common soldier.

Life on the march was far different. One had to do everything for oneself. From squatting in the trench dug behind the tents to empty one's bowels, to bathing in meagre water, dressing, and keeping one's armour and weapons cleaned, a soldier did it himself. It was the life he had known since childhood. This luxurious life in the palace was new and felt much too simple in contrast. The harem women were ever present to take care of his every need. If he wanted to drink water, they were there to offer him a goblet. If he wished to relax on a *baithak*, they were there to fan him with exquisite large fans. If he preferred to play *Shatranj* or *Chausar*, they were there, trained to play the game. And if he yearned for a goblet of wine and the touch of a woman while he drank it, they were there. When he grew bored with the company of his wives, they were there to invite him to their beds, knowledgable in the arts of seduction.

His duties as Samrat were meagre as well. He attended the Council meetings, but only those he was informed about. *The Samrat need not concern himself about lesser issues,* Prime Minister Chanakya would tell him. Asoka did not dare to object for the man was almost a hundred years old and had served his father and grandfather ably before him. In truth, he felt rather wary of the old man; someone one could not question or object to. After all, the old man had helped him win his throne.

The woman in the water moved her hands over his belly, washing away the foam she had made with her aromatic powders. Asoka suddenly became aware of his distended belly. He had become corpulent in the last year, a result of palace life. He tried to remember the last time he had been on the back of a horse. This life of luxury was making him soft. It had'nt always been so since his coronation.

Even after being hailed as Samrat, he had been continuously on the march. His brother, Sushem, had been defeated and his *Ashwamedha* foiled, but he still had supporters in Uttar Bharat. The nobles of Taxila had gathered in the city under the banner of his chief wife, Divija, and her firstborn son. The Prime Minister had sent Asoka all the way to the north with his army, to destroy these enemies. He had hoped that, like old times, his friends Shiva and Kanakdatta would ride with him, but the Prime Minister had kept them in the capital on the pretext of teaching them to manage the empire on the Samrat's behalf. *This is something you must do yourself,* he had told Asoka.

Asoka sighed despondently. The last time he and his two friends had had a drink together was years ago, when Sushem had been defeated. The war against the rebels had kept him busy for two years. And when he had returned, he had found them engrossed in managing the affairs of the realm for him. The Prime Minister sent them to far corners of the *Samrajya* on one mission or the other.

Asoka closed his eyes. The days of the siege reminded him of Devi again; a chapter of his life he had tried hard to forget. The one true love of his life had been taken from him. He still remembered the fateful day. It was to have been the best day of his life, but turned into a nightmare of despair. The day of his coronation. He had promised to share it with Devi, to marry her that day. But she had chosen to turn way and forsake him in his moment of glory. He remembered the Prime Minister's lined face when he delivered the news to him. Devi, who had been trying to help the poor of the city, affected by the fire in the eastern quarters caused by

Sushem's arrows, had been caught in a burning hut. He remembered how heartbroken he had been when the burnt, unrecognizable body had been placed before him. He had fallen to his knees and held the blackened corpse in his arms, refusing to accept what had happened. And the worst was they had argued and disagreed the last time he had seen her.

Sushem's men did this. The Prime Minister had placed a comforting hand on his shoulder as he sat on the ground, unable to let go of Devi's charred body. *Sushem is dead, but his men still live in the North. Go and eradicate their kind from this world. Go and burn their cities. Go and pillage their lands. Avenge what they have done to you. You are now the Samrat, lead your men North.*

He had done exactly that. For three years he had devastated the North-west, destroying all of Sushem's supporters. He had raided Taxila twice, destroying the remaining guerrilla army which continued to fight against him. At the behest of the Prime Minister, he had even invaded the Northern Kingdoms, bringing them under his rule. When he returned to Patliputra, he had been given a hero's welcome. They had hailed him as their saviour and leader. But all that killing and violence had not brought Devi back.

Gentle hands rinsed his neck-length hair. Asoka opened his eyes. The sun had risen and was casting its first rays over them. The women giggled and splashed water over him. Suddenly Asoka realized that both the women were in the pool with him, so who was washing his hair? He turned his head and smiled. It was his wife Asandhimitra, whom he had spent the night with and lovingly called Asandhi. "So you are awake," he said.

She bent and kissed his wet cheek. Asoka walked up the steps, out of the pool. Rivulets flowed down his body, making puddles at his feet. The two women who had also emerged from the pool hurried away, their places taken by two more, who brought a cotton cloth to dry him with, and another to tie around his waist.

"How manly you look!" Asandhi smiled as the two harem women pulled a full length mirror, decorated with bronze, in front of him.

Asoka frowned. "I am not half the man I once was," he said, observing his pot belly. His shoulders, arms and legs were still taut, but his once lean and lithe frame had vanished and he had developed a slight stoop from sitting all day.

"Nonsense!" said Asandhi dismissively, placing a hand on his shoulder.

She looked beautiful as the early rays of the sun fell over her, lighting up her brown eyes. For a moment, Asoka wished it was Devi standing there. Quickly, he brushed the thought away. It was not fair to his wife, who loved him so much.

The harem women worked quickly, bringing him a fresh *angarkha* and cotton shorts. When Asoka tried to take them, they leapt back, giggled like nymphs. Asoka gave in and raised his arms. The women quickly dressed him.

"You are still very handsome," Asandhi assured him, placing her hands on her hips.

"Handsome?" Asoka laughed as the women tickled him on the thighs while putting on his inner clothing. "You should have seen me in armour!"

Asandhimitra flashed him a coquettish look. "Why not let me see for myself now?" she quipped, clapping her hands. Two slave boys appeared. "Bring the Samrat's bronze armour to us," she ordered. They bowed and departed.

Asoka smiled at his young wife. She had the enthusiasm of a child. And of course, she was beautiful. Her fair skin was said to rival the fabled Greek beauty, Helen. The match had been arranged by the Prime Minister when he saw Asoka was still grief-stricken after his return from the northern campaign. *You must forget her*, he had said. *You need a wife. A Samrat cannot be celibate.*

I promised Devi she would be the only woman in my life, Asoka had said. *But* Asoka had protested in vain. *She is dead,* the Prime Minister had said with finality. *There are no promises to keep to the dead.*

The Prime Minister had sent out letters seeking suitable matches. Portraits of eligible Princesses from all over the *Samrajya* and neighboring kingdoms had arrived at Patliputra. Asoka had watched with disinterest, having made up his mind to reject them all. But he had been unable to resist Asandhimitra's beauty. She was a Princess from a small northern kingdom, one that had helped him against Sushem's rebels.

When the Prime Minister had invited the Princess to visit Patliputra, Asoka had been dumbstruck by her allure. And so he had agreed. After all, who could resist such beauty when he had not felt the love of a woman in three years? The marriage ceremony had taken place in the capital and since then, Asoka had spent most of his nights by her side. But even Asandhi's beauty had not been able to make him forget Devi, whom he still saw in his dreams.

"Here it is," Asandhi said cheerfully as the servants brought in the heavy bronze breastplate Asoka had not donned for a long time. It bore the insignia of a roaring lion, the insignia of his father. The servants walked up behind him and Asoka stretched out his arms as they put the armour on him carefully. He immediately felt the weight of the metal, something he had not felt in some time. It brought back old memories, of riding his horse and swinging his sword in battle.

As one of the servants pulled the leather straps that tightened the armour around his body, Asandhimitra stepped forward saying, "I will handle the Samrat's armour." The servants bowed and retreated.

Asoka smiled. "Have you ever handled armour before?" he asked as she struggled with the leather straps.

She shook her head, answering saucily, "But you can certainly teach me, my Lord."

"You must pull like this." Asoka put his hands over hers and showed her. "Then you need to tie a knot, like this." He tied the uppermost strap across his chest.

"Like this?" Asandhimitra took the second strap and tied it across his chest. She was a fast learner.

Asoka nodded as she took the third strap and pulled, struggling to make the ends meet across his stomach. Unfortunately, they were not long enough to cover the expanse of his large belly. "Looks like you need bigger armour, my Lord," she said, giving up.

"It would appear that our Samrat is bent on giving his old friend, Kanakdatta, competition," said a gruff voice from behind them.

Asoka smiled. He had not heard that voice for a long time. He turned to look at his friend, Shiva, who stood at the entrance of the Rang Mahal. In all these years, Shiva of Avanti had not changed, except for his title. He was the same well-built, bearded man Asoka had known since the Southern Wars. But now he was Maharaja of Avanti.

"You are back!" Asoka said, spreading his arms in welcome and walking towards the door.

But Shiva moved back and bowed low. "Indeed, my Samrat," he replied. "I returned this morning from our military fort in Vanga. I was there to arrange for the annual training of our soldiers. I am pleased to report it was a success."

"How many times have I told you not to bow to me, Shiva?" Asoka removed his armour and handed it to the waiting servants.

But Shiva seemed not to have heard. He was bowing again, this time to the the fair Asandhimitra.

"I apologize I am not dressed to receive you, Sir," Asandhimitra said, her hands joined in greeting.

"It is I who should apologize," Shiva said, "for intruding upon you like this."

"You know you are welcome any time, Shiva. And I must insist...no bowing." Asoka watched his wife retreat towards her chambers.

Shiva shook his head. "Protocol dictates everyone must bow before the Samrat."

"I make an exception for you, my friend."

"But I am your Senapati first," Shiva averred, folding his arms. "You should not make an exception for anyone."

"Then, perhaps you should not be here either," Asoka said, an eyebrow lifted. "No Councillors are permitted to enter the Rang Mahal."

"Indeed, I too wished to avoid bursting in on your loving morning," Shiva teased, "but I am here on urgent business."

Asoka looked at his friend. "Urgent business? That can mean only one thing these days."

Shiva nodded. "The Prime Minister has called for an urgent Council meeting, in secret. That is why he has sent for me."

"Is it even the first *prahar* yet?" Asoka asked, looking at the faintly lit sky. "Does the Prime Minister even sleep?"

"I would never dare to ask," Shiva said. "And trust me, it must be something important for him to summon me two nights ago by sending a fast rider to Vanga. And guess whose horse I just saw in the stables when I rode in, the stirrup decorated in gold and gems of the costliest kind?"

"Kanakdatta's here?" Asoka asked, his mouth wide open in surprise. "This is highly irregular. The Prime Minister loves to keep you two away from me. I don't remember a single Council meeting when all three of us have been present."

"The Prime Minister keeps us busy governing your kingdom for you, you mean, while you get fat in this place." Shiva grinned at his friend. "The last I heard, your spymaster was away in the northern mountains."

"Oh Kanaka hates that job," Asoka laughed. "We both know he wanted yours. Be that as it may, I am glad I am awake and dressed, so I will not have to keep the two of you waiting."

"And I am pissed I could not rest in my warm bed with my arms around a sweet woman for the last two nights, riding all the way from Vanga," Shiva said. "But you don't see me complaining."

"This calls for a celebration." Asoka gestured to the servants, who quickly filled bronze goblets with wine.

"Wine this early in the morning?" Shiva laughed. "I now understand where that belly has come from."

Asoka chuckled as the servant handed them goblets. "You certainly look odd in the company of Kanaka and I, O Sober One!"

"Well, one of us at least has to be fit when our enemies come marching at us," Shiva said, taking the goblet.

"Have I left any enemies for you to deal with?" Asoka asked, slapping his friend playfully on the back.

"If you did not, what is this urgent meeting for?"

Asoka emptied his goblet and sighed. "It has to be something sinister," he agreed.

"Whatever it is, I am glad it has brought the three of us together once again after a long time. Let's get this meeting over with so we can sit and talk."

"Let's go to the Council chamber then, Senapati." Asoka held up his refilled goblet. "For old times' sake."

Shiva raised his own goblet. "For old times' sake."

3
KANAKDATTA:
DRUMS OF WAR

For years folk had called him Kanakdatta, the Buddhist. Earlier, when he had been a common foot soldier, he was known to his friends only as Kanaka. No one else cared what his name was due to the beliefs he had chosen for himself. He was just an untouchable Buddhist to steer away from. Later, when he became a famed weapons dealer, people could no longer igore him or keep away. In a world so treacherous that everyone needed weapons to defend themselves, he had the best on offer. The nobles who bought from him coined a new name for him then; not that he had ever minded. The name brought a certain gravitas to his persona and his enemies trembled at its mere mention, the same enemies who had once called him an untouchable Buddhist.

Kanakdatta clenched his teeth and bent over his desk. He held a small knife in his hands, the black iron blade stained with dried blood and scratched with marks. He reached for the leather quiver he had carelessly flung upon the table when he had entered the chamber a few hours ago. He moved his hand over the leather pouch, pulled out an arrow and placed it on the desk, its plain iron head pointing away from him. With the blade of his knife he scraped against the edges of the arrow head. After a while he examined the head and then began to rub the knife back and forth again. It was a ritual he followed whenever he returned to the city from his assignments. Sharpening his arrows needed a good source of light, a good wooden surface to rest upon, and some free time, none of which were usually available on his assignments.

These assignments were of a sinister nature. Sometimes, the Prime Minister would send him to a vassal Rajya to extract information about supposed treachery. Sometimes he traversed forests, deserts and mountains to destroy hidden bandit strongholds. Sometimes the Prime Minister even ordered him to disguise himself and his men as bandits and hijack some foreign caravan travelling through Maurya lands. And as the nature of his work changed, so did his name. Now folk called him Kanakdatta, the snake.

Kanakdatta sighed as he sharpened his arrows one by one, careful not to cut his hand with the lethal knife. *How can anyone compare me to a snake?* he wondered as he sat back and moved his free hand over his enormous stomach. *If I am to be compared to an animal at all, surely it should be the elephant?* But he knew that his strange new nickname meant he was doing his job well, for who is more dangerous as a Spymaster than a Snake?

He picked up the last arrow and held it up. His eyes lingered on its length, where a set of parched brown feathers sat majestically on its tail. It was the best arrow in his quiver, the one with the eagle feathers – the one he used on special occasions when he had an impossible target. Its arrowhead, unlike the others, glistened in the sunlight that filtered in through the wall alcoves. Kanakdatta polished its copper edges with his fingers and then sharpened it quickly, one slash at a time. Then he put it back in the leather quiver and got to his feet.

There was a knock on the wooden door; three soft taps followed by two quick ones. He knew it was Dhanush, his most trusted aide. "What is it?" he called softly.

"The Samrat and your old grizzled friend are here to see you," Dhanush said from behind the door.

The scoffing words brought a smile to Kanakdatta's lips. Dhanush had been in his service for half a decade and knew all the nicknames he had for his friends. "Well then, send them in already!" he replied. "You should know better than to keep the Samrat waiting."

"I know better than not to ask for your permission first." Dhanush's footsteps moved away from his door.

Kanakdatta glanced into the giant mirror by the side of his bed. He was dressed in the silken robes he habitually wore for all occasions. It was his habit to awaken at first light, even though he had not had much sleep, having reached the city late at night. He had been riding for over a *saptaha*, from the foothills of the Himalayas. When he had received the Prime Minister's summons, he had been on a sensitive mission to neutralise a certain belligerent warlord who had led his tribe from the foreign lands across the snowy mountains, across the Mauryan borders, to loot and pillage in the northern *Rajyas*. Kanakdatta had been surprised by the sudden summons, for he could not think of a more important task than the one he was engaged on. But he knew the Prime Minister had his reasons.

He held the wooden door open and watched as his two friends walked down the corridor towards his chamber. The sight of them, engrossed in deep conversation, made him smile. It was over a year since he had last seen them. He looked disapprovinglyly at Asoka's rotund figure. When had his lithe friend become obese?

"I'd doubt your intentions if I didn't know better." Shiva grinned as he saw Kanakdatta view Asoka's belly.

"And I'd be afraid if I were you," Kanakdatta retorted, laughing and embracing his friend, "because that would be a sure way to get him to rid me of my wretched job."

Asoka watched them, his arms folded. Then Kanakdatta turned and pulled him into a shoulder grip. "You still require something to match my size," he said.

Shiva looked at them disapprovingly. "We are not supposed to embrace the Samrat," he said, tapping Kanakdatta on the shoulder.

"Oh bollocks!" Kanakdatta chuckled, letting Asoka go. "We were the ones who made him the Samrat."

"Look at you," Asoka observed, surveying his friend. "All those days out on the land and you have not lost a finger width! You are still as large as I remember."

Kanakdatta bowed with his inimitable grace. "I have a reputation to protect. Unlike you, who seems to have lost all control of your physique in just one year in the palace."

"If I am the Samrat, I must look the part, must I not?" Asoka smiled, patting his friend on the shoulder. "How goes your assignment?"

"My men tracked the bandits all the way to their camp," Kanakdatta replied quietly. "I was about to attack them when the Prime Minister's envoy summoned me. It was a shame I could not be present to see the bloodbath."

"So you were tracking some bandit?" Asoka playfully punched his friend on the shoulder. "So that's what you are reduced to now?"

"Tracking a bandit on your behalf," Kanakdatta reminded him. "Are you so lost in pleasure that you don't even know I am risking my neck for you every day?"

Shiva laughed. "He was out on a long campaign after all."

"I am interested to know," Asoka said, sitting down on a bejewelled chair. "Why don't you both tell me all you have been up to in the last year?"

Shiva smiled. "I'm sure Kanaka here would love to tell his tall tales, but I hate to break it to you that the reason the Prime Minister sent me to fetch you two was to make sure we'd all appear in the Council chamber without delay."

Kanakdatta cleared his throat. "Ummm...well, I would indeed like to know why he dragged me here from my cozy, cold camp up North."

"Let's go then," Asoka said, getting to his feet. "We can reminisce later. We have the whole day to ourselves."

"With the Prime Minister, you never know," Shiva remarked morosely, walking out of the door.

"Yes, I do sometimes have the strongest desire to assassinate the wretched old fool," Kanakdatta joked, following them out.

"He'd have you upside down in a torture chamber before you could even draw your hidden blade," Shiva laughed. "You know how devious he is."

"But I am no less." Kanakdatta put his hands together in a snakelike gesture. "I am after all, Kanakdatta the Snake."

Asoka joined in the friendly laughter as the three emerged from Kanakdatta's chambers into the upper corridors of the palace. The Council chamber was not far, just three turns away, nestled in the western part of the building, overlooking the whole city. The corridors here were out of bounds for common courtiers, and guards stood at every turn. They bowed to their Samrat as the three men traversed the stone flooring.

When they reached the vast Council chamber, they found the Prime Minister was already present; his bald head the first thing they saw as they entered. The chamber was dominated by the vast stone table that stood in the middle. Tall, narrow embrasures overlooked the city, bathing the chamber in bands of glistening light. Asoka stepped forward, catching a view of the western part of the city. The houses looked like small coloured blocks from where he stood. The wind hummed through the narrow casements. The chamber was a clear reminder that the Patliputra palace had been originally built as a fortress.

Against the almost surreal backdrop, the Prime Minister looked as ancient as the fortress itself. But the stone table was an entirely other story. Made of shining black granite, it seemed to have been carved from the floor itself. It was, in fact, the newest addition to the old room.

"Acharya." Asoka bowed, breaking the old man's meditative trance.

Prime Minister Chanakya turned. Asoka took the handlebars of the chair and pushed it towards the table. Kanakdatta observed the stone table with interest. Its acquisition had been one of the first tasks for the Prime Minister as Spymaster, a job he had not wanted. 'You and I are the only men in this Council who have travelled across the vast expanse of this land multiple times,' the old man had told him. 'We must create a model of what we have seen, a map to plan our moves by; a miniature version of our great lands, something the likes of which has never been made before.'

And so he had found the best sculptor he knew, far away in the South, and brought him to the capital. For many days the three of them had sat in this hall as Asoka campaigned in the North, describing to the sculptor their travels and explorations as the man followed them with his chisel. The thing had taken months to complete and he had left on another assignment before the sculptor allowed anyone to lay eyes on the finished product. Now, as he entered the chamber, Kanakdatta finally saw it in all its austere dominance. He saw the Prime Minister looking at the table with a strange sparkle in his eyes. Sometimes, the old man's enthusiasm about such things encouraged him. The man was decades old, yet planned his conquests like a youth about to go carve his legacy. At other times, the same enthusiasm frightened him.

The Prime Minister cleared his throat and all eyes fell upon him at the head of the table. "Behold your *Samrajya*, Prince," he said, raising both palms upwards to indicate the table. "Do you like what you see?"

"It is exquisite," Asoka said admiringly.

Beside him, Shiva nodded, lost in wonder. Kanakdatta smiled. The sculptor had done his job well. From the rough mounds of the Himalayas, painted in milk white, to the green plains of the South, the stone table was indeed a good representation of the Mauryan lands and beyond.

The Prime Minister wheeled his chair to the eastern side of the table. "However, we are not here to admire the table, but to use it," he said.

The place where he stopped his chair, left no one in doubt what was to come. Shiva coughed slightly and stood with arms folded. Asoka walked to the Prime Minister's side and stood with his hands on his waist. Kanakdatta took a deep breath and looked around, trying to find a place to sit. But in the vast chamber, there were no chairs.

"Kalinga must fall." Prime Minister Chanakya's raspy voice tore through the chamber like a knife through skin.

At his side, Asoka looked interested. Shiva's face was wrought with worry as the Samrat's Senapati. Kanakdatta sighed. It had been a long time coming. He was sure Asoka longed for battle once again.

"Word has it that Kalinga is having elections," Chanakya said, tapping his frail, freckled hand on the map. "The erstwhile ruler of Kalinga is dead. As the contenders squabble amongst themselves for power, we will fall upon them like lions on a herd of butting bison."

"Is it really necessary?" Kanakdatta was surprised at how quickly the words came to his dry throat. "The Kalingans have been paying tribute to us. My men tell me the toughest contender is a military General, interested in power for himself. We could simply buy him off in return for helping him win."

Chanakya gazed at the map. "That would be a merchant's way," he replied laconically. "But this decision must be taken by Kshatriyas." He looked up at Asoka.

Asoka nodded. "It must be done," he agreed. "Kalinga is the only kingdom that remains outside our control. We must have it. We must have it forever. And the only way to accomplish that is through conquest."

"Kalinga is not a kingdom," Chankya breathed, "but a *Mahajanpada*. A blot on the body of our Samrajya." He turned his piercing gaze on Shiva. "How much time will you require?"

Shiva seemed unaware of his hands tugging at his beard. "It is a big chunk of land," he said thoughtfully, weighing every word. "Too many rivers, rolling hills. Equipment will have to be cast. More men will have to be recruited."

"You will have as much time as our Spymaster will provide." Chankya said, cutting him in, "No more."

Kanakdatta nodded, understanding the Prime Minister's meaning. "We will need all the regular information, of course," he said. "The size of their army, the contenders in the elections, their motivations. My men will be able to extract all that in less than two new moons, like a babe at her mother's breast."

Chanakya looked thoughtful. His eyes moved gently across the stone table, as if bathing it with his vision. "I must speak with each of you alone," he finally said. "It is of vital importance. We have decided in council the course of action, now I must talk to each of you alone."

Kanakdatta turned to leave, but the old man coughed and said, "You first."

Asoka nodded and smiled at his friend. "We'll be in the corridor," he said, "planning how to conquer this seafaring country."

As he and Shiva walked out, Kanakdatta turned to meet the gaze of the old man. Alone with him, he realized how uncomfortable he felt in the strange gaze from the Prime Minister's half-dead eyes, sunken deep in their sockets.

For a time neither man spoke. Then the Prime Minister cleared his throat. "I know what ails your mind," he said. "I also know the answer you seek."

Kanakdatta nodded. "Why now? It's been a year of peace."

"You know why. The Kalinga elections. They will be most vulnerable. It is the opportune moment to strike."

Kanakdatta shook his head. "There has to be more. I am sure of it."

A sly smile came to Chanakya's toothless lips. "Do you know why I never made you Senapati, Buddhist?

"Because I failed in the first assignment you gave me," Kanakdatta replied.

"And what was that assignment, if you remember?"

Kanakdatta felt uneasy; his legs had gone suddenly numb. "I do not wish to talk about it," he said.

"They are there," Chanakya murmured, his voice a gravelly whisper. "My men saw Radhagupta there, as clear as day. You have another chance to succeed."

"And the Prince Tissa?"

"They did not see him, but he must be with his uncle."

Kanakdatta sighed. "So you want me not to just send spies into Kalinga, but assassins."

"No, I do not," Chanakya said harshly. "But I have always known you to be sharp and sure."

"Is that why we are attacking the Mahajanpada?" Kanakdatta asked quietly.

"We must bring it into our Samrajya," Chankya said. "Kalinga's ports will bring much wealth to our treasury. We can kill two birds with the same arrow. Precisely the kind of antics I'm told you are good at."

Kanakdatta nodded. "I will tell you all that my men see and hear…" He took a deep breath. "And do…in Kalinga."

Chanakya looked him in the eye. "What I have told you never goes outside this chamber."

Kanakdatta nodded in silence.

"Ah, it is good we understand each other so well." Chanakya nodded. It was the signal that the meeting was over. "Send in your friend."

"Asoka?" Kanakdatta asked, turning his head as he walked towards the door.

"He is no longer your friend," Chanakya hissed from behind him. "He is your *Samrat* now."

Pushing the door open, Kanakdatta emerged into the passage. He found Asoka and Shiva at the battlements, gazing out over the city. "He wants you next," he told Shiva, who grimaced and left.

Kanakdatta walked up to stand by Asoka's side. The sun was up in the sky now and the whole city had come alive. An amalgam of countless sounds hung in the air.

"Do you like it here?" Kanakdatta folded his arms and stood with his back against the stone spikes.

Asoka nodded and then looked down at himself. "But I must start riding again and get out of this damned palace."

"I have not met your wife."

"Asandhi is well. She grows lovelier with each passing day. And she is very fond of me."

"Do you like the court?"

Asoka shrugged. "I don't. Sitting on that throne the whole day hurts my bottom. I yearn to be on horseback. But the Prime Minister insists."

"It's your duty as Samrat."

"The peasants bring me all kinds of puzzling cases, my friend," Asoka told him, "from family disputes to gruesome murders. Most of the time I know not what to say. My word is law. The crown feels heavy on my head."

"So do you leave the judgments to the Prime Minister?" Kanakdatta asked.

Asoka nodded. "Sometimes, I wonder what I will do when the Prime Minister passes away. Being Samrat is difficult. I was not trained for this." He paused for a moment before saying quietly, "Sometimes I think Sushem would have made a better ruler."

"You are just starting out, my friend," Kanakdatta told him. "Do you imagine I learnt archery in one day? These things take time."

"Indeed they do," Asoka agreed. "Ye gods I miss her, Kanaka!" Asoka sighed, his eyes on the horizon. "I still see her in my dreams, you know. Somehow, I feel if she had been at my side, everything would have been different."

"You have your wife. You have Asandhi."

"Asandhi is a child," Asoka sighed. "She is a good wife; she does her duties well. She loves me. But she isn't a pillar of support."

"Don't let her hear you say that."

Asoka looked at his friend. "Losing Devi was the greatest sorrow of my life."

Kanakdatta did not speak. He had seen a worse kind of sorrow when he had taken the news of Devi's death to the other man he respected most in this life. "I must go," he said to Asoka.

"So soon?" Asoka grasped his friend's hands. "You should wait. The three of us have so much to talk about. We have not met in so many moons."

"I know, but I must hasten back to camp. If we are to act on the Prime Minister's orders, there is no time to lose."

Asoka smiled. "The coming war is the only thing that brings a smile to my face. When I am in the thick of action, I will feel happy again."

"Then let me go." Kanakdatta patted Asoka playfully on the shoulder, "so I can bring the war to you sooner."

"Will you not wait for Shiva?" Asoka asked, looking at the closed doors of the Council chamber.

"I'll see him on my way out."

"When will I see you again, my friend?" Asoka asked, holding Kanakdatta's shoulders.

Kanakdatta smiled. "Let us hope it is soon, my friend."

The two men embraced against the backdrop of the city. Kanakdatta bowed and walked away. He did not look back. If what the Prime Minister had said was true, there was no time to lose.

4
HARDEO:
THE ELEPHANT ON THE MINARET

VIDISHANAGRI, 263 BC

He felt as though he had lived a thousand years. The wind blew in his face, bringing tears to his eyes as Hardeo looked at his city from the top of the highest tower in Vidishanagri. It was his latest addition to the Guild building – a tall minaret akin to those seen at the palaces of the Farsi Kings. It had been designed by foreign architects, and constructed using the best materials, with a spire of pure gold on top. It told the world that Vidishanagri was no longer a mud-and-dung hell-hole, but a power to be reckoned with, as beautiful as any other ancient city.

The soft rays of the morning sun bathed the city in a golden glow as Hardeo admired his creation from his perch. From here, he could see far beyond the walls of the city to the forests that lined the horizon. The minaret was open on all sides, meaning he could look everywhere, in all directions, presiding over his hegemony. Indeed, he felt like a God.

How many things he had achieved in his meagre life that his predecessors had taken millennia to reach? How many experiences he had had; how many lands he had seen. Hardeo raised his palms and looked at them. Suddenly, he was back in the Northern wastes, holding silken ropes in his hands, ready to capture the wild beasts they called horses.

He took a deep breath. So many accomplishments in so little time! From being a slave, he was now standing atop the tallest minaret in the whole of Madhya Bharat. How many of his brethren even came close? Was he not just like a God who lived for a thousand years?

Hardeo sighed. He was not here to enjoy the view and indulge in hubris. He breathed deeply to clear his mind. He was here to check the finishing of the construction work. He turned to find a host of engineers, ministers and servants standing before him, waiting anxiously for his speech.

One of his Chiefs of Construction bowed before him. "Does the Maharaja like our work?" he asked.

Our work? Hardeo smiled as he remembered the vast number of gold chests that had been required to build this minaret, the many friends he had sent letters to, imploring them to send him their best architects, designers and engineers to build what he called 'a monument to the new era that had fallen upon their tribe'.

"It is indeed exquisite," Hardeo agreed. The men before him had toiled tirelessly for days and nights to complete this wonder and deserved his praise.

As the men bowed in unison and Hardeo felt the wind tug at his lapels once again. "Is everything ready for today?" he asked his Chancellor, who stood behind him.

"Aye, Maharaja, the count is complete. All have arrived in our camps. The last caravans to reach the city came in today. Those unable to attend have sent letters with their choices. You have quorum, Guild Master."

Hardeo smiled. For four years now he had held two titles. The young Samrat had kept his word and made him the Maharaja of Vidishanagri, giving him command of all the neighboring Rajyas. And for a decade before that, his brethren in the subcontinent had affectionately called him Guild Master, acknowledging his leadership of their Merchant's Guild. But today, he would hand over that title to another man.

"Good," Hardeo said, nodding. "I will change and then let the Council begin."

Before descending the spiral staircase, he once again gazed at his city from atop. Outside the walls, he could see numerous tents put up exquisitely and hastily put up stables. He saw people like small ants, and donkeys and horses, wandering about them, some appeared to be too foreign in their clothes and appearances. These were the camps of the Preferetti of the Merchant's Guild. Five New Moons ago, he had sent letters all over the lands, calling important members of the Guild to a Council to the city, his city. And it was here that he would announce his retirement today and let a younger man take up the job.

He walked down the staircase slowly, holding on to the stone wall for support as his entourage followed him. Hardeo took his time to descend the flight of stairs, putting one foot after the other one slowly. He had been running all his life. He deserved to be slow now. The walk down to his chambers would be a short one. Even after being hailed as the Maharaja, he still preferred his old quarters in the Guild building. They did all the official business in the palace, but Hardeo hadn't moved and still lived on the topmost floor, overlooking the city. *I already live at the tallest place in Vidishanagri* he had told his Chamberlain when he would request him to make the shift, *why are you dragging me two levels down*.

He changed into simple cotton robes that flowed down to his ankles. Usually, he would wear ornate clothing on such occasions, but today he was stepping down. Hardeo wanted to look simple, like a man who had enjoyed his days of glory but was no longer in the light now. He wanted to exude the aura of an advisor; a wise man who would know when to step down instead of carrying on till people hated him. He had already started to hear criticism that he paid more attention to his Maharajya than the Guild. He wanted to step down in grace, and to be remembered as a great leader.

"The Council is called, Guild Master." His Chamberlain bowed from the entrance to his door, "The Merchant leaders shall await you soon in the main hall."

Hardeo nodded, tying his waistband into a knot. It was a part of his Buddhist traditions to wear his clothing on his own. *Another man shall not assist you to breathe, eat, and cover yourself.* The Great Noble one had said and Hardeo was true to his ways, even after he had been hailed as a Raja of Rajas. "Please ask my favorite Merchant to see me before the Council." Hardeo told him as he bent down to put on his boots, "I have much to discuss with him."

The Chamberlain coughed uneasily. "He is not here, Maharaja. He sent a letter to say he would be unable to attend."

"Kanakdatta is not here?" It was highly unusual.

"His letter says the Samrat sent him away on some important business of State," the Chamberlain informed Hardeo. "Nothing more."

Hardeo tied his bootstraps and waved the Chamberlain away. *Important business of State.* Kanakdatta always visited him to discuss important matters at hand. He would also bring news of the Royal court and what was happening in the capital. Sometimes, Hardeo would use the information to make important changes to the Guild policies based on the new royal laws that were about to be passed. What was of such priority that he hadn't come to attend the Council nor discuss the same?

He walked out of the room and emerged out in the corridor that led to another spiral staircase downwards. The Main hall was on the lowest level. He walked through the corridor through which he had walked countless times in his life. As he neared the chamber that adjoined his own, he suddenly stopped in his tracks. Hardeo sighed. This was where Devi once resided. He would always like to see her every morning, before he would set out on important business. He had still kept her old chambers as they were, a servant would clean and dust it once each day. It still felt like she lived there, and had gone out for some of her adventures in the forest.

Hardeo breathed in to fight a tear and walked along. Sushem's siege of the capital had taken away his daughter from him. She had been the apple of his eye, the only one in this world whom he had loved so much. And now she was gone, all of a sudden. *Wars are cruel* Hardeo knew that. He should never have let her ride off to the capital in face of upcoming siege, but she had volunteered. And once Devi had set her mind on something, she would listen to no one. He smiled at the thought of her smiling face as he descended the stairs that led to the lowest level. Here, he could hear the murmurings of the people from outside the streets. Hardeo looked through the *jali* on the wall and noticed a sizeable crowd at the gates of the Guild House, talking amongst themselves. It was not every day that a Council of the Merchant's Guild was called and the local traders knew that something was afoot. They were waiting on the streets to hear news of what was to come. Hardeo paid them no heed. The decision of today would not affect the common men. It did not matter to them who led the Guild and who didn't as long as the new Guild Master would stay true to the laws of the Guild.

When Hardeo entered the Main hall, he found that it was already full with people. Most were sitting on the stone of the floor as their tradition dictated. Hardeo sensed the noise in the hall die down slowly as people caught sight of him entering through the bejeweled double doors. He saw familiar faces as he walked towards the front where a single chair stood at the end. He caught sight of some of his old friends from the North in their woolen heavy clothing. He saw a group of men wearing high turbans, the kind they wore in the lands far across the western sea. Some of them bowed to him as he walked and he acknowledged them with a nod of his head. The younger ones just watched him in awe, no doubt wanting to be him in their coming years. A few of the older men who were still part of the trade, waved to him, a reminder of when they had traded with him as equals.

By the time Hardeo reached his chair and took his seat, the hall was silent. Only the noise of the city could be heard from the streets. "My fellow brethren," he said, addressing the crowd. "Many of you may be wondering why I have called this council, disturbing you in your regular business." His eyes moved over the crowd, noticing that everyone was listening to him with bated breaths. "Let me not keep you wondering any longer." He said loudly, "You are here to elect your new Guild Master."

The air of silence suddenly transformed into that of a fish market as all of the Preferetti began talking amongst themselves hurriedly. It did not affect him. Hardeo knew that some amount of surprise was to be expected. He had not discussed his plans with anyone, nor could anybody have guessed what was in his mind. He raised his voice to get their attention. "For five years I have juggled the role of your Guild Master and Maharajya of Vidishanagri," he said loudly as they began to quieten. "I have brought immense wealth to the Guild through our businesses, and have uplifted the name of this city." He raised both his hands above his head and pointed towards the ceiling. "Above our heads now lies the tallest tower in the entirety of the Subcontinent, a token of what we have achieved over these years. All of you must have seen it in all its glory when you rode to the city. Tell me, fellow Brethren have you seen sights like it anywhere else?"

The men began to talk again, but Hardeo continued unabashedly, "Now, time has come for me to step down and lend the leadership of the Guild to someone younger, so that I can spend my old days in peace as the Maharaja of Vidishanagri."

To his surprise, the roar of the crowd increased, as fists were banged in protest. *Traitor!* some voices called out. The men began talking agitatedly in groups as Hardeo's guards looked around uneasily with their hands upon their weapons, ready to strike if something untoward was to happen.

"There is no call for disorder." Hardeo said loudly and tapped his walking stick with strength upon the ground, "You are here for new elections. It is time to elect a new Guild master."

"Silence!" a strong voice said imperatively.

Hardeo looked towards its direction and noticed that a very old man standing up in the corner, his frame supported by two servants holding him up by his arms. "Guild Master." He said loudly, "It is highly irregular. Why were none of us given any notion of this?"

Hardeo narrowed his eyes to look at the man whom he recognized quickly. He was called Dhanush, one of the oldest merchants in the subcontinent, specializing in spices and condiments. "Master Dhanush, I did not give any premonition because I did not want any group to plot to place their man in the top position," Hardeo said. "Now, when each member votes, it shall be without prejudice, and the best man shall be elected."

"That is not what I mean." Dhanush said with vigor, "It is highly irregular that you should take such a decision when our Guild is in immense danger."

"Danger?" Hardeo's questioning gaze moved over the room. There were voluntary nods by many to Dhanush's call. "Brothers, this has been one of the best years for the Guilds."

Best year for you perhaps! A rowdy shout came from the back.

Hardeo stamped his foot angrily and stood up, holding onto his walking stick. "If anyone wants to make allegations against me, I implore he do so openly."

"That is exactly what I am doing." Dhanush moved his closed fist in the air for effect, "How come it is that you, Guild Master is able to build a huge minaret when some of our own Brothers and their families were ruined this year."

"Business is a game." Hardeo stared down the old man. "Sometimes, some people lose. If this is about the trade blockade of Kalinga I have said before and shall say so again that I support the Samrat regarding the same. We can do business without trading with the Kalingans and if some of our brothers lost their fortunes for having invested heavily into foreigners, they themselves are to blame."

Dhanush returned his gaze. "Who said anybody about ruin in business?" He said defiantly, "Our Brothers were killed, Guild Master."

"Killed?" The surprise clearly showed on his face as his right hand involuntarily began to shake. He had had these tremors for some days now and they would come when he would suddenly feel shock of any kind.

"Aye, killed. Or should I rather say, murdered." Dhanush now turned to face the other persons in the room. "Some of our best; our most promising members. Shrivardhan from Taxila, the most successful trader who traded with the Greeks, killed in his bed. His wealth looted by supposed thieves." The crowd gasped in horror as they listened on, "Another one, Dantes of Tezpur, attacked when his caravan was travelling to the Far East, disappeared in the far deserts along with his carvan. Ghatkarpara of Vanga, a fierce man who was famous to have crossed the northern mountains to take trade to the lands of the Hunas, disappeared without a trace with his treasury looted not some time later."

"Master Dhanush," Hardeo said from his chair, "I have no knowledge of this."

"We wrote to you, Guild Master." A young chamberlain sitting on the opposite side got to his feet, "We sent couriers, letters..."

"I never saw any of them." Hardeo clenched his fists.

"Nor did we!" Dhanush nodded from his place. "Our messengers never returned."

Hardeo breathed in deeply. "This is grave news."

"Indeed, Guild Master." Dhanush coughed, exhausted from speaking. "As I said, our Guild is in grave danger. Someone is after us."

Hardeo stared at the men in the hall all watching at him. For a moment, he felt that he was watching them in slow motion. The thought in his mind swirled like leaves of trees blown down in a high wind.

"Someone is killing our best merchants. Something evil is afoot. You cannot step down at a time like this, Guild Master," the Chamberlain said emphatically. "We need you!"

"You need to find who is after us, son," Dhanush roared from his corner. "And you need to teach them a lesson."

"Wait..." Hardeo said suddenly looking around. "Did you say that all the messengers you sent me were killed?"

"Aye," Dhanush nodded in affirmation. "Not a man returned."

"And yet nothing happened to the men I sent to invite you to this city."

Dhanush nodded, his eyes as big as marbles.

"And then how come those who killed all your messengers let you all come here, to this city today, if they wanted to keep this information from me?" Hardeo asked sharply.

Dhanush opened his mouth to respond, but closed it as the realization dawned upon him. "Oh Lord Buddha!" he exclaimed. "This is a trap."

"Run!" Hardeo shouted. "Run for the doors!" Suddenly, there were screams from outside. *Fire, Fire!* People screamed as the guards quickly came to him and Hardeo's heart missed a beat. How was this possible, in his own city? Suddenly, two arrows swooped inside the hall breaking the glass tiles of the windows. They hit the wooden floor with a singular crackling sound and Hardeo realized that they were lighted arrows to his horror. The blaze spread in circles, around the place where the arrows had hit slowly. 'Get them out of here.' Hardeo told the guards, pointing to the old members of the Preferetti. "I can take care of myself."

He walked past two of the Preferetti who were trying to revive Dhanush, who had slunk to the floor in shock, his servants had run away at the first sign of danger. The guards helped the others move towards the doors, as another barrage of arrows entered the hall, this time pointed towards the ceilings. They stuck in the wooden trusses and the flame doubled. "Watch out." Hardeo held a Preferetti by the hand and pulled him away as an arrow closely whizzed past his face.

"This place is going to collapse." Hardeo said with worry as they emerged out of the double doors into the hall, "We need to get to the streets right now."

The captain of his guard met them with another detachment of soldiers at the entrance to the Guild building, sword in hand. "Maharaja," he said, worried, "there are attackers in the city. They captured a building close to the Guild Hall and begn firing arrows."

"Did you kill them?" Hardeo asked as the reinforcements ran for the hall to rescue the others.

"My men have surrounded the building." The Captain coughed from the smoke that had filled the place. "They will have them in few more moments but we need to evacuate the hall for they are continuously firing lighted arrows at it."

"Do that." Hardeo nodded. Then, a wooden truss above them cracked due to another impact as a loud bang shook the grounds beneath their feet. "Watch out." The captain yelled and pulled Hardeo aside as a wooden beam creaked and broke above their heads, dangling over them. Hardeo kicked the doors of the Guild House angrily and they emerged out in the courtyard. The crowd watching the Guild House from earlier had disappeared, having scampered off at the first signs of fire. Hardeo watched men of the City watch forming a chain outside, carrying wooden buckets filled with water.

"Put out the fire!" he yelled at the men, turning to look at his building, "Put it out before it reaches the minaret!" But the captain had already held him by the shoulder tightly. "Guild Master, look!" He pointed and Hardeo followed his finger. The Golden dome atop the minaret had collapsed sideways into the roof and the wooden pillars that had held it up were burning with flames. The golden dome was half dug inside the wooden planks with only its bottom half now visible over the top. Hardeo clenched his fists with anger. His minaret, the pride of his city had been toppled over before he had even had chance to inaugurate it for the people.

Hardeo watched as the Preferetti were brought out of the building, one by one. Last, he saw Dhanush being carried out by two guards. As they passed him, Dhanush reached out and held his hand. The soldiers carrying him stopped, unsure of what to do. Hardeo looked down at the man's face. He was badly injured, the side of his leg was clearly burnt and there was immense pain visible in the line of his face. "Guild Master," The Old man said weakly, "You know who did this. No one else would dare."

Hardeo clenched his teeth and nodded, "I do," he said.

"The Order." Dhanush closed his eyes. "They wanted to kill us all."

"Well, they have failed." Hardeo looked up. *Had they?* His great creation now lay dangling from the Guild House, having destroyed its own foundation.

"We must strike back," Dhanush said. "This is a war."

This was indeed war. Hardeo looked at his men who were throwing water from the buckets at the walls, one by one and then moving back to let the man behind them raise his bucket. The entire building was burning letting up a huge pillar of smoke. The soldiers carried Dhanush away as the captain turned to him.

"What do you want me to do?" He asked, looking palely grim.

"Escort these men to their camps outside the walls." Hardeo ordered, pacing around the courtyard, deep in thought, "Tend to the injured and place guards on each and every corner."

"Aye." The Captain bowed, "When my men find the attackers who did this, I will kill them with my bare hands."

"No, I will." Hardeo lifted his cane into the air angrily. "After we have had a confession out of them."

"Look there, Guild Master." The Captain pointed towards the streets where a man in armour was running towards them. "That is my Sergeant, leading the men who encircled the attackers. He must have captured them."

The armoured man reached them and bowed. "Report, soldier," the Captain said sternly. The man opened his mouth uneasily and then looked down at his feet.

"What's the matter, son?" Hardeo's questioning gaze bore into his face.

"I don't know how to say it," the man stuttered. "The attackers...we managed to encircle them and breach the house they were holed in. But..."

"But what?" the Captain shouted.

"They were carrying Kalkoot, Sir." The man bowed his head in shame. "We could not get even one of them. Their bodies now lie atop the building. My men are bringing them down."

"Bollocks!" the Captain cursed, then looked apologetically at Hardeo. "I am sorry, Guild Master."

"It is done," Hardeo said calmly, looking away. "See to it that no other attackers are present in the city."

"I will comb every alley and house," the Captain said through clenched teeth.

"And prepare my palanquins, Captain. And a detachment of your best guards," Hardeo ordered.

The Captain's mouth opened in surprise. "And where should I prepare them for, My Lord?"

"For the capital, Captain," Hardeo said, walking away. "I am going to Patliputra."

5
CHANAKYA:
ONWARDS TO KALINGA

When the Council chamber was finally empty, Chanakya looked towards the dark alcoves in the walls. A sudden bout of fatigue had overcome him after talking to the Spymaster and Senapati, answering their questions, and explaining stratagems to them. Breath did not come easily to him these days, and he had to fight for each gasp of air. He raised his hands and signalled for what he wanted. Shadows moved across the walls eerily. But they were merely the Brothers of the Order in their black cloaks. It had become an unwritten custom of the Order that two Brothers would follow him at any given hour, light or dark, rain or shine. Today, it was the turn of two of his favourite veterans.

Nikumbh was the first to emerge from the darkness. Thin lines of light fell on his bearded face from the strip windows to the east, all the way down his cloak. In his hand, Chanakya caught sight of a wooden pitcher, lines etched into its surface. Prajapati followed him slowly, his robes flowing behind him along the ground, holding a wooden tray with a silver goblet which shone at intervals as he walked through the patches of light and dark.

Chanakya felt a sudden bout of coughing overcome him like a bolt from the blue and covered his mouth with his palm. He felt his chest heave with each cough, his weak heart pounding against his ribs. When the fit had passed, he found Prajapati standing before him, holding the goblet as Nikumbh poured a dark glistening liquid into it from the pitcher

"Drink quickly, My Lord," Prajapati urged as he placed the silver rim against Chanakya's lips.

The ancient closed his eyes and gulped down the liquid they poured into his mouth. He could not feel its taste upon his numb, hardened tongue, only its wetness. Taste had been lost to him a few years ago. He felt the liquid travel down into the confines of his chest, between his lungs, which suddenly felt on fire. He forced himself to take a deep breath, but it did not feel complete. Finally, he gave up and looked at the two men with him.

"Do you feel better?" Nikumbh asked anxiously, placing the vessel on the stone table.

Chanakya nodded. Indeed, he felt a burning sensation in his chest. The liquid was a special potion, a secret brew of the Order, to bring strength to his old limbs. It began like a fire burning in his belly, the warmth of which slowly flowed towards the tips of his fingers, giving him the strength to keep his mind and body awake.

Prajapati hunched forward and holding the wheeled chair by its ivory back, turned it, moving towards the dark alcove in the wall. Chanakya closed his eyes as the wall came upon them. But the chair did not strike it even as it kept moving forward. He opened his eyes to the blackness around him. His weak eyes could no longer adjust to the dark. He felt the lack of air with each breath he drew and the sudden heaviness above him. They were indeed inside the tunnels. It would have been impossible for him to enter them now without consuming the brew.

"You should not have told the Buddhist that we found Radhagupta in Kalinga." Nikhumb's voice sounded strange in the narrow space.

Behind his chair, Chankya heard Prajapati grunt in affirmation and smiled. These men did not understand his stratagem. *Was he a fool, to trust the fat Buddhist?* "It is a test," he said. "What he does now will decide whether he lives or dies."

"You mean whether you send us to kill him or not," Nikumbh laughed. The hoarse laughter echoed against the walls in a receding spiral.

"The Buddhist is not the problem," Chanakya told them. "It is the Senapati. He thinks that preparing the army for this invasion will take at-least half a *varsha*."

"Half a *varsha?*" Prajapati muttered, turning the chair.

They had now reached a circular slope, like a minaret that went below ground instead of above into the sky. He carefully maneuvered the chair down the curved slope as Chanakya held onto the ivory handles to avoid falling.

"The Senapati is a fool!" Chanakya felt his head spinning as they went down in slow spiralling circles. "He does not understand the time to move is now, when the elections approach."

"There are three contenders, Grand Master," Prajapati said. "It is chaos there. I have seen it with my own eyes. If we attack now, no one will stand against us."

Chanakya nodded slowly. "Let the Senapati take his time. When the time comes, I will force the invasion."

"What about the Buddhist?" Nikumbh asked. "How much time will he take to gather the information necessary for the attack?"

Chanakya laughed but stopped abruptly when he realized that it sounded like the babbling of a baby from his toothless mouth. "Let the Buddhist bring information or not," he said. "We already have all the information we need. We know all the rivers in and out of their country, their forts, their best defensive positions, their towns and cities, the kinds of weapons they use, and more. And our Brothers who ventured into their territory recently have brought us all we need to know about the changing political situation."

Behind him, Prajapati appeared confused. "But how? We have never invaded Kalinga. How do we know so much about them?"

Chanakya chuckled. "We almost did."

Nikumbh laughed. "We almost invaded Kalinga decades ago," he recalled. "You were a mere boy then. I was one of the spies sent to the frontlines to learn about the country. Rivers, hills and roads do not change much in fifty years, do they?"

Prajapati looked at them both in amazement. They had reached the tunnels below the palace, and torches adorned the walls on both sides. The yellow light flickered on their faces as well as the rough walls. "Did Great Chandragupta invade Kalinga then?" he asked, awestruck as realization dawned upon him.

"As I said," Chankya muttered as they moved along the tunnel towards the Order's Headquarters, "he almost did..."

FIFTY YEARS AGO.

'The bigger an army, the slower it marches,' Generals of yore had famously stated. I had experienced it first hand, time and again and seen it with my own eyes. The soldiers would wake at different hours, each troop governed by the amount of discipline its Captain demanded. The tents were huge, requiring at least two *prahars* to set up and two more to remove the next morning. The elephants, though extremely powerful beasts, were as lazy and getting them to rise from their slumber each morning was a tedious and time consuming task. When we marched with our meagre army from Taxila to Junagarh, almost six hundred *kos* away, it had taken a month. Marching from Patliputra to Kalinga had taken longer.

Around us were rolling hills covered with waist high grass, and no trees as far as the eye could see. The Daya River, which formed the Eastern boundary of our new Mauryan Samrajya, lay a few *kos* behind us. We were barely fifty *kos* from the border, yet it felt like we had marched to the end of civilization itself. This region was called Dhauli, barren grasslands inhabited only by small tribes of hunter-gatherers and Nagas. We had seen no villages since crossing the river. But it was not these barren grasslands we were interested in, but what lay beyond.

"I see you are awake, Guru."

It took me some time to recognize the voice. I washed my face, splashing water from the large brass vessel outside my tent. Since the end of the Nanda Rajya, almost everyone had taken to addressing me as Guru. When the battle for the city had subsided, Chandragupta and all of us had gathered in the town square, where he had made his great speech. *You are hereby liberated!* he had declared to the people. *I shall be your new Samrat and govern with the principles of efficiency, compassion and humility*. He had taken my hand and raised it up into the air. *Guided by my Guru, who is a guru not just to me but our entire nation*. Word had spread, the common folk taking his words literally.

"The Samrat is looking for you."

I recognized him as Sunga, a Kshatriya youth Chandragupta had found during the march to Patliputra and made a Captain. "It is against his nature to disturb me thus early, when I perform my meditation. Surely it must be something important." I wiped the contours of my face.

The young and muscular man nodded. "It is the scouts. One of their groups is riding towards us from the east. He wants you to be there when they make camp, to learn what they have seen."

"Then it seems I have no business meditating today." I raised my hands above my head and tied my hair into a tight knot.

Sunga nodded, gesturing for me to follow him through the dirty, noisy surroundings of the army camp. The air carried an amalgam of smells, from horseshit to burnt meat in the kitchens where the cooks were preparing the morning meal for the men. The army was a disorganized mass of men held together by the weak order and discipline we were able to impose.

The only disciplined units were those of the cavalry. The horses were a rare breed, intelligent and noble, and the riders felt superior in mounting them. They also possessed the desire to distinguish themselves from common foot soldiers. Giving a man a cavalry rank was a trick Chandragupta had used well, raising common soldiers to become cavalrymen through promotion. The result was that we could count on the cavalry corps to carry out important missions when on the march. Missions like scouting ahead of a slow, stubborn army.

We had sent out the scouts, dividing our four-thousand cavalry into six distinct units. The scouts went in six directions across the grasslands, and beyond, to bring back information. For beyond lay Kalinga, the 'land of sailors', the last Mahajanpada of our subcontinent.

Following Chandragupta's coronation in Patliputra, we did not have had to think long and hard as to what our next steps were. It was obvious what needed to be done. If we wished to achieve our aim of *Akhanda Bharat*, we had to move quickly. Our armies were riding high on a wave of confidence after the great victory over Patliputra. I wanted to ensure their high enthusiasm helped me achieve two or three more victories before it subsided.

I had wasted no time in sending royal decrees to all the independent Rajyas left in the subcontinent. Those that were part of the Nanda Samrajya were already ours, secured through the support of the Ancient Brahminical Order, in the tunnels below the city. Those that were not, lay mainly to the south of the Narmada. The small Rajas were quick to send back replies with fast riders, accepting our leadership and assuring us of their tribute. The North was ours, but the stubborn kingdoms of the Far South refused to acknowledge us, too proud in their high and mighty ways. A Southern War had to be undertaken, but before that we had to secure the East.

Kalinga had, on paper, long been a vassal of the Nandas. The same arrangement carried on when we took over. In return for tribute, the Nandas left them alone. But on close inspection, I found the Kalingans paid tribute only on their earnings through trade on land. The Kalingans were seafarers. The sea was their goldmine and we received no part of its bounty. Furthermore, they still governed themselves as a Mahajanpada, with the common folks electing their rulers even in this day and age. Kalinga was a cancer that had to be uprooted. So I sent them an order to surrender. As I had expected, the young, headstrong and newly-elected Governor Navin, had ignored my letter, giving us a strong *casus belli* to attack.

The Nandas had never been able to subdue the Great Mahajanpada of Kalinga. Nor had they ever tried. Whether they were afraid of the strong-headed seafarers or just too dull witted to understand the huge wealth that was being hidden from them, I do not know. But the fact remains that when I had decided to invade Kalinga as our first step after capturing Patliputra, I had to start with intelligence gathering. Nothing at all was known about the mysterious land in the beautiful delta region. So I had sent spies to gather information, and waited till we knew enough to attack. As we marched against them today, I was still unsure that we knew enough.

"Look, the scouts are returning!" Sunga pointed as we walked through the camp towards Chandragupta's tent.

My head turned expectantly. We watched the small group of horsemen emerge from the tree line and gallop towards us lazily, their mounts tired by their labours. Their strides slowed until, by the time the Captain had reached the first tents, his horse was walking.

"What news do you bring?" I asked him, a rugged middle-aged man whose eyes looked like they had seen a dozen battles.

He took his time to answer. He descending from the back of his mount as stable boys ran to catch the reins tossed to them. "Prime Minister!" he said in surprise. "Our foray has been most successful. We scouted the location of each Kalingan army fort from here to the Eastern Sea. I can assure you that I can lead our army right to the capital of Kalinga without one enemy patrol spotting us."

"If what you say is true," I said, "you are worthy of receiving a reward."

The Captain bowed. "I thank you for choosing me for this scouting expedition, for my old eyes saw today, what I would never have seen elsewhere."

"What is it that you saw that was so wonderful?" I asked, observing the look of wonder on his swarthy face.

"I felt like Lord Hanuman must have done on seeing Lanka for the first time," the Captain said.

"Don't speak in riddles man, for now is not the time."

"Gold, Prime Minister!" the man breathed. "Never in my life have I seen so much gold! In the town we scouted, I saw a golden circlet on each man's arm. And the women...heavy necklaces and bangles, dangling earrings, shining *kadas* on their ankles..."

"And why does it cause you such delight since the gold does not belong to you?"

The voice spoke from behind me. I turned. Chandragupta stood with his scabbard slung across his back. He was barechested, and droplets of water dripped onto his torso from his wet hair.

The Captain immediately snapped to attention, visibly awed by the appearance of the Samrat. I admired the effect Chandragupta had on his soldiers. It was one of the things that made him a natural ruler.

He surveyed the soldier from head to toe, like an eagle scanning the land for prey. "How much did you take?" he asked calmly, every syllable causing the meagre hair on the Captain's scalp to rise.

The Captain bowed low, his teeth clenched. He pulled out the pouch that hung from his waist. It clunked of metal.

Holding it in his upturned palms, he brought it forward, offering it to his Emperor. Chandragupta picked it up and tossed it to me. I caught it awkwardly. The pouch felt heavier than I had expected. I opened it to reveal shimmering, golden coins.

"From a caravan outside the village we surveyed." The Captain spoke slowly, his voice riddled with shame. "My soldiers were tempted. I was tempted."

Chandragupta pulled off the golden circlet he wore on his left wrist and tossed it to the Captain, who caught it uneasily. "Make sure this is the only gold you and the men of your unit take from this campaign," he said, his eyes fixed on the man's face, "or I will cut off the hand that holds that ornament."

The Captain nodded silently and backed away. Chandragupta dismissed him with a wave of his hand. "Go to your tent. Rest. When you wake, tell us everything you saw."

When the Captain had gone, I walked with Chandragupta back to his tent and showed him one of the Kalingan coins from the pouch. It gleamed bright in my hand. "Solid gold," I said, tossing it to him. "Not even a trace of any other metal. If such coins are found on the roads of Kalinga, imagine what we will find in their treasuries."

"We have come a long way, Guru," Chandragupta said, holding the gold coin up so that it sparkled in the sunlight.

"You are a scion of the Ajatshatru dynasty," I told him. "You are bound to do great things."

Chandragupta smiled, flipping the Kalingan coin. I looked at my pupil and felt a strange sense of joy. Kalinga would be merely the first conquest. Then we would march south. I was so near my goal now. Soon, the lands of the Aryas would be united and no power in the world could stop us.

My thoughts were disturbed by a sudden commotion and shouting outside the tent. Chandragupta was the first to get to his feet. "What in the God's name?" he demanded, lunging for his scabbard. "Are we being attacked?"

"I do not think so," I said, standing up. The sounds were of our own men shouting. I drew aside the fabric of the tent and stepped out. Chandragupta followed, sword in hand. A group of our men were gathered near the stables.

"What is it?" Chandragupta's loud shout immediately contained the noise.

The men turned towards us slowly. Sunga was standing in the centre, holding a long roll of parchment. Another man stood in front of him, but I had never seen him before. Nor was he in warrior garb. Instead, he wore a long blue tunic, like the ones I had seen worn by the Greeks. But this man was no Greek. He was fair and his rugged face left no doubt that he was a Kshatriya.

"We have a messenger here, my Samrat," Sunga said, raising the scroll in his hands. "From the North, he says."

Chandragupta looked at me. "Who can it be?"

"Let us find out."

Sunga gave a shrill whistle and tossed the roll of parchment to one of his men, who caught it and ran towards us, bowed and handed it over to me. As I took it, I saw that it was yellowed and its sides were tattered, which meant it had been on the road for some days. The red seal embossed on the ribbon was one I had seen only once in my life, and had hoped never to see again.

"This is the symbol of Baselius Alexander," I said, looking sideways at Chandragupta. I knew he had recognized the seal as well.

"Sunga, you and the messenger come to my tent," Chandragupta ordered.

I looked at him and nodded. There was no point in reading the message in the open and causing panic. The seal meant it contained bad news.

"What are you looking at? Disperse!" I heard Sunga order the men as we walked back to the tent.

Chandragupta held the flap aside for me to enter. Once we were inside, he took me by the shoulders. "Guru, it is impossible! Baselius Alexander passed away due to illness in Faras. Your own spies brought the news to us not six new moons ago. There is no way he could have sent this missive to us."

"I do not think it has been sent by him," I agreed.

"Then who?" Chandragupta's fingers tightened on my shoulders.

I forced away his grip and sat down on the cotton bales, suddenly realizing that my heartbeat had started to gallop. "There is only one way to find out," I said.

Sunga entered, dragging the messenger by the arm. Now, at close quarters, we could see him clearly. There was no doubt he wore Greek garb, for no one in our lands wore those pointed, bronze boots. His face was smeared with dust, no doubt by long and constant riding.

"Who sent you?" Chandragupta asked.

The man chuckled, looked to his left and spit on the floor. Immediately, Sunga's hand hit him on the back of his head. The man gave a grunt and fell to his knees. "The Samrat asked you a question, fool!" Sunga hissed. "Answer!"

I unrolled the parchment and ceremonial letters, written carefully in a rich ink for the letters had not faded even after many days of braving the sun and wind.

Chandragupta stared at the man and asked in the cold voice his men feared, "From where do you come?"

The messenger remained on his knees, one wary eye on the figure of Sunga standing over him. "I come from the North," he said. "From beyond the Sapt Sindhu."

Chandragupta looked at me, noticing my eyes moving over the scroll. "Who has sent this?" he asked.

I did not answer for I simply could not believe what I read.

"Guru?" Chandragupta raised his eyebrows.

"The man speaks the truth," I finally said. "He does indeed come from beyond our lands."

"What does the letter say?"

"That a great Greek army has amassed at our borders, led by the great Seleucus Nicator, Diadochi of the East, foremost heir of Alexander the Great."

"So the Greeks are back?" Chandragupta asked, surprised. "What else?"

"It orders us to withdraw all our armies from all lands to the west of the Beas River."

Chandragupta clenched his fists. "But there lies Taxila, our home! The Greeks cannot threaten us in this way!"

"The letter was not sent by the Greeks," I said slowly, placing it on the desk for Chandragupta to see. The official name was scribbled neatly at the bottom: *Sent by the Prime Minister of Maharaja Malayketu of Paurava.*

"That treacherous swine!" Chandragupta trembled with rage. "We thought he was our friend! We fought together in the campaign. First, he betrayed me by leaving our camp without informing us. And now, when we have captured Patliputra, he dares to stab us in the back?"

"It would appear that Maharaja Malayketu, as he fashions himself, is the least of our problems," I sighed, pointing to the bottom of the letter. There lay a hastily scribbled signature below the line that I recognized at first glance: *Amatya Rakshasa*

6
RADHAGUPTA:
THE DECEPTION OF ENEMIES

KALINGA, 263 BC

The woman moved like wildfire, her sword flashed like lightning. At times it was difficult to say which moved faster. Radhagupta had been watching her practice for the better part of an hour, yet he had still had not caught the colour of the sword's hilt, or the number of bangles she wore, which clinked with every move of her right hand. She seemed to have noticed him watching though, for she glanced in his direction at intervals, as if to see whether he was still there. Radhagupta did not move an inch.

They were in the courtyard of the Dantapura palace, the seat of the Late Governor of Kalinga. Radhagupta stood in the corridor that led away from the throne room to the gates, while she was in the wide open space between the two wings of the building. The air felt cool and fresh as the sun prepared to set; the heat of the day long past. At first, the woman paid him no heed, ignoring his unflinching stare, but Radhagupta knew that if he stood there unabashedly for a length of time, she, like any woman, would definitely budge.

And indeed she did. She stopped moving and looked at him with finality. Radhagupta looked away immediately but there was no doubt she was now walking towards him.

When she did reach him, she found him leaning against one of the wooden pillars that held up the roof, his arms folded.

"Were you watching me?" Her tone was sharp and direct, without any hint of small talk. The sword she carried remained unsheathed.

Radhagupta noticed that its handle was made of black iron. "It seems you do not waste time with your words, just as you do not with your sword," he said, bowing courteously.

"And it seems you do not with your eyes," she retorted, playfully moving her sword through the air, "for they remained fixed as soon as you caught sight of me."

"May I say that you handle your blade exceptionally well?" Radhagupta settled back against the pillar.

"Should not we all?" She sheathed the sword in its scabbard with an air of finality. "In this treacherous world, it is the only true friend we can really count on."

"You choose a peculiar place to practice."

The woman laughed mockingly. "Only place in the city where no one gawks to see a woman with a sword. Or so I thought till now."

"Are the people in this palace blind?" Radhagupta laughed. "How can one not look when one sees a beautiful woman performing a man's art so well?"

"The truth is that here in the palace, they are afraid of me." The woman raised her eyes to look directly into his face. "You see, I have worked here under Governor Navin for almost a decade as his right hand."

"I know who you are, Lady Karuvaki," Radhagupta said. "It is why I was watching you."

Karuvaki looked amused. "But I do not know who you are, Brahmin."

"You may not know my face," Radhagupta told her, "but you surely know my name. I am called Radhagupta."

That was enough for her manner to change abruptly. "If you are the man called Radhagupta, we should not be having this conversation," Karuvaki scoffed as she turned to walk away,

"Wait!" Radhagupta was quick to block her way. "I have been trying to see you for many days now, but your officials tell me that you will not see me."

"If they have told you that I do not want to see you, then why do you think that watching me practice like a hungry dog will change my mind?"

"You do not do me justice," Radhagupta said. "While watching you, all I did was admire your courage and skill. No base thought entered my mind."

"Whatever you wish to ask of me, the answer is no," Karuvaki said angrily. "You know I cannot talk to you. As Minister to the Late Governor Navin, I am honour bound to support his son in the elections. I cannot converse with his opponent's right hand."

"If you do not, My Lady, the Late Governor's son will lose an opportunity, something he cannot afford to do, especially in the time of elections."

Karuvaki glanced around to see if there were any onlookers. "Not here," she said softly. "Follow me at a distance. We shall talk where nobody can see us."

Radhagupta nodded and watched her walk along the corridor and then turn left to go up a staircase. He waited till she was well ahead and then followed. Karuvaki led him up one level and then another till they emerged onto the terrace of the palace. Radhagupta admired the view of the palace gardens, where the trees surrounding the palace rose to meet them. Colourful birds flew around, chirping. "Quite a romantic place for such a unromantic discussion," he said, smiling.

"This way we will have a cover," Karuvaki told him. "No one would doubt a couple was having a rendezvous in this beautiful place."

"You Kalingans are quite the liberal lot," Radhagupta observed. "From where I come, such rendezvous would be frowned upon."

"Are you going to speak, or just flirt?" Karuvaki asked. Irritated by such trivia.

Radhagupta nodded. "I am here to talk to you about the day the candidates declared themselves. Did you see us coming?"

Karuvaki's face flushed as blood rushed up into her fair cheeks. "No. In fact, General Bheema was the only opponent we imagined would stand against us. But alas, it appears the Gods had something else in mind."

"But it is not the Gods who decide these elections, is it? It is the people."

Karuvaki shook her head. "I never took your master for a political person. He's a foreigner, just like you. How many years has he lived here... three...four?"

"He has been here long enough, if that's what you ask." Radhagupta folded his arms.

"And after *enough* years, he desires to be Governor of Kalinga?"

Radhagupta smiled and shook his head. "He does not. That's why I am here."

"Oh you sly bald devil." Karuvaki pursed her lips. "You are here to make a deal, are you not?"

"Devdatta is a merchant at heart, My Lady. All he wants is to have friends in high places."

"And what does he want those friends to do for him?" Karuvaki asked curtly. "Grease his loins while he penetrates our holy motherland with his business deals?"

"I know you do not think highly of his smuggling raids," replied Radhagupta. "But you forget your Late Governor owes him much goodwill for his work in bringing essential goods to your ports; something no one else could do."

"The Late Governor is dead," Karuvaki snapped. "Navin and I did not see eye to eye on many occasions. The fate of your master was one of them. Navin wished to cut a deal with him and make him the State's exclusive trader. I refused. Kalinga's official face to the world could not be that of a smuggler. Navin died soon after."

"I know," Radhagupta nodded. "And that is precisely why I advised him to contest the elections."

"So it was you," Karuvaki whispered. "You knew that after Navin's death, his son would stand in his stead."

"And I knew you controlled his son."

"And that I would never give Devdatta what he wanted."

"So I made him stand against you, Karuvaki." Radhagupta moved a step closer.

She laughed. "What happened to My Lady?"

Radhagupta stopped when he was just a step from her beautiful face. "Now you listen to me closely," he murmured. "Governor Navin ruled Kalinga for half a century. Before him, his father was Governor, and before that, his grandfather. Navin's family has ruled these lands for centuries. The people want change. And Devdatta did one hell of a job in his declaration speech at the docks that day, presenting himself as that change."

"Did he?" Karuvaki wondered. "He advocates peace with the Mauryans. Any wise man would stand for the same. We have the same stand as he as Navin Kumar clearly said in his speech."

"The problem is nobody in the crowd was listening," Radhagupta pointed out. "Navin Kumar is a child, and you Kalingans are a country of sailors. The Late Navin was a famed pirate in his youth, his forefathers were even fiercer ones. It is a shame Navin did not give importance to teaching the ways of the sea to his only son."

"I know the people do not look up to Navin's son as a leader." Karuvaki pursed her lips. "But they do look up to me."

'Who is, again, not a sailor."

"I am a fisherman's daughter."

"But one who has not been on a boat in the past decade," Radhagupta stated. Karuvaki flushed again.

"Accept it or not, that day, Devdatta won the respect of the merchant class. He won it fair and square, by advocating a policy that would benefit them."

Karuvaki's eyes glittered in anger. "Yes, some merchants will follow him for that purpose. But what of our nobles? The nobility carry more votes than the commoners. The nobles will never follow a foreigner."

"And that will result in a hung House," Radhagupta noted, walking away towards the edge of the terrace."

"We will take our chances." Karuvaki held her ground.

"The first rule of politics is not to take chances," Radhagupta observed. "Why divide your votes when you can get the support of both the nobles and the merchants?"

Karuvaki looked at him directly. "I assume you have a proposition?"

"Indeed, I do." Radhagupta walked back to her. "It is simple really. In the upcoming rally, declare Navin Kumar's admiration for Devdatta, and acknowledge the immense contribution he has made to Kalinga."

"And if I do that, what will your master give us?"

"He will respond in kind and appeal to his followers to stand behind the governing family of Kalinga."

Karuvaki's face gave no clue to her thoughts. Radhagupta admired her ability not to show her emotions on her face. No doubt, her years as an Ambassador had helped her cultivate the art. "What if I say no?" she asked finally.

"Then we part never to meet again," Radhagupta shrugged. "After a hung House, there will be a re-election. Messy things re-elections. If Kalingan elections are known to be bloody, imagine what re-elections would be! Is that truly what you want for your country?"

Karuvaki raised her chin. "And if your master betrays his word?" she asked.

"I admire how you are straight about matters of importance," Radhagupta said, bowing. "I give you my word and swear upon my caste, that if you keep your end of the bargain, Devdatta will step down and join your camp. Where I come from, a Brahmin never breaks his vow."

"Devdatta is not a Brahmin, is he?"

"Which is why it is I who stands before you." Radhagupta said. "You would never trust my master, but you can trust me, Karuvaki. We are not too different, you and I. We do what needs to be done, but we have values."

"I have heard you." Karuvaki nodded. "Now let us part ways."

"When shall I have your answer?" Radhagupta asked.

"On the day of the speech in Dantapura." Karuvaki smiled sweetly and walked away.

***

When Radhagupta emerged from the palace, he saw a large and familiar man standing with his back against a tree, staring intently at the palace gates. When he saw Radhagupta walking towards the gates, the man stood up straight and went towards him. As Radhagupta stepped out, the man stood blocking his path.

"A pleasant surprise, General Bheema," Radhagupta said, bowing. "I had not expected to see you here."

"But I had expected to see you," the corpulent man grinned. "What were you doing inside, if I may ask?"

"I'm here to meet an official," Radhagupta said calmly. Whatever it was the General wanted, Radhagupta knew it could not be good.

"Did that official have a nice ass?"

Radhagupta opened his mouth to answer, but the General placed a strong arm on his shoulder and pressed his shoulder blade, to the point of pain, before releasing his grip. "We have a saying in the army," the General said bluntly, "Never toy with a prey you do not wish to kill."

"I do not see how that applies here." Radhagupta held onto his customary smile.

"Oh it does not," the General replied, showing his teeth. "But I can make it apply."

Radhagupta moved to one side. "I am not intimidated by subtle threats. So if you have anything to say to me, say it, else it is time I was on my way."

"Oh, I shall say it," the General laughed. "I know your kind very well, Brahmin. You strut about brandishing your bald heads, thinking you hold true power. I am here to tell you that you do not."

Radhagupta shrugged. "Well, they do say that the quill is mightier than the sword."

The General raised his eyebrows. "Only while the sword is sheathed. And if you get in my way Brahmin, I will draw it before you can even beg for forgiveness."

Radhagupta bowed, "General, the last I heard you were advocating war against the Mauryas, while Devdatta preaches the opposite. So I can hardly say we are in each other's way."

"The support of the merchants was mine to wield," the General snarled. "Your master took it away from me that day in Dantapura."

"It was fate," Radhagupta shrugged. "Both of you were attacked, both survived. It is not my fault the merchants prefer Devdatta's policies."

"But it is your fault your master did not die that day during the speeches." There was a strange gleam in the General's eyes. "It is you who watches over him, who tells him what to say, how to say it; the one who schemes against his enemies like they were your own."

"Devdatta is an illustrious person," I remarked. "I am but his humble advisor."

"Keep doing what you are and you shall be his dead advisor." The General held up a forefinger for effect. "I am warning you, Brahmin."

"I do what needs to be done."

"Then listen to me closely." The General bent forward and pulled him into a hug. Radhagupta felt the strong arms on his back press a little harder than was required. "You stole the merchants from me. It was a mistake but I forgive you. Now, before the next speeches, I shall take back the favour of the merchants. And if you make another mistake, I will not be so gentle."

Radhagupta gave him a smile. "I shall keep that in mind."

"Good." The General walked away, whistling.

Radhagupta sighed and went his own way.

***

It was nearly evening when he reached the docks. The eastern sky was bathed in orange and the seagulls had returned landwards, their flocks appearing black against the bright-hued sky. Devdatta was waiting for him in the stern of his ship.

"You have done well," he said after listening to all that Radhagupta had to say. "So why do you look so gloomy?"

"The General's words..." Radhagupta murmured, looking out to sea. "It does not make any sense. How can he take back the favor of the merchants?"

"Perhaps he will try to kill me." Devdatta shrugged. "We will double the guard. It is not so easy to send me heavenwards, my friend."

Radhagupta rubbed his chin ruminatively. "The General's threat had something sinister to it. He is planning something."

"I doubt that thick head could plan anything." Devdatta laughed, pouring wine for both of them.

"I think he had someone behind him," Radhagupta remarked thoughtfully. "Someone we have already met."

"The Order? Do you think your old friends from the Mauryan lands support his claim?"

Radhagupta nodded. "That would make the most sense. I feel that in a way all this is my fault."

"Hey, I do not hold it against you that you lied to me," Devdatta said. "I would have done the same in your place. You came to Kalinga, just as I did, to escape the past. It is not wrong to change your name and history. That is the whole purpose of starting a new life."

"I feel they are after you, because of me," Radhagupta sighed.

"Don't be so hard on yourself." Devdatta placed an arm on Radhagupta's shoulder. "Besides, whatever it is, old friend, we can handle it." Devdatta handed over a wine goblet.

Radhagupta raised his goblet. "To your success."

"To our's," Devdatta corrected, and drank deeply. "Now take my advice and go home to your wife, Radhagupta."

"My wife?"

"Are you drunk already?" Devdatta laughed, patting him on the shoulder. "You live with your wife in the city, don't you?"

Radhagupta nodded silently.

"Then go to her. Spend the night with her. You deserve some rest."

Radhagupta nodded again and put the goblet down.

***

His house was modest. Built of wood, it stood just across the city square. It was dark by the time he reached it. Devi was waiting for him at the door.

"What happened?" she asked as soon as she opened the door.

"We must talk." Radhagupta put his cloth bag down in a corner against the wall, then looked into the inner rooms.

"They fell asleep," Devi told him. "Tissa has gone into the city, to buy some food for the morrow."

Radhagupta sat down. "Now listen to me," he said urgently. "It is no longer safe for you here. You need to get out of the city."

"Why?" Devi asked, surprised.

Radhagupta sighed. "This election business is getting dangerous. The General threatened me in the open today."

"We always knew it would be dangerous," Devi reminded him. "Yet we decided it was worth it, that it was our only way to beat Chanakya."

To beat Chanakya? Radhagupta looked at her. Even in a simple cotton saree, without ornaments, she looked beautiful. She had grown a little plump since they had come to the city, but he could see why the Samrat had fallen in love with her. "Winning the elections is just the first step," he told her. "We won't be able to beat Chankya if we are not alive after it."

The point was taken. "What is it you propose?" she asked.

Radhagupta sighed. They have had this discussion before and she had not taken it well. He was sure it would be no different now. "You should take the children to your father," he said, waiting for the explosion. To his surprise, it did not come.

"You are right." She looked down at the ground. "If these elections are really going to turn bloody, this is not a safe place for them."

Radhagupta placed a hand on her shoulder. "I am glad you see it like it is, My Lady," he said.

"But *I* am staying."

"What?" Radhagupta looked at her. Surely he had not heard correctly?

"I have told you before and I tell you now, I will not run to my father." She looked him in the eye. "This is my battle. It always has been. He never looked for me."

"Devi, your father thinks you are dead."

"That does not forgive his lack of interest in searching for me."

"You have become a spiteful creature since we came here," Radhagupta said regretfully. "But you do not have a choice now. The children are barely five years old. They need a ward."

Devi stared out of the window into the street. Suddenly, light twinkled in her eyes. "He can take them," she said.

Radhagupta followed her gaze. In the street, a lone and tall figure was walking towards their house, muscular arms carrying sacks, filled no doubt with items from the market. He had to agree that Tissa had grown up quickly.

"His life is in danger too," Devi muttered. "And two young ones travelling through the Mauryan wilderness with their older brother will not raise any suspicions."

Radhagupta kept looking at his nephew, who was now almost at the house. "I still see him as the small child I brought with me from Taxila years ago," he sighed. Devi had a point he had to agree.

"When my father learns about us, he can send help here." Devi nodded. "I will not go to him like a helpless damsel in distress. I will ride back victorious."

Radhagupta smiled. "Still filled with the same fire... It's decided then."

"We are sending three heirs to the Patliputra throne out into the world alone," Devi murmured, getting up to go and open the door for Tissa. "What dark times have come upon us."

"Dark times indeed, Devi, dark times,' Radhagupta agreed as he too, got to his feet, wondering how to break the news to Tissa.

7

KANAKDATTTA:
REVELATIONS OF THE WORST KIND

───────────~───────────

PATLIPUTRA, 263 BC

Their horses rode along the dusty road like bolts of lightning tearing through the clouds of dust their mounts left behind as they galloped forward. They rode without exchanging a word. On the horizon in front of them were the countless lights of Patliputra, clustered below the stars like shining jewels adorning the night sky. The sight was mesmerizing but none of the riders stopped as they passed the small hillock which presented the spectacular view, for they were carrying important news.

Kanakdatta led the way. His two companions, Daruman and Hanuman, followed on either side, trying to keep up. Dressed in full armour, they came directly from the camp in the South, along the Daya River. They had been riding for three days because there was no time to lose.

Kanakdatta pulled on his reins and slowed his beast as they approached the walls of the city. The others did the same. Breaking formation, they passed the southern bridge over the Ganga in a line, one after the other. They could see the guards atop the city walls as tiny moving lights, no doubt coming from the torches they carried. The passage to the southern gate was alight with burning torches on wooden columns on both sides of the road. The high frontage of the enormous iron gate across the moat was now visible to them. Made in a single casting, it had been fashioned with protruding spikes on the outside to discourage attacks by man or elephants. It appeared one with the darkness of the night sky as Kanakdatta and his companions stopped at the moat that separated them from the city.

"Who goes there?" a loud voice asked from above.

Kanakdatta raised his head and scanned the area above the gates. His heavy helmet made it difficult to see clearly. Finally, he caught sight of a sentry carrying a flaming torch just above them.

"I am Kanakdatta, The Serpent, Spymaster of the Samrajya, here to see the Samrat, so let us in."

The man on the battlements watched them for some time, considering the request. "There has been no message the Spymaster will be visiting the city," he declared.

Kanakdatta was irritated by this stubbornness. He kicked his horse and rode ahead of his companions, to the point where the embankment fell into the deep moat below. "I carry important news," he said angrily. "I come with the speed of the wind to inform the Samrat."

The sentry waited, uncertain till another gob of light appeared. "Spymaster!" the other man said loudly, "I know you by face. Pray show yourself, so we can be sure."

Raising both hands, Kanakdatta lifted the helmet off his head. He turned his horse and rode back to a flaming torch along the road, where the light fell on his face. He faced the battlements again, wondering where he had heard the second sentry's voice before.

"It is you for sure, Buddhist!" the sentry declared. "You may enter."

This time Kanakdatta recognized the voice. It belonged to a man called Nikumbh, one of the Prime Minister's closest aides. That man carried nothing but spite for him. The three horsemen watched as lights moved atop the walls. However, the gate did not budge. The men dropped a wooden ladder over the battlements, positioning it over the moat so one could climb it to cross the moat and get to the walls.

"What is the meaning of this?" Kanakdatta asked angrily, "Open the gates! Our horses need food and rest."

"I am sorry Buddhist, but your horses will have to wait," Nikumbh said from the top without any sign of remorse. "We have strict orders the gates are not to be opened at night for anyone."

Kanakdatta clenched his teeth and cursed. He jumped off his horse and began removing his armour. The ladder appeared flimsy and his heavy armour would break it for sure. Behind him, his companions did the same. Kanakdatta placed his heavy chestplate and thigh guards on his horse's back. Only in his cotton clothing, he reached for the ladder and began to climb. His protruding stomach was a deterrent, but Kanakdatta managed the climb deftly, quickly reaching the walls. The sentry on the wall reached out a hand and pulled him onto the walls. As soon as he stepped on the elevated wooden platform, he saw Nikumbh gesture for the ladder to be pulled up. Kanakdatta's two companions looked up, confused.

"My companions come with me," Kanakdatta said loudly. "Lower the ladder."

"No Buddhist." Nikumbh stood tall in-front of him. "I know you by face, but I don't know them."

"I can vouch for them," Kanakdatta said, irritated. "They are my men."

Nikumbh shrugged. "They must wait till morning. This is how we secure the city in times of coming war."

"I bring urgent news of the war for the Samrat," Kanakdatta pressed.

"One man is enough to carry news." Nikumbh whistled and guards appeared below, on the ground inside the gates. "Take him to the Samrat," he ordered.

The soldiers nodded. Kanakdatta used the stone stairs to descend. "Follow me," the Captain grunted as he set off along the street.

"Where are you going?" Kanakdatta asked, pointing. "The palace is in that direction."

"Are you here to see the Samrat or not?" The man spat on the ground disinterestedly.

"Aye," Kanakdatta nodded.

"You will not find the Samrat in the palace at this hour," the Captain said, gesturing him on.

Kanakdatta gave up and followed.

***

The Hall of Pleasures had been built beside the Ganges River, which flowed behind the palace. As they approached, Kanakdatta could smell perfume and sweet oils, and hear the giggling of women. The guards halted at the arched entrance and the Captain declared, "We are not permitted beyond this point. From here you go alone."

Kanakdatta nodded and walked in under the arch. There were creepers with sweet smelling blossoms that slept in the night, on both sides. He crossed the small walkway to enter the hall, which was full of people. A podium had been constructed on the river bank, atop which stood a marble pavilion. He could see women everywhere, some clothed, others only in their inner garments, talking to each other. The whole place was bathed in moonlight. A spiral stairway led up to the lofty pavilion.

Many eyes watched Kanakdatta as he climbed up. His mind registered that these were the women of the harem and that he was setting foot in an area that no man but the Samrat was usually permitted to enter. This was the Samrat's personal area. The women on the upper level were dressed even more skimpily and turned away as Kanakdatta's large figure appeared at the top of the spiral stairway. Some ran to the side with little shrieks of dismay while others jumped into the water with sparkling splashes and laughter. Kanakdatta paid them no heed. His eyes searched for the one he had come to see.

The commotion caused those in the pavilion to turn to see what the noise was about. Between the pillars that held up the domed ceiling, Kanakdatta caught sight of his friend. "Asoka!" he called, to get his attention.

The Samrat's dreamy eyes did not register the call. It did not take long for Kanakdatta to climb up and get a clearer view of his supine friend. Asoka's eyes were red rimmed and hazy. There was the distinct smell of wine in the air, as well as another peculiar odour. Two women sat beside the Samrat, massaging his shoulders, giggling, and touching him in places they should not.

"Asoka!" Kanakdatta called loudly above the noise.

This time the Samrat opened his eyes. It took a while for recognition to arise in his eyes. "Kanaka?" he finally said in surprise.

As the two women moved away, Kanakdatta noticed a smoking pot lying to the side and realized the strange smell in the air was opium. "What is all this, Asoka?" he asked, looking around in surprise.

"You….you caught me unawares." Asoka's voice rasped. "I did not know you were coming tonight."

"Opium? Wine? Where is Asandhi, your wife?'

For a moment, traces of guilt crossed Asoka's face before turning into lines of anger. He stumbled to his feet. "Who are you to ask me anything?" he demanded loudly. "And why are you here?"

"I bring news," Kanakdatta said, hiding his mortification. "But are you in a state to hear it?"

"And who says I am not?" Asoka stepped forward, and suddenly sank to the ground. One of the two women ran to him, and supported him in her arms.

"You make your own case." Kanakdatta folded his arms. "What in the world is all this? Who taught you?"

Asoka pulled himself to a sitting position with an arm around the woman's shoulders. "Do not look at me like that, Kanaka. These are my women. This is my palace. I am the Samrat."

"Who showed you all this?" Kanakdatta looked around again. "Was it the women of your harem? Does your wife know?"

"Silence!" Asoka shouted angrily. Pushing away the women supporting him, he slowly rose and stood rocking back and forth in the breeze that blew off the river. "Do not speak to me like that."

"Then how should I talk to you?" asked Kanakdatta.

"Tell me your news and leave," Asoka snapped.

"This is all the Prime Minister's doing!" Kanakdatta held his ground. "Don't you see Asoka? He is making you a prey to the baser vices so that actual power rests in his hands. He is using you."

"Silence!" Asoka yelled, his bloodshot eyes gleaming furiously.

Kanakdatta realized that what he had said had not registered in Asoka's drugged brain.

"State your news," Asoka muttered.

Kanakdatta sighed. There was little he could do while Asoka was not in a clear frame of mind. "I sent my spies to Kalinga to gather news, as the Prime Minister asked. You will not believe who they saw while infiltrating the Kalingan capital."

"Who?" Asoka murmured, not really interested.

"Devi,"

"What!" Asoka's manner suddenly changed. He backed up and collapsed onto a chair like a rag doll. Kanakdatta stepped forward, worried he had hurt himself in the earlier fall.

"It can't be true," Asoka sighed, his head moving from side to side in a flowing cadence.

"My men saw her with their own eyes, Asoka. They brought me the news, and I came immediately."

"We saw her burnt body with our own eyes, Kanaka," Asoka whimpered.

Kanakdatta noticed there were tears in Asoka's eyes. "My lead man knows what they saw. He knows her face as he has been in my service since my days in Vidishanagri."

"How can it be, Kanaka?" Tears trickled down Asoka's cheek and fell on the silken cushions, forming a wet spot.

Kanakdatta walked forward and placed his hand on his friend's shoulder.

Suddenly, Asoka flinched and pushed the arm away. Kanakdatta was taken aback. "You did not see her yourself, did you?" Asoka asked, his face suddenly blank.

Kanakdatta shook his head. "But I trust my man's word."

"But my mind does not trust your's," Asoka retorted angrily. "Why are you doing this, Kanaka?"

"Why?" Kanakdatta folded his arms. "If Devi is really in Kalinga, we should send for her, bring her here."

"I don't believe you!" Asoka looked his old friend in the eye. "I saw her body with my own eyes."

Kanakdatta took a deep breath. "The body was badly burnt," he said. "It could have belonged to any woman."

Asoka leaned forward and grabbed Kanakdatta by the collar but his friend did not fight back. "The body had unburnt pieces of Devi's clothing," he snarled. "And her ornaments."

"That could have been easily staged."

"By whom? And why?"

"The Prime Minister, Asoka." Kanakdatta spoke hurriedly. "It has to be him."

Slap! Asoka's hand moved swiftly across Kanakdatta's cheek. Even in his drunken state, the slap was powerful, and Kanakdatta stepped back a pace. He rubbed his cheek and looked at Asoka in surprise. *What has gone wrong in you, my friend?* he wondered, staring at the unrecognisable figure before him. Suddenly, rage engulfed Kanakdatta.

"You dare blame the man who placed me on this throne?" Asoka shouted angrily. "You dare blame the man who brought victory to us?"

"Look around you, friend," Kanakdatta pleaded, pointing to the women, the opium smoke. "This is no throne you are sitting on. This is an illusion."

Asoka lunged at him again, but this time Kanakdatta was ready. He dodged the blow and responded with one of his own, hitting Asoka straight in the gut. The women around them screamed as Asoka fell to the floor, vomit dripping from between his lips. 'Guards!' they screamed.

A group of guards arrived, led by a menacing looking man, dressed in light leather armour. "Retreat two steps and raise your hands," he ordered Kanakdatta.

As he did as he was told, Kanakdatta watched Asoka get to his feet and wipe his mouth on the sleeve of his silk undershirt.

"Hold him well, Cuska," Asoka said. "He had the audacity to hit me in the gut."

Cuska's grip on Kanakdatta's arm was strong and firm. "Yes, my Samrat," he replied.

"What do you want Kanakdatta? Barging in here like this and lying to me?" Asoka asked, the opium fumes leaving his brain.

"I do not lie." Kanakdatta tried to move but Cuska's powerful arms were too heavy to throw off. "Devi is in Kalinga."

"Did you see her yourself?"

"I already told you, my man…"

"Your man could have lied." Asoka took a step forward. "*If* she is alive, why would she not come to me? Why would she hide in Kalinga?"

"How would I know?" Kanakdatta struggled to free himself. "That is what we need to find out. Let me go to

Kalinga with some of my best men, and we shall discover the truth."

'So that is what you really want." Asoka spat on the ground. "The Prime Minister was right about you after all."

"Right about me?"

"I loved Devi with my life," Asoka sighed. "I never imagined that you of all people would try to use that against me for your own selfish motives."

The blood rushed to Kanakdatta's head. "What are you saying?" he gasped. *Was it the wine and the opium talking?*

"What he is saying is that we know the truth about you," a raspy voice said from behind them.

Kanakdatta did not have to turn to realize they had been honoured with the Prime Minister's presence.

"Tell him, Samrat." The Prime Minister wheeled his chair forward. "Let him hear it straight from your mouth. Let him know that *we know*."

Kanakdatta looked at Asoka, who walked up and stood to his side. "What is it that you claim to know, my friend?" Kanakdatta shrugged. "Tell me so I know it too."

"Do not make me say it out loud." Asoka sighed and leaned to his side, putting his mouth to Kanakdatta's ear. As Asoka's lips moved, slowly speaking the words, Kanakdatta could feel his warm breath upon his ear. His eyes widened in horror.

"You misunderstand, my friend!" he pleaded as Asoka retreated back to his seat, visibly tired by the effort. "You are mistaken."

"Take him from my sight." Asoka waved his arms and Cuska pulled Kanakdatta away.

"Asoka!" Kanakdatta shouted as they dragged him down the pavilion steps. "This is a mistake! I am your friend. I would never betray you!"

As they moved him along the path that led to the arched entrance, Kanakdatta caught one last sight of his friend, sitting atop his seat, head flung back against the headrest, eyes closed. The women had returned and were once again moving their hands over his shoulders. "Asoka!" he screamed again as they brought him out in the open.

Like an apparition, Chankya appeared from the darkness beside the flowering archway, his chair moving over the walkway. "A word with the man," he said, and the guards moved away from him, except Cuska, who kept his iron grip on him. Chanakya wheeled his chair closer and observed Kanakdatta's face.

"You did this!" Kanakdatta spat at him, but Chanakya only smiled. "Look what you have made of him!"

Chanakya smiled, amused. "Did I really do it, Buddhist? All I did was introduce him to the wonderful summer wine we have here in the palace. All I did was show him how potent the effects of opium smoke was on the mind. All I did was tell him he was the Samrat, and all the world was his for the taking, that no one could stop him, not even his wife."

"You evil bastard!" Kanakdatta cursed. "Why did you do it? Why put him on the throne at all if all you wanted was to exploit him like this?"

Chanakya's smile turned into a frown. "The Maurya line is cursed," he declared angrily. "I dreamed great dreams for this Samrajya, but the Gods never did bless me with another Chandragupta. Your friend has no qualities to be a Samrat. His quick addiction to physical pleasures proves my point.

He is just a soldier. But now I will use him as best I can till the subcontinent is united under one rule."

"You will pay for this." Kanakdatta was calm now and had stopped struggling in Cuska's hold. "He does not understand me now in his drunken state but I will see him again and convince him I speak the truth."

Chanakya laughed. "He doubts you now, Buddhist. I cannot blame him after what he knows about you now."

"And how long have you known?" Kanakdatta looked the old man in the eye.

Chanakya nodded. "For ages. Did you take me for a fool? I built this Samrajya from the ground up, my boy. Me!"

"Why did you not tell him before?" Kanakdatta asked. "Why keep it a secret?"

"In politics, one of the greatest qualities is patience." Chanakya smiled. "Nothing is more potent than a deadly blow at the right time, not early, not too late, but just at the right time."

"He is my friend. I will convince him."

"Oh I have no doubt of that," Chanakya nodded.

"I have my two spies who saw her in Kalinga. I will bring them to him. They will describe her to him. He will believe me then."

"You mean those two poor souls you left outside the gates?" Chanakya clapped his hands imperatively.

Nikumbh walked towards them, carrying a sack slung across his back. When he reached them, he let it drop to the ground at Kanakdatta's feet.

Horror etched itself on Kanakdatta's face as he realized what the blood soaked contents of the sack were. "Daruman!

Hanuman!" he cried in vain. Their heads had been cut off and now lay at his feet like so much offal. Then it all came to him. "You knew about her, didn't you?" He glared at the old man. "You knew she was in Kalinga."

"After my men found Radhagupta there, it did not take much time to realize she was there too," Chanakya replied, shrugging.

"And you wanted me to find her and bring the news to him so you could use that precise moment to make him distrust me."

"How predictable you have been," Chanakya laughed. "Alas, there is no longer a reason to keep her alive. My men shall attend to her, and to Radhagupta, after they have attended to you."

Kanakdatta looked up. "You will kill me?"

"I gave you a choice, Buddhist." Chanakya folded his arms. "Like the one I gave you years ago when I told you to take Radhagupta to his death, but you disobeyed me. I gave you one more chance, but again you failed. Had you come to me with the news of Devi, had you been loyal, I would have let you live. I have always liked you, boy. Even though I hate Buddhists, I was always gentle with you, for I see something of me in you. You are sharp like me, intelligent. You do what needs to be done. Alas, you leave me no choice." He looked at Nikumbh. "Finish him and throw his body in the river," he ordered.

Kanakdatta watched Chanakya wheel his chair away, then turned to see Nikumbh smiling at him devilishly.

"At last, Buddhist," Nikumbh said. "I am glad it is I who gets to sully the streets with your blood."

He drew a bloodied knife from the scabbard tied to his waist. "This is the same blade with which I killed your men," he said. "Now it is your turn. Hold him well, soldier." The command was for Cuska, as he walked towards them, brandishing his blade.

Kanakdatta closed his eyes in the face of impending death, trying to clear his mind as he remembered the teachings of the Buddha. *Life is full of suffering,* the Wise One had said, *and it is death that finally ends it.* As he waited for the blade to fall upon him, his final thought was of his friend. *I failed you, Asoka.*

Suddenly, he felt Cuska's grip on him loosen. Kanakdatta opened his eyes just as Cuska's hands left him and he lunged at Nikumbh. The surprising attack was so unexpected that Nikumbh fell to the ground, unbalanced, his blade flying from his hand.

"Quick!" Cuska whispered to Kanakdatta, bending to see if Nikhumbh was really knocked out. "There are horses in the southern stables. If we get to them before anyone catches us, we can jump the wall."

Kanakdatta looked at the young guard. "I thank you."

"Thank me later for now we must run like the wind." Cuska dragged Nikhumb's body into the bushes.

Kanakdatta followed the young guard through the streets to the southern stables.

"Take the black one," Cuska said, pointing to one of the horses. "That one is already saddled."

Kanakdatta did not waste any time. He climbed onto the horse with the agility his men knew well. To his surprise, he saw Cuska get onto another horse. "You are coming with me?" he asked.

"That depends, Lord." Cuska looked at him. "Where are you going?"

Kanakdatta closed his eyes and thought. "North. Shiva's army training camp is in Chitrakoot. I must go there."

"Then I am coming with you." Cuska grabbed the reins of his mount and pointed. "We can jump the wall there."

The stables were built along the elevated platforms along the river. Cuska rode out in front and made the jump first, his horse flying over the wall. Kanakdatta took a deep breath and followed. He could feel the blood rush to his head as his mount leapt into the air and then landed with a thud. There was no reason to stop now. He had to ride on.

8
HARDEO:
SHOWDOWN IN PATLIPUTRA

———————— ~ ————————

PATLIPUTRA, 263 BC

The voices of the city began to speak to him as Hardeo's carriage moved along the elevated ramp that led through the gates. Patliputra was the largest city in the whole wide world and at this moment it certainly sounded like it. He could hear the chattering of people and shopkeepers yelling to sell their wares above the hoofbeats of his galloping horses. At junctures he could hear the pleas of beggars, roused by the sight of a passing bejewelled palanquin. Hardeo did not peer through the curtains even once. He hated large cities, especially the ones he did not control.

As they moved through the market area, his nose was assaulted by various odours. There was the overwhelming stench of horse-dung. Perhaps a horse merchant was in town. The rotten smell of summer wine lingered between the quarters. Obviously the famed Bootlegger's Guild in the city still flourished. When they passed the markets, the foul stench of excreta and waste flooded the carriage, doubtless emanating from the large *nullah* that took the city waste out to the East.

"How much farther?" he asked loudly, fidgeting in his seat. The carriage driver had been required to lay down his weapons at the first checkpost before the gates. Not that he had expected anything less, but all of a sudden, he felt exposed in this large mass of houses and people.

"We can see the palace walls up ahead, Guild Master," the man dutifully informed him. "We shall be out of the civil quarters shortly."

Hardeo nodded uneasily, wishing to get out of the crowded streets as soon as possible. He had seen his share of crowds in his life. Now, when his hair had turned grey and his knees started to trouble him, he had no wish for more. The carriage finally stopped outside the palace gates, seeking entrance. Hardeo could hear the driver talking to the guards on duty. Someone was at the curtained window of his carriage, moving about. Hardeo took a deep breath as the fabric was moved aside, but it was only a city guard.

"Name and purpose?" the guard asked in a gruff voice, eyes elsewhere.

"I am the Maharaja of Vidisha, here to pay homage to the Samrat and update him on important issues."

A sly smile crept onto the guard's lips as he heard the declaration. 'Vidisha, you say?" The smirk turned into a furious snarl. "You cannot go in!"

"What in the name of..." The driver tried to argue. 'He is a Maharaja. He has a right to go in."

The city guard did not seem to care. "I have my orders. He does not go in."" He walked away.

"Orders from whom?" Hardeo's driver called after the retreating figure.

"Orders from me," a smiling voice said. A new person seemed to have joined the fray.

"And who are you?" Hardeo's driver asked rudely as Hardeo himself sat back in his seat, waiting anxiously to hear the answer. But the new entrant had no interest in speaking to the guards. He came to the carriage door and pulled away the curtain, revealing a handsome face. The young man smiled courteously and bowed. He had sharp blue eyes and a strong jawline which etched his clean, shaven face. Nothing about the man's manner was hostile.

"I am called Prajapati," he smiled. "Welcome to the capital, Maharaja. I regret you had to be greeted like this."

Hardeo nodded in acknowledgement. "Let me inside the palace," he ordered, "so I can meet the Samrat."

"I regret I cannott do that." The smile did not leave Prajapati's face. "The Council has passed a new law."

Hardeo leaned forward. "And does it say Maharajas are not allowed to meet their Samrat?" He had expected resistance, but not of such a strong nature. "I have not heard of any such law."

Prajapati shook his head. "It says that no non-believer is allowed inside the palace walls, or in the presence of the Samrat." He stopped to look into Hardeo's face. "Not that it should matter to a Maharaja, but you are a special case."

"It is imperative I see the Samrat." Hardeo coughed. "I have important, rather vital business to discuss with him."

"I do not doubt it." Prajapati suddenly let go of the curtain and opened the door of the carriage. Hardeo could now see his whole form, his torso covered with armour. "You would not visit here if you did not have something important to discuss."

"Master!" Hardeo heard the cry of his driver and felt sudden movements in the front of the carriage.

"What are you doing?" he asked angrily.

Prajapati paid no heed and climbed into the carriage. He sat down opposite Hardeo and leaned forward, looking into his eyes, still smiling like a fool. "You have nothing to worry about. We are just taking a detour. Your driver will not know the way so I have replaced him with my own man."

The carriage began to move. Hardeo watched through the open door to where his driver stood by the city guard post, looking helplessly at the moving carriage. Hardeo looked ahead again once he was out of sight. "Where are you taking me?" he asked, still composed. *They wouldn't dare kidnap me*, he thought. *Not in the capital*. Though they had indeed dared to attack him in his own city.

"Relax, Guild Master." Prajapati sat back and smiled calmly. "There is nothing to fear. We shall return your rider to you when your business here is done."

"That does not answer my question," Hardeo snapped. "Where are you taking me?"

"Well, you do have important business to discuss, don't you?" Prajapati folded his arms and smiled.

***

When the carriage stopped moving, Hardeo could smell a strange mixture of fragrances. It was like the place full of flowers of all kinds. There was the *Nishigandha*, the *Jai*, the *Jui*, and the *Mogra*. He knew these flowers because Devi had loved them and adorned her room and the corridor outside with them. He would always awaken to their fragrance. This place brought back those memories.

"What is this place?" Hardeo asked loudly as Prajapati opened the carriage door and stepped down.

"Patience, Guild Master, patience." Prajapati offered his hand as support.

Hardeo did not take it and bent to place his own cane on the ground outside. He descended from the carriage and looked around. They were standing in some sort of alleyway, with high walls on both sides. However, there were no flowers. The floral perfume emanated from behind the wall in front. Above the wall, the arched roof of a tall building loomed. Hardeo stretched his neck to see and realized it was higher than his own Guild House.

Prajapati tapped on a door in the wall, barely the height of a man, too small to accommodate Prajapati's large frame. A spy-window opened in the door and a guard's face appeared. The aroma of flowers became stronger. The eyes peered at Prajapati and lines of recognition etched themselves on his face. The spy window closed and the small door opened. Prajapati doubled over, hand over head and squeezed through. Hardeo followed, his frail form passing easily through. The guard closed the door immediately.

Prajapati gestured for Hardeo to follow and walked in through a corridor even narrower than the alleyway outside. Only one man could pass at a time. As they moved ahead, Hardeo heard the sounds of the city fade. Instead, they could hear someone playing on the strings of a *Veena*. The same intoxicating perfume was everywhere. The place was cloaked in eerie silence except for the music. Ornate double doors loomed before them at the end of the corridor. Prajapati pushed them open and walked through. Hardeo followed him.

Light filled his eyes. They were standing in a large hall with round, stone pillars holding up the massive ceiling above them, from which glass chandeliers dangled, carrying candles and spreading light. A flight of stairs in one corner led to the upper level. As they walked in, Hardeo noticed there were women standing in the corners, eyeing them strangely; women dressed in revealing attire, goblets of wine in their hands. The eyes of the women followed them as Prajapati walked towards the stairs that led up. Hardeo caught sight of a woman licking her lips with her tongue as she gazed at him seductively. "You have brought me to a brothel!" he muttered angrily.

"Not just any brothel," said Prajapati. "I have brought you to Kautilya's brothel. It is the largest and best in the whole subcontinent."

"I don't care if it is the biggest in the world," Hardeo declared, placed his hand on the wall to help him get up the stairs. "My faith does not permit me to be in such places."

"Relax, old man," Prajapati said as he climbed. "You are not here to partake in the activities this establishment provides, but to meet someone."

They climbed to the second level. Hardeo panted, trying to catch his breath. He was not used to such steep climbs anymore. It was the reason all stairways in the Guild House were spirals. They were easy to climb, easier on both the knees and the heart.

"Through here." Prajapati led him down another corridor, a darker one with fewer torches on the walls. As they turned once again, they walked into another corridor, dark and devoid of light. Prajapati stopped before a closed door. "We are here," he announced. He pushed the door open and gestured to his companion to walk in.

Hardeo walked into a room engulfed in darkness. As his eyes adjusted to the meagre light, he saw they were in some kind of study. A desk stood in front of them, and a large wooden board was nailed to the wall behind it. As Hardeo looked more closely, he saw that something was painted on it.

"Sit here," Prajapati said curtly, pulling out a chair from the darkness.

Hardeo obeyed and sat down, resting his cane on his knees. Prajapati went to a corner and Hardeo heard the sound of liquid being poured. The sound stopped and Prajapati handed him a goblet. "Drink this," he said.

Hardeo sniffed the liquid. It smelt of berries and grapes. "I do not consume wine," he said loudly, about to hand the goblet back to Prajapati.

A raspy voice spoke from behind them. "Do you not, Guild Master? I thought that you made an exception on cold nights."

Hardeo breathed in. The strange voice made his skin prickle. He heard the creaking of wood, as if something was moving over the floor. Hardeo sniffed the liquid again, wondering if this was it. *Would they poison me?* he wondered. The hand holding the goblet shook at the thought. It was those tremors again.

"Drink up, Guild Master!" The voice spoke again, its source now directly in front of him. "It is only wine. If I wished to poison you, you would be dead already. Besides, you are going to need it."

Hardeo raised the cup to his lips and drank the liquid slowly, feeling the sour sweetness roll over his tongue and turn into a slow warmth as it moved down his throat.

Prajapati walked in again, carrying with him a crackling torch which bathed the room in firelight. As he lit the lamps in the corners of the room, one by one, Hardeo observed the figure of the man sitting in front of him grow clear. He was very old, his toothless mouth looked horrid in the light, and his frail arms lay to his side, almost lifeless. He sat in some sort of wheeled chair, with contraptions tying him to the seat. His round, hairless head was larger than any human head he had ever seen.

"I know who you are, Prime Minister." In the small chamber, Hardeo could hear his own words rebound from the walls and gallop back towards him.

"So you know who I am," Chanakya smiled. "But the question at hand is, do you know what I can do?"

Hardeo played with the empty goblet in his hands, avoiding the old man's gaze. He had not expected to sit across from the most powerful man in all Bharatvarsha. But here he was. He realized there was no point in silent deliberation. "I wish to see the Samrat," he said loudly, looking up.

"Alas, you will have to make do with me." Chankya smiled. "Rest assured the Samrat carries out all his actions through me. You, being a businessman, should appreciate that by coming straight to me, you have cut out the middleman."

Hardeo felt a sudden chill run down his spine, but he did not let it show on his face. "I have come to ask for justice," he said. "My brethren, myself included, were attacked in Vidishanagri."

A sly smile crossed Chanakya's face and was gone in an instant, like a flash of lightning. "A city you claim to control," he remarked.

"I am a Maharaja who serves the Samrat." Hardeo bowed. Perhaps humility would soften this man. "Hence an attack on me is an attack on the Samrat."

"Do you know who attacked you?" Chanakya raised his hands and crossed them under his chin. The flames in the lamps on the wall fluttered in an unseen gust.

"The Ancient Brahminical Order," Hardeo muttered. "The attackers had Kalkoot. It had to be them."

"No, Buddhist." Chanakya turned his wheelchair and moved towards the other side of the room. He now faced the wooden panel on the wall behind the desk, his back to Hardeo. "It was I who attacked you. The Ancient Brahminical Order works for me."

Hardeo felt his heart thudding in his chest. His throat felt dry, but he gulped some saliva to hold his composure. "You wished to kill me?" he asked slowly. "Why?"

At the question, Chanakya began to laugh. The hysterical laugh echoed in the small room and Hardeo could feel vibrations in the wooden floor. "Kill you?" The raspy voice pierced his ears. "I did not want to kill you. If I wanted to kill you I would have sent assassins in the middle of the night instead of arsonists in the middle of the day."

Hardeo swallowed his words. He had to hold his ground. Here, of all places, he could not afford to look afraid.

"All I wanted to do was scare you. I trust I succeeded, Guild Master?"

Hardeo felt no fear. The tremors in his arms had disappeared. Instead, he felt rage – deep, burning rage. "Your men broke my minaret," he said through clenched teeth, "destroyed the monument to my life's achievements, which I worked five long decades to raise."

Chanakya waved his arms. "An unfortunate occurrence, but not one that I regret."

Hardeo clenched his fists in fury. "You will regret it," he said clearly. "You threatened me in my city and now I am threatening you in yours."

"Are you?" Chanakya laughed, sounding genuinely amused. "I did not threaten you in *your* city, Guild Master. I threatened you in mine. All cities in this subcontinent are *mine*." He spread his arms towards the panel on the wall.

Hardeo saw in the light that it was a map of the subcontinent, from the pointed mountain peaks drawn on the top, to the sea below. Hardeo did not respond.

Chanakya wheeled his chair back and faced him again. "The men I had killed were traitors, working for the Kalingans. They were smugglers who did not respect the blockade on the Mahajanpada and were smuggling goods into Kalingan trade routes by sea. In light of the current situation, they had to be killed."

"It is a lie." Hardeo banged his fist on the handle of his chair. "They were honest merchants, some of our best. I have supported your blockade, and they would never disobey me."

Chanakya stared into Hardeo's eyes and then nodded. "Yes, a lie," he said, his face expressionless. "But a lie which the Samrat believes is magically transformed into the truth. Do you see? A war is coming, Guild Master. We will invade Kalinga soon, and all enemies within must be dealt with first."

"You kept me in the dark." Hardeo said angrily, "Killed those messengers my Preferetti sent to me."

"And you stayed in the dark." Chanakya said, "Years of success brought you hubris. It was easy rather. I couldn't believe my luck when you called all your Preferetti to Vidishanagri."

"How did your men enter my city?" Hardeo leaned back on his chair. "No weapons are allowed inside. All unknown visitors are checked."

"And yet, my men entered your city, carrying enough firepower to destroy your entire Guild House and your wretched minaret." Chanakya smiled.

"Five of my Preferetti are heavily injured." Hardeo said angrily.

"Fire does that." Chankya said pitifully. "We don't really have the power to fight nature."

"Damn you!" Hardeo got to his feet but Prajapati was instantly between him and Chankya, naked sword in hand. Hardeo did not advance. There was nothing he could do to hurt the old man.

"For five years you thought that you had finally managed to bring power to you and your brethren." Chanakya said. "I let you become Maharaja of Vidishanagri. I let your lot trade, only waiting for the correct opportunity. And now I have got it."

"This wasn't the first time your Order has tried to kill me." Hardeo said, "Try again. We shall endure. Now if there is nothing else, and if you have called me here just to threaten me, I would like to leave now."

"Oh, but there is something else, Guild Master." Chanakya murmured. "Pray sit down for I am not yet finished. Furthermore, I have a proposition for you and your brethren."

Hardeo sat back down on his chair. He did not have a choice. In this dark room, he was at their mercy. '*I have to play their game*' he thought uneasily.

"So, now do you see that nothing in this subcontinent happens without my will?" Chanakya coughed. "You became Maharaja because I allowed it. You set up your Guild because I permitted you to. Furthermore, you now sit in front of me alive, because I wish it."

Hardeo did not respond nor did he lower his gaze.

"And anything that you think that you control, I wield the strings to control it, Guild Master," Chanakya laughed.

"Let your own Spymaster come to know of what you have done." Hardeo said menacingly, "When Kanakdatta will know, he will set his wrath upon you."

"Kanakdatta the serpent." Chanakya smiled, looking at Prajapati, "He's no longer the Spymaster. Sure, Word takes time to travel to Vidishanagri. You for sure must have missed the courier that I sent to you along the way."

"What do you mean?" Hardeo's face was entranced with surprise. His eyes were widened. His heart had started beating fast. This was something he hadn't expected at all.

"He is a declared enemy of the Samrajya." Chanakya smiled mockingly. "And is currently on the run, alone."

"But he is Asoka's…"

"Friend?" Chanakya laughed, "*Rulers* don't have friends. You of all people should know that."

Hardeo sat transfixed on his chair, looking down at the floor. '*They have seen the surprise on your face*' He told himself. They knew that he had been outsmarted.

"Alas, Guild Master." Chanakya chuckled, "You thought that you had it all figured out. Arranged for your daughter to wed the Prince. Managed to place your right hand in the closest circle of the *Samrat*. What could go wrong, for sure? What would?"

Hardeo stared at the floor, his eyes into nothingness. His hand was shaking once again. The base of his cane rattled on the wooden floor with each wave of the tremors.

"And this is what I can do." Chanakya's arms fell back to his side as he closed his eyes, 'I can make the right turn into wrong. I can make black into white. I can make day into night," He opened his eyes again, "And I can make fire into wind. Am I really the kind of person you would want as your enemy?"

The sentence made Hardeo recoil in horror. "Why are you doing this?" he tapped his cane on the floor, "I helped the *Samrat* break Sushem's siege. I helped him to his throne. I gave his cause precedence over my own at Junagarh. I even sacrificed my own daughter for his sake."

Chanakya smiled. "Our *Samrat* owes you." He said, "However, what you don't see Guild Master is that I do not."

"What do you want?" Hardeo asked, looking up.

Chanakya clapped slowly. "Finally, the businessman in you awakens. Where was he? I was looking for him from the very start."

Prajapati folded his arms. 'We want conversion." He said, "You and all of your Preferetti leave your ways and come back into the Aryan fold. You start worshipping the Gods once again. You force all of your merchant brethren to do the same."

"And why would you want that?" Hardeo stared at the Prime Minister aghast.

"After we conquer Kalinga, the subcontinent will be unified in land, but not in soul." Chanakya closed his eyes. "We cannot have two faith in a united Samrajya. I have to end your doctrine, now." Chanakya spoke from his side, "As most of you are now traders, we will accept you all back in our fold as Vaishyas, irrespective of what you were before. The rules that apply to Vaishyas shall apply to you all irrespective of your births. That is the compromise that I am willing to make."

Hardeo shook his head. "This is impossible." He said, "The Buddha taught us the one true faith. He showed us the truth. He told us that there are no Gods, only men. My brethren would lay down their lives than do as you ask."

"Not such good businessmen, are you then?" Chanakya folded his arms. "We will kill all of you if you refuse. You will not get a better offer."

I need to get out of here! Hardeo thought urgently. He looked in the old man's eyes and suddenly, he knew what would make him tick, "And you will not get a better chance to kill me than now." He said, looking him in the eyes, "Kill me now, for if you let me out of here today, Next time we meet, I shall be sitting on the other side of the table."

"Silence!" Iron grazed iron as Prajapati drew out his sword.

"No!" Chanakya held Prajapati's hand weakly. "Stay your blade." Then, he looked up at Hardeo. "The man has given us his decision." He said, "Let him walk away."

Hardeo breathed out. It was done. Chanakya had reacted to the slight as he had expected.

"I say kill him now." Prajapati still held the blade.

"No." Chanakya waved, "He thinks that we cannot catch him if he runs. So let him run. Go to your city, Buddhist. Go to what you think is your Stronghold. We will come for you there. We will make an example out of you and your brethren and then the rest of your kind shall either surrender or die. I will send an army to your city. Make your last stand there if you must. Or run away, if you can like cowards. For wherever you go, I shall find you."

Hardeo got to his feet. He walked backwards, his eyes on Prajapati's blade. "I thank you for the audience." He said as he pushed the doors open wide and let them slam behind him with a bang as he walked out.

9
CHANAKYA:
DISTURBED RELATIONS

———————∼———————

PATLIPUTRA, 263 BC

"I don't understand your thinking!" Asoka shouted, banging down his half-empty goblet on the brocade covered armrest of the great stone throne. The clang of metal could be clearly heard in the empty audience chamber. Ruby droplets fell onto Asoka's silken garments.

Seated in his wheel chair at the foot of the steps leading up to the throne, Chanakya hid a smile. Introducing the Samrat to wine had been a good idea. Asoka was a military man, used to the street-spill the small folk considered liquor. He had never tasted the fine wines consumed by the elite of the city, nor had he ever felt their potent effects. But once he had, there was no stopping. Chanakya knew it was the wine speaking now.

"My thinking is for your welfare," Chanakya said, wheeling his chair forward until he was right below the stone steps that led to the throne. "All I do as your Prime Minister is for your benefit."

"You confuse me." Asoka's speech was noticeably slurred. He shook his head, trying to think clearly. "You say one thing now, having said something entirely different before."

"Do you feel I have changed my stance on some issue?" Chanakya asked.

Asoka pointed his finger straight at the old man. "Yes, you have. Three years ago, when you sent me north to destroy Sushem's rebels, you told me that taking the fight to them was my job as Samrat of the people. Now you tell me that, as Samrat, my place is not on the battlefield."

"Our actions are in response to the situation around us, My Samrat." Chanakya coughed. "If I have changed my stance, it is because the situation has changed. Three years ago, there was civil war. The people needed to see their leader go into battle to save his Samrajya from breaking up. Now, however, it is an entirely different situation."

'Wars are all the same, Guru," Asoka sighed, "whether fought up north or down south."

"But this war is an act of aggression," Chankya said. "It is to add territory. It is not your honour that is at stake. You have an able Senapati to take care of this for you."

Asoka leaned forward. "But that is not the actual reason for keeping me away from the battlefield, is it?" The half empty goblet slid from his hand and rlled down the steps making a clatter and leaving a trail of wine. It hit Chankya's chair and lay at his feet, empty.

"That is one of the reasons, though not the most important," Chankya agreed. "You are aware of what is most important."

Asoka laughed. It was a mirthless, drunken laugh. "You will not allow me to go into battle because I have no son and heir yet," he stated.

Chanakya smiled. *He learns fast*, he thought. "We cannot risk your life when you have no heir. Nor can we risk the Samrajya's stability because you have a thirst for battle."

"A thirst!" The shout echoed through the vaulted chamber and sent a rush of adrenaline through Chanakya's heart. The Samrat had not sounded like that for many days.

"A thirst, you say?" Asoka asked, his voice cold and hard. "I do not have a thirst for battle, Guru. No sane man does. All I want is that if my men are risking their lives for me, I should risk mine, fighting beside them."

"Your life is no longer your own," Chanakya told him. "You are Samrat of Bharatvarsha. Your life belongs to the people now."

"Well said." Asoka clapped loudly, raising both hands high. When the clapping stopped, an eerie silence filled the chamber. "I know what you are going to ask me next," Asoka said, his words dropping like stones into still water.

"If you already know, I need say nothing," came the guarded response from the old man.

Asoka sighed. "I promised Devi she would be the only woman in my life. But then she died, and I married another. I promised Asandhi the same thing. Strange creatures, women. How their faces lit up when I made this promise. And now you are telling me to break my word a second time."

"If she cannot give you a child, My Samrat, you must find one who can," Chanakya said sternly.

"Has it ever occurred to you that the problem may be with me?" Asoka asked. "That it is my *virya* which cannot produce a child, and not her womb?"

Chanakya smiled slyly, but the shadows hid much of his face. "Yes, it has," he said. "But let me assure you it is not so."

"How do you know? Have your vaids performed some experiment on me in my sleep?" Asoka laughed.

"Not my vaids," Chanakya replied softly. "My women."

Asoka sighed. "She will not like it when I tell her." He closed his eyes and sat back. "She will throw a tantrum. She is like a child. I do not know how to tell her."

"This is the battle you must fight, My Samrat." Chankya said, "while your army fights another in Kalinga. Both are for the sake of your people."

"My people?" Asoka muttered. "Sometimes I think it is not the people my life belongs to, Guru, but you."

Chanakya felt his heart skip a beat. These words had been spoken to him once before. "I beg your pardon," he said in mock humility, but no reply came from Asoka. The Samrat had passed out on the throne, his head fallen to one side.

Chanakya clapped and men appeared from the shadows. "Carry the Samrat to his chambers," he ordered curtly.

They walked up the steps and carefully lifted the Samrat's limp body. Chanakya followed them out of the room, wheeling his chair. His mind remained on the words Asoka had spoken, stirring a long lost memory. *It had all begun with those words*, he thought. *But this time, it will end as it did the last time.*

50 YEARS AGO

The upper corridors of the Patliputra palace appeared eerie after nightfall. The crickets made their homes in the high stone ceilings and filled the air with their chirping. The flaming torches on the walls leapt and crackled, creating larger than life shadows as one walked by. The wind whistled through the emptiness like the flute of some invisible bard.

I had walked through here on countless occasions, but each time I did so at night, it brought a chill to my spine. It was one of the reasons Chandragupta's chambers were on the upper level. Dhanananda occupied the lower rooms in the palace, not that he had a choice, given his enormous size. The upper rooms had always been used as military barracks for the ruler's bodyguards. One of my first actions as Prime Minister had been to renovate them for the Samrat. An assassin was sure to feel unnerved sneaking through here, and in such matters, any safeguard, however small, helped. Chandragupta had not complained, for he loved the view from high places. When he was a boy, he and his friend Dileepa would secretly climb the western tower in the old Taxila Academy.

I shook my head to remove these thoughts. The past was long gone. And the future was full of uncertainty. I found him standing at the edge of the large elevated balcony, gazing down on the city, which appeared like a thousand illuminated *diyas* at this hour. Chandragupta looked royal, even in his simple cotton nightclothes.

"You summoned me?" I said.

Chandragupta did not turn around. "What days have come that I must summon you to see you."

"I have been busy." The breeze blew in our faces. "It is not that I have avoided seeing you." I folded my arms.

"We should be out there, Guru," Chandragupta said, turning to look at me. "We should be in a camp somewhere, on our way to Paurava, to teach those traitors a lesson. In Kalinga, we had an army. We should have turned it and marched right back to the Northwest. But you had me turn and bring it here."

"We will teach them a lesson," I told him, "just not through war. We did not march on Patliputra and defeat the Nandas only to have war amongst the Aryas."

Chandragupta laughed. "Those Aryas have betrayed us. Must I remind you of your own lessons about how to treat betrayers?"

"Malayketu betrayed us," I said sternly. "Rakshasa betrayed us. Perhaps they have Councils and Ministers to back them. But if we go to war, it is the common people who will die."

"Then let us do something!" Chandragupta urged. "Let us send spies into their lands. We still have brethren in Taxila. Let us move them towards another revolution."

'Revolution causes bloodshed," I reminded him. "And that is what we are trying to avoid."

"But I am the Samrat," Chandragupta declared, slamming his fist down on the stone of the battlements. "I cannot do nothing. I cannot sit here in the palace like a puppet. You do not even let me go outside the city walls."

"Yes, you are the Samrat, but you are a Samrat without an heir. For that reason you must remain where we can protect you."

Chandragupta opened his mouth to argue but shut it again, knowing it would be futile.

"Everything I do, I do for a reason," I told him. "And you should do the same. You are not the first born son of a long reigning Raja. If you die, there is no one to take your place. You do not have sons or brothers, no family. Your life is the most valuable thing in this whole Samrajya."

Chandragupta folded his arms. "I can beget an heir," he said grimly. "You need to find me a bride."

"That is not so easy," I sighed. "Your heir cannot come from any common womb. The lady has to be from a noble house. And with Malayketu's open rebellion, the old houses of the Aryas are afraid to pledge their daughters to you for it would mean taking sides."

"My own vassals! They would rather wait it out and see who the winner is before committing."

"So, until we find you a wife and she has borne you a son, I cannot permit you to go out of the city. You are not safe out there."

"And I am safe here?" Chandragupta laughed mockingly. "How many attempts on my life have you saved me from, Guru? Two...three?"

"Four, to be exact."

Chandragupta shrugged. "Four attempts, right in the heart of our own city."

"Rakshasa has tried," I agreed, "but he has failed each time, has he not?"

"He came pretty close the last time." Chandragupta walked to a bronze desk in the balcony and picked up a cask and poured me some wine.

Rakshasa had indeed made numerous attempts to kill him as soon as war had been declared. It was one of the reasons I halted our Kalinga campaign and brought him back to the city. The first assassination attempt had been made just as we were about to enter the city gates.

Chandragupta was riding a large black female elephant called Chandralekha. I had never liked elephants, but the Samrat needed to look Royal. On elephants, the rider sat back in the *ambari* on the elephant's back and the *mahout* controlled the beast's movements. Hence, he also controlled the rider's life.

When we returned to the city, we found the western gate decorated beautifully with exquisite woodwork.

Chandragupta wondered who the artist was. I wondered too. The man was revealed to be one of the old palace carpenters named Daruvaman. But something about the man set me thinking. I suggested to Chandragupta that Daruvaman be honored as the first to enter under his own highly decorated gate. The man showed no trace of fear as he was led to mount an elephant. If the carpenter was anything, he was brave, or perhaps he hoped to somehow get off the elephant before they reached the gate.

Even as Chandragupta placed a bag of coins in the carpenter's hand, I placed another in the hands of the mahout. *Hit your ankush hard,* I instructed. *Make the elephant run.* The mahout did exactly that. Daruvaman never understood what had happened as the elephant charged forward and the huge carved contraption fell on him as his mount set foot inside the gate. It had been a death trap designed to kill Chandragupta. As we watched the horrific spectacle, Chandragupta sighed. The war had begun.

"Why not beat them at their own game?" Chandragupta now suggested, offering me a goblet. "Send in our own assassins."

And have the bards say Chanakya was so afraid of Rakshasa that he had him killed? I bit my lip. I needed a convincing response. "Do you wish people to say the mighty Chandragupta stooped to the level of his enemies to win?" I taunted.

Chandragupta sighed and shook his head. "We have to do something," he said, swirling the wine in the goblet. "I cannot even take a sip of wine without being afraid someone will poison me."

"You need not fear," I said. "I shall taste the wine first." I put my goblet to my lips and drank down one gulp. I was thirsty and I sighed as the warm fruity liquid travelled down my throat.

Chandragupta seemed satisfied and sipped from his own goblet. He was right to be afraid. The second assassination attempt had been made through wine. Our Vaidya had served in our camp for years and been with Chandragupta since we marched on Junagarh. I never knew how Rakshasa turned him, or perhaps he had some secret grudge we were unaware of. When Chandragupta was ill, the Vaidya dissolved the required potions in wine and brought it to his chambers. Fortunately, I was sitting right by Chandragupta's side. The Vaidya greeted the Samrat and made his regular checks. Then he offered the wine.

Chandragupta was about to drink it when I stopped him. *You are the Samrat*, I told him. *Drink from a golden goblet.* I had studied poisons in my time at Taxila, and knew gold made them change colour. When poured into the golden goblet, the crimson liquid turned dark blue. We looked at the Vaidya questioningly. *Drink it first,* I said to him. When he hesitated, Chandragupta grabbed him by the collar and emptied the liquid into his mouth. The Vaidya lay shivering on the floor not two minutes later.

"Did you not wish to check it in a golden cup this time?" Chandragupta joked, returning to look out over the battlements.

I smiled. "I personally supervise every cask of wine brought to you since the incident."

Indeed, the poisoning had made me realize it could happen again. So I had begun to supervise every cask of wine sent to Chandragupta. Not only that, I put minute doses of a mixture of known poisons into the wine. I made the mixture myself. Beginning with extremely small doses, I increased the quantum each week. The idea was that Chandragupta would slowly become immune to the poisons. And to make sure my prepared mixture was not fatal, I would drink a goblet of the wine myself before sending it to the Samrat's chambers.

"We cannot remain on the defensive," Chandragupta said, finishing his wine. "When Malayketu brings the Greek and his own army here to Patliputra to lay siege, we must fight him, even if we do not wish to. At that time, innocent Aryas will die. Are you just trying to delay the inevitable, Guru?"

"It will not come to that," I said, pouring another round. "We will destroy them before they march."

Chandragupta took the goblet from me. "We cannot destroy our enemies sitting silently in Patliputra, Guru."

"If we can't, then maybe we have no business sitting in Patliputra as rulers."

"I'll tell you what will happen." Chandragupta looked at me. "Rakshasa will make another attempt to have me killed, like he almost did last time."

I sighed. The third time had almost proved charmed for Rakshasa. A Council room was to be built for the Samrat, a place where he could meet in secret and carry on clandestine discussions. This was a time of war. We could not trust the old palaces chambers; those walls had ears. I had chosen the site on the western ramparts, away from the hustle and bustle of the city, and commissioned the building before we left on the Kalinga campaign. It was a small place and had been ready on our return. I never understood how Rakshasa's men managed to infiltrate the construction, but they did. In the prahar before Chandragupta was to use it, I went to inspect the building. I looked in every corner. Everything seemed normal. I was about to leave when I noticed a trail of red ants on the floor. Curious, I followed the trail to a wall. Immediately, I ordered the chamberlain to burn the place down. As the flames took hold, armed men ran out from hidden chambers behind the walls. We slaughtered them. They had been sent by Rakshasa to kill the Samrat when he came without bodyguards to attend one of his secret meetings. If not for the ants, all would have been lost.

"He will never kill you as long as I am here," I told Chandragupta with finality.

"He will kill you first." Chandragupta finished his wine. "Then he will kill me. We must do something."

"We are doing things," I said carefully. "I have my men looking for any more spies inside the city."

"I mean go out and actually do something." Chandragupta burst out. "Not cower in the house like women."

"Do you belittle the role of women?" I asked, surprised. Chandragupta did not reply. I had caught him. "You must trust me." I said. "Listen to what I say, as you have done before. We will rise above these problems as we have before."

"How can I trust you when you do nothing?"

I sighed. "I am *not* doing nothing. I am finding ways to beat Rakshasa at his own game without any bloodshed. It will take time, but I will do it."

"Without going out of the city and without gathering an army?" Chandragupta slammed his goblet down, splashing wine all around.

"Indeed, yes."

Chandragupta raised his brow. "You realize I am the Samrat. If I wish it, I could force *you* to sit in the palace and ride out myself."

I took a deep breath and said nothing.

"But I am not going to do that for I trust your actions Guru. I always have, until now. Why do you give me reason to doubt? Now of all times."

"What actions of mine have planted the seed of doubt in your mind?" I asked.

Chandragupta shrugged, "You tell me nothing of your plans. You simply instruct me to sit inside the palace."

"The less people who know about a plan the better."

"You do not trust my discretion?" Chandragupta asked, his eyes glittering with their strange fire.

"I do, but you may not prefer my methods."

Chandragupta raised his hands in defeat. "Have it your way, Guru. I will respect your wishes and remain inside this palace. But be warned that I am watching you. If you give me any reason to doubt, I will take matters into my own hands."

"I would expect nothing less from you, *Vrishala*," I said, using the old Sanskrit word for 'son'. Chandragupta did not respond. He looked away, dismissing me with the wave of his hand.

When I returned to my chambers, I found Dasharath at my door, pacing the corridor uneasily. He rushed to me saying, "Where have you been?" he asked. "I was worried and had men looking all over for you."

"I was with the Samrat," I told him.

"Discussing what?"

"Nothing of importance." I opened the door to my chambers. "Did you find them?"

Dasharath stamped his foot and swore. "I looked in every alley, every house in this cursed city, every cellar and building, but Rakshasa's family cannot be found."

"But they are not with him in Paurava, so they must be here." I sat at my desk and poured oil into the lamp which had almost gone out.

"If they are in the city, we would have found them," insisted Dasharath.

"Perhaps he hid them where we will not look," I suggested.

Dasharath shook his head. "Impossible! I have looked everywhere."

"Pride is the fall of men, my dear friend," I said. "They are in this city. I am sure of it. Rakshasa would keep them where we would least expect them to be. That is how he would think they would be safe."

"If he has, he has hidden them well." Dasharath muttered, folding his arms.

"Then that is the way to beat him," I said, getting to my feet and walking to the window. The lights of the city flickered outside like a thousand fireflies. Looking for one family in this city was like looking for a needle in a haystack. Maybe the only way to find it was to use the magneto stone which the ancients said attracted iron.

"Look again, everywhere in the city," I told Dasharath. "Only, this time, let word out that you have found his family and will be imprisoning them at midnight."

A smile came to Dasharath's face. "And if they hear, whoever is hiding them will move them."

"And you will be waiting."

"Why did I not think of this?" Dasharath cursed.

I shut the window. "Because you do not think like me. Find them, Dasharath. Our whole plan depends on you finding them."

Dasharath nodded and left the room. I sat at my desk and did something I had not done for a long time. I prayed.

10
RADHAGUPTA:
A STRING OF BETRAYALS

~

KALINGA, 263 BC

"Our first goal today is to discover what the General plans to do." Radhagupta's words were drowned in the chaotic sounds that filled the docks as he and Devdatta made their way back to the city along the wooden boardwalks.

"We don't have any time, friend." Devdatta shook his head, pointing to the dock, clearly visible from where they were. A mass of people had already gathered where a wooden podium was being hastily raised by a group of labourers. "If I were you, I'd rather worry about what your friend Karuvaki will say today."

Radhagupta shook his head. "She is not the problem. It is the General I am afraid of."

"Well, she better not be," Devdatta said, raising his arms. "Look at the number of people here."

Radhagupta had to agree. A huge populace had arrived at the docks that day. The numbers were ten times the crowd they had seen on the day of the candidates' declaration. "It is working," he told Devdatta. "Your men have been visiting the small fishing villages along the coast, telling the small folk of your exploits and giving them a chance to see the man who brings food for their bellies in these troubled times."

"You glorify me too much." Devdatta shook his head. "These crowds could be here to see the feisty Karuvaki or the strong-armed General for all we know."

"That can hardly be the case," Radhagupta told him. "Karuvaki has been busy wooing the nobles, and Navin Kumar's clan has never visited the countryside. As for the General, I doubt the poor fishermen would dare to stand and listen and not run away when his men knock on their doors."

"So you are telling me all this is for us?" Devdatta appeared incredulous but pleased.

"Aye, Master," Radhagupta nodded. "The Captains tell me that your men have visited dozens of villages this past fortnight. It is people from those villages who form the bulk of the crowd today. They are here for you."

"Do not forget the nobles hold more votes than commoners," Devdatta pointed out. "That is why I tell you it is Karuvaki who worries me."

"It is true the nobles hold more votes, but the country has more commoners," Radhagupta countered. "An average fishing village in Kalinga has one hundred fisher families. Each carries one vote. Word of mouth spreads fast among commoners, for they mingle. You win the hearts of a dozen in each village and they will win over the rest for you through their weekly festivals and meetings in the village centres. On the other hand, the noble families are much tougher to win over. Though they hold a hundred votes each, they do not mix and have to be won over individually. There are all manner of noble families in the cities of Kalinga, and each has to be won over in a different way. Some want underhand deals, some want bribes, some vote only as their ancestors did, guided by noble traditions, and some will not vote at all, declaring the whole exercise is futile and Kalinga should be a hereditary Maharajya like Patliputra. Commoners can be wooed more simply. All they desire is a little respect, some attention, and most of all, food in their bellies, and peace in the land."

"You have studied the Kalingans well in the short time you have been here," Devdatta remarked admiringly. "I am counting on your strategy."

"'The second rule of politics is never count on anyone'," Radhagupta quoted a *subhashit*. "That is the reason for the speeches today. Today will confirm that it is not my stratagem alone that you will be counting on in these elections."

Devdatta smiled. "Just tell me where I can get more like you. Will I have to search in the depths of the Ancient Brahminical Order?"

"I would worry more about the General than finding men like me," Radhagupta said sombrely.

"What is it about General Bheema that worries you so much?" Devdatta asked. They had reached the dock area where Devdatta's Captain was standing, dutifully ready to escort him to where the speeches would take place.

Radhagupta closed his eyes. "General Bheema is unpredictable. In my life I have learnt that the most dangerous enemy is not the one who is most powerful but the one whose next move you cannot predict." The bald face of Arya Chanakya floated before him in the darkness behind his closed lids.

"We don't have time to spy on the General," Devdatta shrugged. "All that mutt head can think of is an assassination attempt. I will take my best bodyguards with me and thwart whatever he throws at us."

"As you wish, Master." Radhagupta breathed in.

"Speaking of best bodyguards, where is my man, Anirbandha?"

"He is supervising the loading at the eastern docks," Radhagupta answered. "A number of your ships are due to sail out today, carrying goods for Java."

"Tell him to stop whatever he is doing and grab his sword and be at my side immediately."

"Master, sending the ships out is important," Radhagupta protested. "We have even held up the goods of other merchants who use your ships to trade in order to send your goods first. We need coins flowing in to carry on the election campaign."

'Who said anything about not sending the ships?" Devdatta wiped the sweat off his forehead with his palm. "You replace him at the eastern docks and supervise the loading. Besides, if things get bloody here today, I would want you as far away as possible. You are too important."

"Allow me to stay at your side," Radhagupta pleaded. "We know not what the General will do. Mingling in the crowd, I can perhaps find out."

"Enough, Radhagupta!" Devdatta raised his hand. "If the General is going to attack me, Anirbandha and his sword will be of more use to me. So go now, we do not have much time."

Radhagupta watched Devdatta and his entourage move towards the crowd. It was going to be a long day.

***

As he hurried along the walkway that led from the western docks to the eastern, Radhagupta could not help but notice the two small galleys floating in the mid-section of the harbour. It was the strange colours that made him notice them, the hull painted a shining scarlet and the body in silvery white. They were like no other ships he had seen in the Kalinga docks. They did not even have the regular slits where archers stood while firing arrows at enemy galleys. Instead, its bow was strangely made with protruding wooden rods pointing ahead, like half penetrated arrows.

For a moment Radhagupta stood watching, rubbing the back of his head. Galleys were supposed to be warships, but he did not understand how these small boats could serve that purpose. He was about to walk away, remembering the urgent task at hand, when he saw the face. It appeared on the deck of one of the galleys. The beard had turned white and the head was bald, but there was no forgetting that face.

It was the man called Nikumbh, barking instructions to two sailors. When Radhagupta saw what the sailors were carrying in their hands, it all came to him in one flash. He ran towards the eastern dock, leaving the galley behind. Out of the corner of his eye he made sure Nikumbh had not spotted him yet as he ran for the archway that led to the eastern docks.

Devdatta's ships were docked along the first two boardwalks. They were huge beasts, with high wooden pillars to hoist the large sails upon open waters. He caught sight of Anirbandha by the first warehouse across the road, barking instructions to a line of labourers, who were carrying wooden crates and jute sacks upon their heads to the ships. Anirbandha looked up, surprised at his arrival and greeted him with a slight bow.

"Devdatta wishes to have you by his side," Radhagupta explained quickly, catching his breath. "You should leave at once."

"But these ships must leave today." Anirbandha looked around. "And they cannot leave before these goods have been loaded."

"Devdatta will not get up on the stage until he sees you." Radhagupta shrugged. "I don't give the orders here, he does."

Anirbandha did not look pleased. "These fools slack off if no one is standing over them," he complained.

"I'll take care of it," Radhagupta said, looking around. "You get your weapons and run for the podium. The Master is anxious."

Anirbandha cursed as he grabbed his helmet and scabbard from a nearby table. "Remember," he told Radhagupta, "only the goods that belong to Devdatta are to be loaded. They are in the first warehouse. The goods that belong to other merchants will go next time; those are in the second warehouse and are not to be touched."

Radhagupta nodded. "I understand."

Anirbandha looked around and then walked away towards the archway. Radhagupta waited till he was completely out of sight before looking for the ships' Foreman. He soon found the corpulent man, standing just inside the first warehouse, pointing the cargo out to the loaders, who walked in a long line.

"Listen to me closely," Radhagupta said to the man. "Order your men to unload the cargo in the holds."

The Foreman looked at him as if he had taken leave of his senses. "But Me Lord," he coughed, "we just spent the whole morning loading the cargo."

"Now unload it in half the time," Radhagupta ordered. He pointed to the second warehouse, adjoining the first

"Then fill the holds with the cargo from that warehouse."

"But that cargo belongs to the other merchants," the Foreman declared. "The Captain told me precisely that the Master's cargo was to be loaded first."

Radhagupta nodded casually. "There has been a change of plans. Now will you do as I ask or must I ask the Captain to come here and tell you himself?"

The Foreman watched him for a few moments, unsure what to say. If he was about to argue, those few moments made him decide against it. Radhagupta knew that all the sailors were aware of his standing with Devdatta. The Foreman let out a sigh. "Aye, we will do it."

"Good," Radhagupta nodded. "And do it quickly."

***

The speeches began late that day on the western docks of Dantapura, for the huge crowd present made it hard to set up the podium. Proceedings were about to begin when Radhagupta arrived. Anirbandha was standing behind the podium and the candidates and were already on the wooden platform. He threw Radhagupta a questioning look as he walked up and stood by his side.

"Is it done?" he asked, twirling his moustache. Radhagupta nodded. "When will the ships set sail?" He looked concerned.

'I have asked the Foreman to time it for when Devdatta takes the stand," Radhagupta told him. "It will send a powerful message as he gives his speech with two of his mighty ships setting sail in the background."

Anirbandha smiled, satisfied. Radhagupta nodded and retreated to the back, from where he could have a clear view of the people standing behind the podium. From the corner of his eye, he searched for Karuvaki on the podium. He soon found her and saw that her eyes were on him too. Radhagupta's brows lifted in inquiry. Karuvaki simply nodded.

The first to take the stand was Navin Kumar. He came forward to moderate cheers from the crowd. Radhagupta saw well-dressed individuals, both men and women, standing at the very front of the crowd. So the nobility was well represented in today's gathering. As Navin Kumar began delivering his speech, Radhagupta retreated to the small wall separating the sea from the dock and looked eastwards. The two strange galleys still stood roughly in the same spot they had been. Their entire crew stood on deck, as if waiting for a signal to set sail. A few yards behind them, Radhagupta caught sight of the high masts of Devdatta's own ships, which had finished loading a short while before.

He glanced to one side and saw General Bheema's piercing eyes staring at him as he strained his neck to see. Radhagupta returned his gaze steadily but soon realized the General was not looking at him, but at the galleys. Their attention was diverted by loud applause and Radhagupta saw that Karuvaki had taken the stage. The clapping stopped as she raised her hand for silence. "People of Kalinga," she declared loudly, "we believe in achieving a clear result in our elections. A hung House is of no advantage to anyone and the ones most affected are the people who have to face an extended period of ineffective governance."

Radhagupta waited with bated breath as she opened her mouth to speak again. Her next sentences would tell him if he had failed or succeeded.

All eyes focussed upon her, knowing that she was about to make an important announcement. "Keeping that in mind," she said clearly, "Candidate Navin Kumar and Candidate Devdatta have reached an agreement."

Radhagupta looked quickly towards the General but his face was devoid of any emotion. It was almost as if the General did not care what she was saying, though it apparently threatened his position in the elections. *I've seen through your plan, you bastard!* Radhagupta thought. *And I am using it against you.*

"We have all come to know Devdatta in the last few years. He has helped our country immensely by bringing goods to our shores during the Mauryan blockade."

'Aye! Aye!' Radhagupta heard the crowd cheer. It was going well.

"The Late Governor Navin extended the hand of friendship to this exceptional sailor, and now his son Navin Kumar will do the same," Karuvaki stated. "They have agreed to work as friends, and not be competitors. Devdatta will address this in his speech, so all of you keep your attention on him." She bowed and backed out as Devdatta stepped forward to a huge burst of applause. Karuvaki walked down the steps, off the stage. Her eyes searched for him again. Radhagupta nodded at her. She had kept her part of the bargain.

"We all heard what Lady Karuvaki and Navin Kumar have said." Devdatta's booming voice soared over the gathering. "I completely agree with what she has said."

Radhagupta looked back to watch the spectacle taking place on the eastern docks. Devdatta's ships had raised their sails and he could hear the distant cries of oarsmen as the ships moved forward towards the western docks, from where they would turn towards the open sea. And then, as Radhagupta looked back at the stage at General Bheema, he saw that the General was not even listening to the speech. He was staring intently towards the eastern docks.

"I too, declare that I am a friend to Navin Kumar and his clan," Devdatta continued. Radhagupta's eyes moved to Karuvaki, who was listening to every word intently.

"I hereby accept their support of my candidature," Devdatta declared loudly. "I ask the nobles of Kalinga to vote for me too, as the Late Governor's family now stands with me."

What! Radhagupta saw Karuvaki's mouth form the soundless exclamation as her face changed abruptly. Navin Kumar's other advisors began talking to each other hurriedly as the young man himself looked back at them from the podium, visibly confused. Radhagupta made his way through the crowd and touched Karuvaki on the shoulder.

"You bastard!" she shouted. "You betrayed me!"

Radhagupta shrugged. "You never gave me a clear answer to my proposition. We never did have a deal."

"You liar! You just made me look like a fool!" she spat.

"That or I just saved you from losing face when your candidate lost the elections."

She retorted angrily but her vitriolic words were drowned by a huge cheer from the crowd as Devdatta raised his arms. His two ships had by now reached the western docks and now sailed in the direction of the open sea, providing a wonderful backdrop.

"You are a lying and deceitful..." Karuvaki suddenly stopped, her eyes wide. "What in the name of..." Her face had turned pale.

Radhagupta turned to see what she was looking at though he already knew what he was going to see. The two galleys were now sailing at breakneck speed towards Devdatta's ships. But they were on fire, flames licking their frames.

"It is the General's doing," Radhagupta said.

Karuvaki turned to look at the stage. Devdatta was stepping back and the General coming forward to address the crowd.

"We must warn the men!" Karuvaki turned quickly towards the boardwalk, but Radhagupta grabbed her arm.

"There is no one on board," he told her quickly. "The sailors pushed the ships into the water and the tide took them out."

"But the goods on the other ships?"

"Just watch," Radhagupta said in her ear.

They heard scattered slogans as the General took the stage. He brought his hands together, clapping deliberately. "Such mighty words," he said, looking at Devdatta, "from a man who claims to be the best in this land of sailors."

Radhagupta watched the crowd. Some people had begun to notice what was happening out in the sea.

"By the Gods," Karuvaki sighed as the first of the burning galleys collided headlong into one of the ships. The flames immediately leapt to the large cargo ship, like dancing devils. The ship was soon engulfed.

People began to shout at the spectacle as the second galley collided sideways, setting the other cargo ship on fire. Those on the platform were now looking back at the sea, and Radhagupta caught sight of Devdatta watching, his fists clenched. He pushed his way through the crowd towards the podium.

"Fellow citizens, look ahoy! There go the ships of the man who claims to be the best sailor in Kalinga...on fire!" the General roared from the podium.

Radhagupta saw that those on the right, especially the merchants, had not moved from their positions and were listening. He finally reached Devdatta's side.

"I will kill that bastard," Devdatta whispered angrily.

"You need not," Radhagupta replied. "He just killed himself."

"What do you mean, man?" Devdatta asked, surprised. Radhagupta leaned over and whispered in his ear. The expression on his Master's face changed radically.

"This amn, who calims to the best sailor among us, could not even save his own ships from attack," the General bellowed at the crowd. "Two of his large cargo ships have been brought down by just two of my small galleys. How will he fare on the open sea? Is this man, who can be deceived like a child, the man to lead you, in charge of protecting us from deceitful enemies like the Mauryas?" The merchants in the crowd were nodding in agreement. The General smiled as he looked behind him, admiring his handiwork. Turning back to the crowd he roared, "Or do you want me, who has just proved I am the toughest in Kalinga? I, who can deceive but not be deceived. Who can protect my own, unlike this man."

Devdatta walked towards Bheema. "Mock all you want, General," he said loudly, so the crowd could hear, "but you have just made a grave mistake." He turned towards the merchants in the crowd. "The ships General Bheema has just set on fire contained *your* cargo, that which you wished me to take to Java and sell in the markets there," he declared.

Sudden silence descended on the crowd as realisation began to dawn on some of the merchants. "Bheema did not attack me," Devdatta continued, "he attacked you! He has burnt your goods. But because they were my ships, I will give each of you who lost your goods, full compensation. But what will General Bheema give you?" He looked at the General, whose face wore an ugly grimace.

'Get the bastard!' Shouts erupted from the crowd. Rotten fruit came flying toward the podium. People began to push forward and some of the merchants drew out their daggers. Bheema watched, his chest heaving in fury as his guards jumped onto the stage to shield him.

Radhagupta watched Devdatta quickly retreat from the stage. "It's done," he said. "This crowd has now turned into a mob."

"The General is furious," Radhagupta said, looking to where Bheema stood, staring down at them, his fists clenched. Eyes locked on Devdatta, he slowly moved his index finger across his throat.

"We should leave," Devdatta said. "There are too many of his men here but the crowd will keep them engaged. We can slip away quickly."

Radhagupta nodded and the two men swiftly made their way towards the chaotic streets.

"Look for Anirbandha, I can't see him," Devdatta said to Radhagupta. The guards had formed a protective circle around them.

As Radhagupta turned to go, Devdatta suddenly caught hold of his arm. "You did good, friend. You turned disaster into victory."

Radhagupta bowed. "It is what I do, Master."

"Find Anirbandha and come to the mansion. Then we celebrate."

Radhagupta nodded and moved out of the protective circle and was soon lost in the crowd. Anirbandha was nowhere to be seen. Radhagupta moved through the crowd, looking for him. Finally, he caught sight of him at the mouth of an empty alleyway leading out of the docks, away from the crowds.

"Anirbandha!" Radhagupta called as he made his way towards the alley.

"Radhagupta!" Anirbandha exclaimed on seeing him. "Quick, I have a carriage for Devdatta in the alley."

Radhagupta shook his head. "Devdatta moved towards the docks," he said. "He'll take a boat out of the city."

Anirbandha appeared disappointed at this information but quickly grabbed Radhagupta's arm. "Then let *us* take the carriage," he said.

Anirbandha ran into the alley and Radhagupta followed. There it was, a carriage standing in the shadows of the alley, with two horses hitched and ready to go.

"Quick, jump inside!" Anirbandha yelled, holding open the door.

Radhagupta climbed in, wishing to get as far from the carnage on the docks as possible. He turned to give Anirbandha a hand, but the young Captain was now facing him, smiling, sword in hand. "We told you not to meddle in our affairs," he snarled.

Radhagupta tried to jump out of the carriage but the opposite door was locked.

Holding his sword, Anirbandha climbed in. "Now suffer the consequences of your own actions," he said, and hit Radhagupta with the wooden hilt.

Radhagupta tried to defend himself, but he was unarmed and the Captain was fast. The sword hit caught him on the back of his head and Radhagupta fell to the floor of the carriage. The noise around him faded away as a blanket of darkness fell over him.

11
KANAKDATTA:
THE VALLEYS OF CHITRAKOOT

~

CHITRAKOOT, 263 BC

They rode through the dark grasslands unseen, like snakes slithering through hay. The wind carried away the sound of their horse's hooves. Kanakdatta led at the front, his eyes wide, looking for any tiny speck of light in the distance. When they stopped for water, at a long line of trees that separated the forest from the waist high shrubland, all they could hear was the incessant chirping of crickets all around them. The sky loomed above like a dark inky mass, filled with tiny twinkling stars. There was no sign of the white moon along its expanse.

"This is a bad idea, Lord," Cuska said between quick gulps of water from his leather pouch. His horse whimpered, as if in agreement.

Kanakdatta did not reply. He put his own goatskin pouch to his lips and felt the cool liquid fill his mouth. He drank slowly, feeling the coolness travel down his throat.

"We should not be going in this direction," Cuska continued as he prepared to get off his horse. "There is nothing but doom for us in this direction."

"You do not trust my friend, Cuska?" Kanakdatta asked, tossing his goatskin pouch to him.

Cuska caught it in a reflexive movement and jumped down to the ground. Only his upper body remained visible among the dark grass in which he stood. "Not a time you should be putting our trust in any more friends of yours, especially after how the last encounter went." Cuska patted his horse gently on its neck. He reached for the saddle bag tied to the saddle and ruffled through it, looking for something.

"That will not happen this time." Kanakdatta gazed into the distance. There was nothing to be seen except darkness all around. From the forest came the call of a distant predator.

"You said the same thing the last time." Cuska drew out a wide-mouthed bronze vessel from his saddlebag. Supporting it on his saddle, he carefully poured some water into it and held the vessel for the horse to drink. The animal lapped at it eagerly, as thirsty as the men.

Kanakdatta tightened the leather straps that secured the bow on his back. It had become loose with the hard cross-country riding. "All the more reason to trust me now. A man bitten once does not make the same mistake twice."

"For our sakes, I hope you are right," Cuska remarked.

Kanakdatta did not answer. He pulled the last leather strap tight before tying it into a knot at his waist. It had been a while since he had ridden out on such a toilsome journey. He could feel the fatigue as he stretched his arms above his head. The clicking of his joints did not bring him the relief he sought. As a merchant, he was used to palanquins and large decorated tents. When forced to ride, the journeys had been no longer than half a day, and never at night. He sighed as he realized that his years of inactivity were bearing down upon him. He brushed away such thoughts. He would endure. He always did.

"How much further?" Cuska asked as he brought over the refilled vessel to Kanakdatta's horse. The mount drank greedily, snorting in relief.

"We should reach them by first light if we keep riding," Kanakdatta said, looking up at the starry sky. They had ridden keeping the North Star in sight for two days and one night. Shiva's camp was said to be in the foothills of the mountain the bards called Chitrakoot. Once they had crossed the grasslands, they would come upon the massive waterfall that fell into the ravine like a foaming cloud.

Cuska tossed the vessel back into his saddlebag and climbed into his saddle. He adjusted his seat and picked up the reins. "And what do we do once we get there, Lord?" he asked, giving his horse the signal to start.

Kanakdatta breathed in deeply and did the same. "Survive," he said succinctly.

They trotted together into the darkness.

***

When the two men reached the ravines of Chitrakoot, the eastern sky was illuminated by the early glow of the rising sun. They rode into a small grove of Kadamba trees and stopped. Cuska got off his horse to hack at some branches that blocked their path. Holding onto his saddle, Kanakdatta climbed down slowly. When his feet were on the ground, he felt a tingling sensation as blood flowed back. The horses stood still for a moment, too tired to bend down and graze. Kanakdatta realized he was as exhausted as they.

They had outridden any messengers from Patliputra. There was no doubt in Kanakdatta's mind that Chanakya would immediately send riders in all directions, publicizing his supposed betrayal to all the Rajas of the subcontinent. It was why he had insisted on riding without rest. The fastest men in the Samrajya were his own men, and he was sure none of them would ride out to compromise their own master. Chanakya would have had to use his own men. Kanakdatta was sure none had matched their own speed.

"Here." Cuska tossed a thorny round fruit at him.

Kanakdatta turned but the fruit hit his shoulder pads and fell to the ground. Kanakdatta cursed silently. *You are getting old*, he told himself. There had been a time when he would never have missed a catch. He stretched his shoulder muscles and then sat down on the ground beside the fallen fruit, stretcheing out his legs. They felt stiff from all the riding.

Cuska joined him, digging his nails into the thick skin of the fruit and then putting his lips to it and sucking out the flesh. Violet juices streamed down his cheeks as Kanakdatta observed the man closely.

"Why did you choose to save me?" he asked, holding his own fruit in his hands.

"It took you a while to ask that question." Cuska spit out the seeds that had entered his mouth.

"Not that we had any time for conversation with the bloodhounds on our trail," Kanakdatta laughed. The fruit tasted strangely satisfying and sweet.

"I asked myself the same question as we rode through the night." Cuska nodded. "Did not make any sense to throw away an honourable position and assist a man who was declared to be an enemy of the Samrajya."

Kanakdatta laughed. "You honour me, my friend. The Prime Minister would merely call me a vile Buddhist who had finally showed his true colours."

"But I am not the Prime Minister, am I?" Cuska had finished his first fruit and moved to the second. "I am a simple soldier. Always have been. Never liked that old fool if truth be told."

"It still does not answer my question." Kanakdatta stared at him.

"You do not give up easily, do you?" Cuska coughed. "Well, I helped you because I had to do something."

"What do you mean?"

"How do you think I became the Samrat's personal bodyguard?" Cuska sighed, looking up at the sky. "I have been with him since the beginning. I was with him when he rode to Vidishanagri the first time to meet you. I was with him when his bodyguard was injured in an attack at night. I rode by his side when he went into Maharaja Avarak's camp to get him to stop his rebellion. Hell, I was the man who rode out from Patliputra when Sushem laid siege, to send word to you."

Kanakdatta closed his eyes, trying to recollect. "How come I do not remember you?"

"It is all the same with you noblemen," Cuska said. "You have no eyes for common soldiers. We all look the same to you."

"Do not have love for me, do you?"

"I am a mere soldier." Cuska looked down. "I do my duty. Do not have much love or hate for anyone."

"Except your Master. Except Asoka."

Cuska turned away. Kanakdatta knew he had touched a raw nerve. He put his hand on Cuska's shoulder, seeing the young man was fighting tears.

"He was a great man." Cuska trembled as he tried to sound composed. "I would have followed him into battle blindfolded. I was there when he rode north to teach the rebels a lesson. I was at his side in each camp, in every skirmish."

"You have been a loyal servant," Kanakdatta said.

"I still am," Cuska sighed. "Something changed when he came back to the palace. The Old Man did some kind of magic on him. He had never drunk an excess of wine. I had never seen him drunk in all our time together, and mind you I am the man who has seen him the most. More than even you."

"I understand," Kanakdatta nodded.

"Something changed in him when he came back to the palace. I felt as if I did not know him anymore, did not understand his actions. He would give orders to kill without thought. He would drink without restraint." Cuskha looked up. "He would take any woman he wanted, even my wife."

Kanakdatta recoiled in horror. "What?"

"I was on duty. She had come to see me in the palace." Cuska closed his eyes. "He was utterly drunk. He saw her walking through the gardens and called out to her. She would not go to him so he ordered me to drag her to him."

"I am sorry, brother."

"As am I." Cuska opened his moist eyes. Tears trickled down his cheeks. "I could not look at my own hands after the day I took my own wife to his bed. I had never thought such a thing could happen. I had heard all the tales of course, of how the Late Samrat Bindusar would do these things, but I thought my Master was different, a noble Samrat."

Kanakdatta rose to his feet and looked down into the valley. A gusty breeze had begun to blow in their faces, bringing the sound of rustling leaves, and wind rushing against unforgiving rock. "So that is why you helped me." Understanding had finally dawned upon him. "You had had enough."

"I have always been loyal," Cuska murmured, looking elsewhere, "and I still am, though to a different man now."

Kanakdatta did not respond. He walked to the edge of the ravine, where the sheer cliff dropped down into the valley. All along the river that flowed below, cutting into the rock, they could see countless tents dotting the landscape, their white fabric fluttering in the morning wind and glistening in the early sun. "We must get going," he said.

"When you brought news of the Prime Minister's wrong doings to him, I dared to hope," Cuska said, holding the reins of the horses. "I knew this was a chance to see my master become his old self again."

Kanakdatta walked back to him. "But then he hit me, his old friend, and your hope was lost."

"No, then he hit you and I knew that *your* hope was lost," Cuska said, handing over the reins. "I knew that for my hope to become true, I had to rekindle yours."

Kanakdatta nodded, climbed onto his horse. "I thank you, Cuska. You saved my life."

"And now I want you to save my Master's." Cuska mounted and rode ahead.

***

They descended into the valley from a small path that curved its way along the cliff, cut out by some old descending stream that had later changed course. The horses traversed the narrow ledges with difficulty but Cuska's skilful handling led them on. When they reached the level of the tents, Kanakdatta looked at Cuska. "It would be safer if no one recognizes us," he said.

Cuska looked down at his scarlet and yellow uniform, covered with dust from the days of travelling. "I will take my uniform off," he said, "but you are Kanakdatta the Buddhist. You are famous across all Bharatvarsha."

"And my appearance is described as silken clothes and shiny ornaments," Kanakdatta nodded, looking down at his own dirty linen cloak. "I daresay we will be fine."

They rode along the line of tents after Cuska had tossed his uniform into the bushes, wearing only his undershirt. Familiar sounds filled the air of a company of archers practicing. 'Shoot!' the Captain would yell, followed by the twanging of a dozen strings, followed by the thwack of the metal tips hitting their wooden targets. They passed an open field where scores of young men stood in line as a uniformed Captain drilled them. "Attention!" he shouted and the men fell into lines.

"This makes me miss my old days at camp," Cuska said as they moved through the narrow paths between the tents. "Old General Sunga drilled us himself once."

"There it is.' Kanakdatta pointed to a tent that rose above the others, emblazoned with the Mauryan colours. "That has to be Shiva's tent."

"Are you going to barge right in and tell him to march on Patliputra instead of Kalinga?" Cuska asked, looking at his companion.

Kanakdatta shook his head. "I would never ask that of my friend."

Cuska shrugged. "I will be here outside the tent with my sword if something goes wrong."

They caught sight of Shiva in his white flowing undershirt, barking orders to some men putting up a canopy outside his tent. Kanakdatta climbed down and handed over the reins of his horse to Cuska. He walked a few steps forward and Shiva caught sight of him immediately. His eyes widened in surprise, but Kanakdatta put a finger to his lips. Shiva nodded and disappeared into the darkness of his tent. Kanakdatta looked around, making sure no one was watching before following him.

Once inside, Shiva looked at his friend in stunned surprise as he embraced him. "Is this one of your disguises, my friend?" he asked. "Is this what you do as Spymaster?"

Kanakdatta went to the table in the corner and poured two goblets of wine. "Listen closely," he said, handing one to Shiva. "Something untoward has happened."

"What is it?" Shiva asked, gulping down the liquid.

"Today, you will receive a messenger from Patliputra, carrying a letter bearing the Prime Minister's seal. He will inform you that from this day on, I, Kanakdatta the Buddhist, am to be treated as a traitor and it is the responsibility of every Mauryan citizen to do me harm."

Shiva's eyes stared at him as if he had suddenly become deranged. "What in the name of…what did you do?"

"I do not have much time, so pay attention." Kanakdatta refilled both goblets. "In Kalinga, my men saw someone we all thought had been dead for years."

"Who?"

"Devi."

"That is impossible!" Shiva's face had turned chalky.

"The man who saw her in Kalinga has known her since she was a babe." Kanakdatta sighed. "If he says he saw her, I believe him."

"You should tell Asoka," Shiva said thoughtfully.

"I did. He did not believe me."

"I do not blame him." Shiva sat down on his narrow soldier's bed. "Even I find it hard to believe."

"There is more," Kanakdatta told him. "My men saw someone else with her, a man both of us are familiar with. A man the Prime Minister told us was a traitor."

"Radhagupta!" Shiva exclaimed, astonished. "But he disappeared on the day of the coronation. He was a traitor, who killed our prisoner, Acharya Hariharan, in our own camp. We did not know it but Chanakya told us later."

"Chanakya told me to imprison him, kill him if I could," Kanakdatta disclosed in a low voice. "But I helped him escape that day. I gave him my horse."

"What in the God's name!" Shiva grabbed Kanakdatta by his shoulders and pushed him away with both hands.

"That is all long past," Kanakdatta said. "But Devi's body was discovered the same day Radhagupta disappeared. Do you see the connection?"

"All I see is that you helped a traitor escape and never told me about it." Shiva looked away. "How could you?"

"Because I owed it to him." Kanakdatta looked down. "That man once had my life in his hands and did not kill me. So I helped him. And I ask you to do the same for me now, for the same reason."

"What do you mean?"

Kanakdatta looked up. "You owe me, friend. When you rebelled with your father against the tyrant Governor of Avanti, I was the one who provided you with the weapons to fight him. Without me, your rebellion would have vanished like a puff of smoke, and you with it. If you still possess your Kshatriya honour, you will help me now."

Shiva shrugged. "What do you want?"

"Nothing that will bring you dishonour," Kanakdatta said, smiling. "I intend to ride to Kalinga to discover if Devi is really there. If she is, I will take her to Asoka. He will have to believe me then."

"What do you need me for?"

"When Asoka refused to believe me, I proposed this same plan to him," Kanakdatta related. "But the Prime Minister insisted I was a traitor, that I needed an excuse to defect to Kalinga. He called it a ruse."

"And did Asoka believe him?"

"He did. Because the Prime Minister told him something that made him believe."

Shiva looked Kanakdatta in the eye. "What did he say?"

"That I am a Kalingan by birth. That I am the firstborn son of Kalinga's late Governor, Navin."

Shiva gazed at him, transfixed. "Why did he believe the Prime Minister and not you?"

Kanakdatta took a deep breath. He did not know how to break it to his friend. "Because it is true, Shiva. I am a Kalingan. I am a son of Navin."

Shiva mouth opened in surprise as he stepped back. "You of all people," he said. "Why Kanaka, why did you never tell us?"

"It was long gone history," Kanakdatta sighed. "My father had banished me from Kalinga even before I had a full grown beard. I had nothing to do with my homeland anymore. I came to the Mauryan lands to make my fortune, and to anyone who asked, I said I was a Shudra turned Buddhist."

Shiva did not speak but kept looking at his friend as if he had seen a ghost.

"You have to trust me, my friend." Kanakdatta extended his hand. "After I related my past to Asoka, he said that I could no longer remain Spymaster and was to be held under house arrest till the war was over."

"So what did you do?"

"I escaped. The Prime Minister's men came after me, but I managed to thwart them and escape."

Shiva took a deep breath. "So you are indeed a traitor. That is how it would look to everyone."

"I do not ask you to trust me blindly. I will go to Kalinga and find the answers. And then you will know. All I ask of you now is to repay the favour I did you."

"And what do you ask me to do?" Shiva asked.

"I cannot make it to Kalinga alone." Kanakdatta touched his friend's shoulder. "Not with the Prime Minister's men and Asoka's vassals looking for me. I need an army."

"I cannot give you one." Shiva shook his head. "If I do, it would be an act of treason."

"You cannot give me one, but you can let me take one from you." Kanakdatta let go and looked outside. "My blood riders, the ones you borrowed to defeat the Shivalik rebels, are my men. They would follow me to the world's end. You tell me where they are and I will go and ask them to follow me."

Shiva sighed and caressed his chin.

"Do this, old friend," Kanakdatta pleaded. "The royal decree has not yet reached you. If you help me now, before it does, your honour will not be stained as a traitorous Senapati, nor for refusing to help a friend."

Shiva nodded. "Have it your way. I used your blood riders to take the monastery in the Shivaliks. A bunch of savages, those brutes are. They are still at the monastery, holding it as a garrison."

"I thank you, my friend." Kanakdatta took both Shiva's hands in his own. "I give you my word, I shall find the answers."

"For your sake Kanaka, I hope you do," Shiva said quietly. "And if what you say is true, I will not regret helping you today."

"I am your friend," Kanakdatta said. "I always have been. You know I would never lie to you."

"Then go quickly," Shiva told him. "Take fresh horses from my stables. You can reach the monastery in two days, three at the most. It is not too far from here." He grabbed a parchment on his desk and scribbled a hurried note for the stable master.

Kanakdatta smiled. "I will reach it in a day."

"And what will you do when you do?" Shiva rolled the parchment into a scroll and handed it over.

"I cannot tell you that because you will be tasked with catching me as soon as the royal decree arrives from Patliputra."

Shiva smiled. "Go with the Gods, my friend."

"You forget that my kind does not believe in Gods." Kanakdatta tucked the scroll under his cloak.

"Then go for the sake of Asoka," Shiva said. "What you do will decide whether we meet as friends or foes."

"Aye, that it will," Kanakdatta nodded. "But for now, we part as friends."

The two men embraced in the pale light that emanated from the tent flap. As Kanakdatta walked out, Shiva could not know that he would never embrace his friend again.

12
HARDEO:
MESSENGERS AND MEMORIES

———————◦———————

VIDISHA, 263 BC

When his carriage rolled in through the gates of Vidishanagri, the skies had turned crimson. Hardeo knew darkness would soon fall, meaning he would not be able to inspect the troops camped outside the city gates. Before he had left for Patliputra, he had instructed his captains to raise the Vidishanagri army. "Not a single man is to be left out," he had told them. "By the time I return, I wish to see every able bodied fighting man from my lands gathered outside the city gates." Now, returning from the capital, he was not sure if even that would be enough.

"Is it done?" he asked his Captain as he climbed down from the carriage.

The captain bowed. "Aye, we have visited every settlement and raised the army and armed them from our own armoury. Several thousand men are camped outside the city walls, ready to obey your command."

Hardeo felt relieved at hearing the number. It would ensure that Chanakya would not capture him easily. If needed, Hardeo would fight to the last man.

"Will these soldiers do as they are told?" he asked the Captain, accepting the tumbler of water an assistant had brought. "For what we ask might be seen as treason."

"The men of Vidishanagri are simple people, Maharaja. They tend to their fields and flocks, and know they are able to sustain good lives because of the fair practices of the Merchant's Guild. They understand only your kindness, not words like treason."

"Good." Hardeo nodded. "Rest them well for we need to be ready soon."

"And what should I tell them to be ready for?"

"For battle, my dear man," Hardeo said ironically.

Chanakya's words echoed in his ears. The old devil had promised he would send an army to attack the city. With his two thousand fighters, Hardeo knew he had a chance to hold the city. Supplies were not a problem. He had ensured the city granaries were full, knowing that the businessman who looks after his people's basic necessities, like food and shelter, is the one who succeeds in the end. He was counting on holding the city long enough for the the Prime Minister to realize that wasting resources on internal battles was not wise when war loomed with Kalinga. He knew the Prime Minister would then make a deal. Hardeo knew that his best option was to get a deal, buy time, and then plan his escape and revenge. These things could not be hurried if they were to be done right.

"There is one other thing, Maharaja," the Captain said. "A visitor has come to the city from down South. His garb looks Kalingan. He is a young lad, who has not even grown a full beard yet. He seeks audience with you."

Hardeo raised his eyebrows. "Did he say who he is? I do not recall any such."

"He says he will speak only to you."

"Bring him to me in the morning," Hardeo nodded.

The Captain bowed. 'We have given them a room near the stables and food and water. They have been travelling for quite a few days it seems, he and the two children."

"Two children?" The wheels in Hardeo's brain began to turn.

"Aye, a little girl and a boy. They are all asleep now, exhausted by their long journey."

"Awaken them," Hardeo said, "for I wish to see them at once."

***

In the meagre light of the lanterns in the stables, Hardeo observed the faces of the three visitors, but his old eyes did not tell him much. It was the voice that did the trick. The young girl, afraid of the sudden number of strangers in the room, clung to the young lad who had brought them to the city. "I want to go home, Tissa," she whimpered. It was when he heard that voice that Hardeo finally understood. The voice reminded of him of long lost years and he felt a sweet happiness tug at his heart.

"Are you the Guild Master?" the young lad called Tissa asked, visibly afraid, holding onto the little girl tightly. The young boy at their side observed everything, sucking on his thumb.

"I am," Hardeo nodded. "Please do not be afraid."

"We come from Kalinga," Tissa muttered, loosening his grip on the girl. "I have a message for you, from your daughter."

"Do you joke at an old man's expense, boy?" Hardeo's forehead filled with lines. "My daughter is dead."

Tissa shook his head. "She is alive. These are your grandchildren." Holding the children's hands, he offered them to him.

Hardeo touched the little girl's hand, but she tugged away in irritation. The young boy, said nothing but watched curiously. Now that they were closer, Hardeo could see their faces clearly. Their brown eyes reminded him of someone he had long presumed dead. "Is Devi really alive?' he asked dreamily, but even as he did, he knew the lad spoke the truth for the girl before him seemed like her mother reborn.

Tissa nodded. "She is in Kalinga. She asked me to bring the children to you for safekeeping for there is soon to be elections. She felt they would be safer here."

"What is your name?" Hardeo asked softly, bending down to hold the little boy's hand.

The child looked at him fearfully, frozen. It was the girl who answered. "I am Sanghamitra, and my brother is Mahindra. My mother says he has your eyes."

Looking at them, Hardeo knew that both of them did. The moment passed. Hardeo straightened, thinking deeply. While his heart was filled with joy, his brain told him the best possible thing in his life had occurred at the worst possible moment.

His Captain bent to whisper in his ear. "Maharaja, if what the lad says is true, the children are not safe here either."

Hardeo nodded. He was expecting an attack on the city. The children could not stay with him. Unless… "We must get them away from here," he said to the Captain. "We leave at first light. Pack their belongings."

"And where will we go?" the Captain wondered.

"To Kalinga," Hardeo said. "To verify that what the lad says is true. If Devi is indeed there, my heart aches to see her immediately. We shall carry the wealth of Vidishanagri with us. When our enemies march here, they will find a deserted city and the only things they can defile are the earthen buildings and wooden halls."

The Captain bowed. "As you command."

Suddenly, the loud tolling of bells came to their ears. Hardeo stood still. He knew it could be coming only from one place. "Did you have the bell tower repaired while I was gone, Captain?" he asked as they walked out.

"Aye, I did. But the man on duty would not just ring the bell."

"Unless he has seen something."

"Do you think it is happening already?" the Captain asked, worried. "Do you think the Mauryan army is here already?"

"There is only one way to find out." Hardeo held up his cane and walked towards the steps that led to the walls. The Captain raced in front, eager to see what the man in the bell tower had seen.

It took Hardeo's old legs a while to climb to the battlements. When he was up, he found the Captain's face had turned ashen. The man pointed wordlessly. Hardeo froze. Hundreds of dark figures had appeared on the horizon, appearing darker than the dark blue night sky. The sound of hooves filled the air.

"Has to be more than a hundred cavalrymen," the Captain guessed.

The truth of his words rang in Hardeo's ears. He knew this must be the advance shock troops carrying the thrust of surprise. He knew the famed Mauryan infantry would soon follow, bringing with them the siege weapons. "Bring the soldiers inside the walls," he ordered calmly. If the fight had begun, he would not let fear or chaos rule them.

The Captain nodded and gave the order. They watched as the sentries blew their horns, awakening the soldiers in the vast camp just beyond the walls.

"It will be too late if the enemy reach the walls first," the Captain said. "I will go down and try to instill some order myself."

Hardeo clutched the wooden battlements as he watched the Captain go. *How cruel the world had become*, he thought. Word of his beloved daughter being alive had been brought to him only to be followed by enemies besieging his city. But Devi being alive instilled a sense of hope in him. As he watched the Captains trying to instill some order in the chaos below, Hardeo sighed. He would not give up. He would fight to the last man. Arya Chanakya would know a real enemy once again in his long life.

13
CHANAKYA:
THE SIGNET RING

———————∼———————

PATLIPUTRA, 262 BC

The exquisite glass vase shattered into a thousand pieces as it hit the floor, the impact sending the shards in all directions. Chanakya wheeled his chair back to avoid injury. "Such a savage display of anger does not become a Samrat," he said. "Your grandfather expressed his anger in words. You should do the same."

On the throne, Asoka did not seem to care. "Maybe you listened to his words. You do not listen to mine."

"So you throw and destroy priceless objects? What if you had hurt me?"

"You owe me an explanation, Guru," Asoka said angrily, banging his fists on the armrests fashioned in the shape of lions. "Kanaka was my best friend."

"And he still left," Chanakya said tenaciously. "You should think twice before calling someone your friend."

"I have known him for the whole of my adult life," Asoka shouted, his voice echoing in the vast chamber, "yet you still branded him a traitor without my permission."

"I did it to protect you. He is a traitor," Chanakya said defiantly,

"That is for me to judge." Asoka raised his finger with the royal signet. "It is my right to look him in the eye and judge him, not yours."

"And that is exactly why I have ordered our soldiers and vassals to capture him and bring him to you, so that you can look him in the eye and pass judgment."

Asoka opened his mouth to speak but closed it abruptly and covered his face with his palms. "My friend," he sighed. "He was my friend."

"It serves no one to cry over spilt milk, My Samrat." Chanakya pointed to a servant carrying numerous rolls of parchment. "We have important matters to discuss."

"Then discuss them," Asoka said curtly, "and then leave me alone."

"I may leave you alone," Chanakya replied, taking hold of the first scroll and unrolling it, 'but the crown on your head never will. Nor the ring on your finger."

Asoka waved his hands dismissively. "What is the first order of business?"

"We must conduct a holy ceremony," Chanakya read, "to ask the blessings of the Gods upon the coming war."

"Damn you and your ceremonies!" Asoka retorted angrily. "You would rather have me sit in saffron robes than don the crimson armor of my grandfather."

"We have already been over this." Chanakya dipped the seal he was holding in the crimson ink in front of him and pressed it onto the parchment.

"What is the next issue?"

"A family dispute, two brothers fighting over their father's ancestral property. They seek judgment."

"Schedule the hearing two days from now," Asoka said, making a quick gesture with his hand. Chanakya dipped his pen into the ink and wrote.

"Next?"

"A foreign poet seeks audience to recite a poem he has composed about you."

"Have him come to the court whenever he desires."

"Which will be never." Chanakya looked at his scroll. "I know this man. He is a Buddhist by birth. Not someone who should be seen with you in court."

"Because it will anger the *pujaris* of the palace?" Asoka mocked. "If you are going to take all my decisions for me Guru, perhaps you should be sitting on this chair."

"I sit on another chair altogether, Samrat," Chanakya said, pointing to his vegetative legs. "I daresay it is enough for me."

"What is next?"

"I wanted to discuss some royal matches I have shortlisted for you." Chanakya looked up. 'Beautiful women from the North. All Princesses."

Asoka shook his head. "If there is no other matters of the State, I would like to rest now," he declared.

"The matter of your second marriage *is* a matter of State." Chanakya stressed every word.

"Yet, I do not see you holding any parchment that says so," Asoka shrugged.

"I have something better." Chanakya clapped his hands and servants entered the chamber carrying large wooden panels, covered with cloths. "Portraits, my Samrat."

Asoka got to his feet. "I will not see them," he said coldly.

"But you must." Chanakya gestured and the servants pulled the covers off, one by one. Asoka hurried down the steps and walked away. But Chanakya caught him stealing a glance at the beautiful faces. It was only a glance but it was a start.

"We should not be fighting." Chanakya rolled his chair after Asoka. "Not in times of war. Our enemies will take it as a sign of weakness."

Asoka stopped in his tracks. He looked back and gave a tired smile. "Perhaps we are weak then," he said and walked away.

Chanakya sat alone in the vast chamber with the portraits of beautiful women behind him. He sighed. He had to regain control. Such arguments had occurred before, but now the Samrat was growing more disrespectful, brasher. He had to do something. He could not lose the Samrat's trust, now of all times. He closed his eyes and contemplated. Suddenly, it came to him, like it had decades ago, and Chanakya smiled.

50 YEARS AGO

"The Samrat wishes to see you," the sentry said, nothing more. I rose from my bed and dressed silently. Outside, the world was dark and rain fell heavily, hitting the rock of the palace like sea waves upon the coast. Tonight was an important night. I had planned to rise at midnight and had hoped to get some sleep till then. But the Gods had decided to withold that moment of peace from me.

Whenever Chandragupta needed me late at night, he usually came to my chambers himself. Today, however, he had chosen to summon me to him. I walked the short distance to his chambers silently, with only the sound of my own footsteps as an accompaniment. But he was nowhere to be seen. The sentry came running after me, panting. "The Prime Minister left before I could tell him the venue." He bowed nervously. "The Samrat is in the audience chamber."

"At this hour?" I said, surprised.

The sentry stood looking at the floor, not knowing what to say. "I was just talking to the rain," I told him and followed him down the corridor.

The walk to the large chamber that housed the throne, was long. We descended several staircases and the torches on the walls made our own shadows dance like devils of doom. The sentry bowed and retreated once we reached the ceiling high ornate doors. I pushed them open and entered. It was dark but for the light coming from the openings in the vaulted ceiling. Chandragupta sat upright on the throne, wearing his crimson armour.

"Welcome, Guru," he said as I walked in.

"What are you doing here at this hour?" I asked, advancing towards the throne slowly, wondering what was happening.

"It occurs to me that you have not seen me on this seat for quite some time." Chandragupta curled his moustache. "So I decided to remind you of who the Samrat of this subcontinent is"

So this was how it was going to be. "How can I forget when I put you on that seat myself?"

"Did you?" A flash of lightning momentarily filled the room with bright light. "I thought this throne was mine by right, having passed to me from my ancestors." Chandragupta raised his right hand on which the royal signet glowed.

"Indeed, Vrishala," I nodded, standing at the base of the steps. "Why did you wish to remind me of your all-encompassing power?"

"Because you have been doing things behind my back, Guru." Lightning flashed again and I did not need to look at his face in the light to know that he was angry.

"Trust me Vrishala, if I wanted to do things behind your back, your ears would never hear of them." I said.

"How do you defend yourself for these actions of which I accuse you?" Chandragupta raised his arm. He was holding a parchment. "Your actions this last week make it seem you are working against me, Guru."

"Why would I do that?"

"Power changes men." Chandragupta smiled. "Your own words, Guru."

I waved my arms. "Let us not dally with words. Tell me, Chandragupta, what you accuse me of and I shall answer."

Chandragupta breathed in and read from the parchment. "I see five names here – Bhadrabhata, Purudatta, Dingaita, Balgupta and Rajasena. All five noblemen defected from our Army and Council and went over to Malayketu. They left the city last week, in the dead of night."

I nodded. "I am aware."

"Then why did you not stop them?" Chandragupta asked angrily.

"For most cogent reasons, Vrishala. Listen to me. Bhadrabhata and Purudatta were Superintendents in charge of our stables. They were addicted to wine, women and chariot racing, a sylvan sport. They neglected their duties with the horses and elephants. So I removed them from their posts. It is no surprise they defected to the other side to try to regain their positions."

"So why did you not kill the traitors?"

"Always kill those traitors who would cause you harm. I chanted a Sanskrit subhashit. "If Malayketu is to make them Superintendents of his stable, I daresay we will have an easy time defeating his elephants and horses when it is time for battle."

Chandragupta looked satisfied with my answer, but he shook his head. "It is not how I would have dealt with them," he uttered. "What about the others?"

"Dingaita and Balgupta were blinded by excessive greed. They were Sergeants in the mercenary division and concluded that the pay they received from the treasury was too meagre. Thinking they controlled the mercenaries, they tried to blackmail us to get their pay raised."

"And you let them go?"

"I sent a strong message to anyone else lusting after the same idea. We cannot be blackmailed. The two left for Malayketu's camp but will not last there long for the greedy are never satisfied and always feel they would be better off in some other place than the one they are in."

"Again, I ask," Chandragupta said, "why did you not have them put to death?"

"It helps to have greedy men in the service of the enemy, and to know who they are," I replied. "When battle comes, we know who will turn sides for a paltry bribe."

"What about Rajasena?" Chandragupta said, his eyes on me. "He was one of our brothers, from the days of Taxila. A fellow student who studied under you."

"Rajasena was a mediocre Councillor." I raised my hand to emphasise my point. "He believed that because he had been with us from the very start, we should confer some important office upon him. But he did not have the talent to attain any position higher than the one he already held. So when we denied his request, he too left, hoping to get what he sought at Malayketu's court."

"And you did not remove him because a mediocre official in the enemy court hurts the enemy, not us."

I bowed. Chandragupta did not smile.

"There is more," he said. "Malayketu is guided by a man known as Amatya Rakshasa. I believe his family was still in city when he left. So you looked for them and found them hiding in the house of a man called Chandandasa."

"Indeed, I did," I nodded. "They were hidden very well, in a secret basement in Chandandasa's house. It took us a while to get to them."

"And yet," Chandragupta said loudly, "you did not act upon what you had discovered."

I folded my arms. "I did act."

"Did you take them into custody as hostages, to use against Rakshasa?"

"No."

"Did you apprehend the traitor Chandandas, who sheltered them, and who is known to be one of Rakshasa's closest friends?"

"It is not yet the right time to do that."

"Then how can you say that you acted?" Chandragupta looked at me with a questioning gaze.

"I am afraid I cannot tell you that."

Chandragupta sighed. "Your silence worries me, Guru. It raises all sorts of questions in my mind."

"You must trust me, Vrishala."

"I would," Chandragupta nodded, "but it is your own teaching that blind trust is fatal. And then there is this matter of the traitor Saktadasa."

My heart missed a beat. The events involving Saktadasa were recent. Chandragupta had obviously been vigilant about what was happening in the city. I could not help but feel admiration for my pupil. "Saktadasa was Rakshasa's Chief Clerk when he was Prime Minister. He is a Rakshasa loyalist, and has been sentenced to death. What worries you regarding his fate?"

Chandragupta leaned forward. "What worries me is that you control it. I have heard talk of a plot to rescue him from prison so he can escape the city. And I have heard your name is behind the plot."

I felt my legs go weak at this speech but I kept my composure. "I do not know what you are talking about."

"Do you not?" Chandragupta adjusted the *uparna* around his neck. "Have you not put your own man, Dasharath by name, on this task? The same man who showed us the way in when I captured the city."

"When *we* captured the city," I corrected him. "It was as much my victory as yours."

"And yet, it is only I who am a descendant of Ajatshatru." Chandragupta got to his feet. "The Ancient Brahminical Order bowed to me, not to you. We managed to forge this Samrajya due to my lineage, not because of your actions."

I clenched my teeth, trying to hold in my anger. The secret of his true lineage was locked in my chest.

"Why do you not share your plans with me, Guru? How am I to trust you if you do not? What do you plan to accomplish by setting Saktdasa free?"

"We will not speak of Saktdasa again." I held my ground. "And I do not share my plans with you because of the cardinal rule of statecraft – do not share a plan with one who has no role in it."

"And why am I not playing a part?"

"Because you are the Samrat. Leave the dirty dealings to me. That way, if I fail, you can simply disown my actions without having the taint of them upon your persona, and continue your iron rule."

Chandragupta laughed. "My iron rule. How do you compare it to iron when it is you who runs the forge?"

"Because I run it for you." I folded my arms. "I run it so the great cause for which we work is not defeated, even if one of us is."

"Listen to me closely." Chandragupta's tone was authoritarian. "You described this greater cause you speak of, after the coronation – to unite all the Aryas against external enemies. It is a noble aim. None has ever before attempted it, and we are close to achieving what we seek. But now your own actions and speech cause me to doubt your devotion to that very cause."

"Do not doubt my dedication even for a fleeting moment, Vrishala," I told him. "For that cause is the only purpose of my life. And it is the only purpose of your life as well, as Samrat of all the Aryas. Your people look up to you. If you betray the cause, I would kill you with my own hands and expect you to do the same to me if I betray it."

Chandragupta nodded. "Do not make me regret my trust in you. If it was any other man in your position, I would have cast him away long ago. But you are my Guru. I know you have never lied to me. I will put my faith in you as I have before, but I warn you, if you ever lie to me, Guru, I shall never trust you again for my faith in you has never been blind."

"But mine has been. I have never doubted you, Vrishala, as you doubt me now." I bowed. "On the day we win, you will have all the answers to the questions you ask, but not today."

"So be it, Guru." Chandragupta walked down the steps and stood in front of me. He hesitated for a moment, then quickly bowed, his hands touching my feet. I blessed him by placing a hand upon his head. His bristly hair pricked my hand.

After he left, I remained standing and alone, for some time, soaking in the history of the place, thinking of all those who had sat on this throne before, from the days of Ajatshatru to now. When I returned to my chambers, I saw the door ajar and the lamp lit. Dasharath was waiting for me inside, already dressed. Under his cloak he wore armour, and on his feet were leather boots made of deer hide that would endure over a long journey.

"The Samrat?" He looked at me, brows raised. I nodded. "Trouble?" he asked.

I shook my head. "Nothing I cannot handle. Now, do you have it?"

Dasharath handed me a small package. It was small, wrapped in cotton cloth and tied with a knot. I unrolled it to reveal a golden circlet, a ring. In place of the stone, there protruded a metallic hemisphere, with lines embossed on it to form the face of a tiger. "A signet ring!" I said in satisfaction. "Just as I had expected."

Dasharath nodded. "Dipped in ink and then pressed upon any surface, it will leave an indelible mark."

"Rakshas' royal seal." I put the ring on my finger "I am sure he misses it. How many times he must have used it. Have you brought the letter?"

Dasharath nodded and reached into the pouch at his belt. He drew out a parchment and placed it on my desk. I moved the candle closer and the characters came to life. My eyes moved over them, taking in every word. Finally, I smiled. "It is perfect. How did you make him write it?"

"Just as you instructed," Dasharath said. "He did not doubt a word."

I uncorked the little bottle carrying my regular indigo ink and poured it into a thin bronze plate. When the layer was thick enough, I clenched my fist and pressed the ring into it. Dasharath unrolled the parchment carrying the letter and held it flat. I pressed the ink-soaked signet hard into the yellowness. When I released it, the mark was there for all to see. "It is done." I said

"Aye." Dusting the imprint with sand, Dasharath placed the parchment carefully in his pouch. "It is time." he said.

It was indeed time. The wheels of destiny would be set in motion today. Dasharath looked me in the eye. "The preparations are made," he said in a low voice. "The Brothers have already taken up their positions in the tunnels. At midnight, we shall break open the door to Saktdasa's cell and bring him out of the palace through the old route."

"Be mindful of the city guards," I warned. "They may sense something is afoot."

Dasharath nodded. "The Gods have blessed us, for a storm approaches. The street patrols will mostly be in the shelter tonight. Those enthusiastic enough to make their nightly rounds despite the rain, will not see us in our black clothing. As for exiting the city, the Brothers have spiked the mead at the inn near the western gate. The guards who are on night duty there are known to drink their fill of it. Tonight, we shall find them not drunk, but asleep."

"The horses?"

Dasharath nodded. "Saddled and ready in a woodcutter's house outside the gates. Two of the best breed. And replacements ready for us in Kuru, and near the River Beas. We shall traverse the distance to Paurava in a week."

"Then I have nothing more to ask." I embraced him. "You have planned well. It is a dangerous mission I send you on. The future of our Samrajya may well depend on you now."

"I have never failed you before, Master, and I will not fail you now," Dasharath's eyes were steady.

"When you send word, we shall make our next move," I told him. "Meanwhile, keep your eyes and ears open while in the enemy camp."

Dasharath smiled. "When are they ever closed? If everything goes according to plan, Master, I will not see you for many days. I seek your blessings."

He bent and touched my feet. I placed my hand upon his shaved head. "Be victorious!" I said.

"Do you think he will recognize me?" Dasharath asked as he rose. "I was in your camp once when we were marching on the Nandas."

"Of all Malayketu's virtues, memory is not one," I assured him. "Besides, you never crossed paths. There is a small risk, of course, but there is no one else I would entrust with this mission."

"Then it begins, Master." Dasharath pulled his hood over his head. "Tonight, we take the first step towards victory."

"And our enemy takes his first step towards his doom."

I smiled, watching him walk out of the chamber.

14
RADHAGUPTA:
DRAWN AND QUARTERED

KALINGA, 262 BC

The wheels of the carriage ground over the dusty road. It was the only sound. In the darkness within, Radhagupta lay slumped on the floor, his hands tied behind his back. His head banged on the floor with every bump in the road. When the road sloped, he would roll helplessly from one side of the carriage to the other.

"What is your name?" he asked the lone guard, sitting above him, visibly bored. They had been travelling down a straight road for quite some time now.

The guard looked down at him lazily and spat out of the window. "How does it matter to you? I don't work for you, do I?"

Radhagupta raised his neck and studied the man closely. He had never seen him before. He looked to be middle-aged, about five to six summers past his prime. There were scars on his brow, which meant he was a veteran. Fighting him would be no use, the man would know how to use his arms. "Do you have children?" Radhagupta asked.

"Aye," the man nodded, "One sweet girl. Beautiful, she is."

Radhagupta smiled. "Married, is she?"

"Still collecting a dowry," the man sighed.

"Listen, my friend," Radhagupta said carefully, "if you untie me, I can help you with the dowry."

The man looked at him reflectively. "Maybe I should gag you," he said, pointing to the cloth tied around his waist.

"But that would not help you with the dowry, would it?"

The man looked to both sides carefully. The window on one side was open. He quickly closed it. Then he bent down. "Even if I untie you," he said, "there are a score of horsemen on both sides. What would you do?"

"I could sit comfortably at least," Radhagupta sighed as the carriage once again went over a bump.

The guard looked seriously at him for a few moments, then nodded. "Alright, I will untie you. But I must bind you again before we reach our destination."

"I ask nothing more."

"Vrag," the guard said. "The name is Vrag."

"I ask nothing more, Vrag," Radhagupta nodded.

The guard reached down and struggled with the knots unsteadily as the carriage continued to jolt and lurch. Finally free, Radhagupta stretched his arms painfully and then sat up straight. The first step was taken. He now had to find a way to sneak out of the carriage. He bent to one side toward the window, to peer through the small gap between the wooden panels.

"Do not move!" The guard placed his hand on the hilt of his sword.

Radhagupta sat back. "Where are we going, Vrag?" he asked, rubbing at the welts that had formed on his wrists.

"Do not know." The guard shook his head. "But we have left the city."

Radhagupta took a deep breath. He already knew from the direction of the light that they were travelling west. And if they had left Dantapura behind some while ago, it meant they were now in the dense jungles that lined the west. He moved his hands along his belt and found the pouch of gold coins, hidden in a secret pocket, that he always kept for situations just like this. Pulling it out, he tossed it to the guard. Taken by surprise, the guard missed catching it and the pouch fell to the floor with a heavy thud. Immediately, the guard bent to pick it up.

"Are they going to kill me, Vrag?" Radhagupta asked.

The guard nodded. He inserted his fingers into the pouch and felt the coins.

"Can you help me?" Radhagupta asked, looking the man in the eye.

Vrag shook his head. "Too risky," he said.

The carriage stopped abruptly. The guard quickly flung the pouch of coins into his shirt and reached for the bonds, but the doors to the carriage were flung open violently. Light flooded the dark interior for a moment before it was blocked by the gruff face of General Bheema. He looked at the scene with interest. "I see you have already managed to talk your way out of your bonds," he said before turning his eyes on the trembling guard.

"I am sorry, Sir," Vrag mumbled in fear. "The Brahmin was talking too much."

"Horseman!" the General called to the man behind him. "Take this fool away and cut off his hands."

Two men immediately entered the carriage. Vrag struggled but they pulled him out roughly. "Mercy, General!" the Guard shouted as they took him away. 'I have a daughter!" But no one seemed to care and his voice trailed off into the distance.

The General climbed into the carriage and made himself comfortable. "Looks like I underestimated you, Brahmin. You turned out to be quite some trouble."

"Why have you kidnapped me like this and brought me here to the jungle?" Radhagupta asked, his voice harsh.

The General laughed. "For all your wits, you cannot deduce something so simple."

Radhagupta looked him in the eye. "What do you want with me?"

"Not so fast, Brahmin, let us talk first." The General folded his arms across his massive chest. "What you did with the ships has hurt me grievously. So much so that I will not be able to get back into the elections."

Radhagupta did not reply. The General's head brushed against the roof of the carriage. "But what you did with Navin Kumar's Council, was very shrewd," he said. "I knew I had to meet you."

Radhagupta breathed in. He had to ensure he escaped this place, for here he was like a monkey with a broken tail.

"I want to make you an offer," the General said, facing him. "Your brains, coupled with my brawn, can beat the shit out of everyone in this election, even your Master, that Buddhist scum."

"I would be honoured to join you." Radhagupta spoke carefully. *If only he can be made to believe I am willing to join him, he may let me go.*

"Alas," the General sighed, "what you did with the ships means I cannot win now, even with you by my side. So you are of no use to me now."

"General," Radhagupta said, "I can mend what I did."

"Can you?" The General raised his brows. "Even if that is the case, I cannot let you go after that speech. I know your true identity, Brahmin."

Radhagupta looked at him in horror as the General grabbed his robe and bared his left shoulder. Radhagupta struggled, but the General's grip was too strong. There, on his shoulder was the mark of the curled snake, burnt into his flesh.

The General pressed forcefully. "Some men have made a deal with me Brahmin," he said.

Radhagupta winced. "What kind of deal?"

"They want you." The General loosened his grip. "And now they are here to collect."

"You are making a mistake, General," Radhagupta said, his heart beating fast in his chest. Had his past finally caught up with him? "When Devdatta learns what you have done to me, he will destroy you."

"Will he?" The General laughed. It sent a chill down Radhagupta's spine. "You see Brahmin, that is the deal. I give you to them, and they help me become Governor of Kalinga."

"You cannot win the elections now, General. The victory is Devdatta's."

The General smiled. "Who said anything about winning the elections? I am going to take my mercenaries to Devdatta's mansion and that traitor Anirbandha is going to open the gates for us. And I will slaughter every last man of your faction."

"That is a heinous crime!" Radhagupta shouted. "The open murder of opponents is against the Mahajanpada rules. When the army learns what you have done, they will imprison you."

"Will they?" The General reached out and grasped Radhagupta by the neck. "The army is going to be busy. The men I have made a deal with speak for the Mauryas. And the Mauryas are coming to Kalinga."

"What!" Radhagupta gasped, taken by surprise.

"The Mauryas are going to invade. And I and my mercenaries will join them after I have made short work of your Master. I am going to be Governor of Kalinga."

"You bastard!"Radhagupta swore. "You would betray your own people?"

"Have you not done the same when you ran away from Patliputra, Brahmin?" The General shook him. Radhagupta struggled but the General pushed him out of the carriage. He fell face down to the dusty ground. They could hear muffled screams in the distance. The General laughed. "It seems your friend has lost his hands. And now I will kill him with my own hands. I would like to kill *you* with my own hands but that honour belongs to your old friends."

Radhagupta felt the impact of the fall in his jaw. The rough ground bruised his skin. He felt the General's foot press onto his tailbone as he trembled with pain.

"Here is your man," the General said loudly.

Radhagupta raised his head and saw a man standing before them, two spearmen to his side, his face covered in a familiar black hood. When the man raised it, Radhagupta saw a familiar face, now old and covered in scars. There was no mistaking those calm eyes and taut cheekbones. Prajapati.

"He is yours," the General said, removing his foot.

The two spearmen moved forward and pulled Radhagupta to his feet. He looked into Prajapati's face.

"Old Brother," Prajapati spread his arms. Suddenly, he hit Radhagupta in the face in a bout of rage. The force of the blow made the Brahmin stagger back.

The General chuckled as he mounted his horse. "If you are going to kill him, better do it in the trees," he advised, pointing to the small dusty trail that led into the forest. "The stench will soon bring the animals and you will not even have to dispose of the body."

Prajapati nodded. "For the Order," he said.

"For your damned Order," the General agreed and gave the command for the convoy to move along. The empty carriage rolled forward, leaving a cloud of dust as Radhagupta watched.

When the dust settled, the General's men were gone and Prajapati stood with his two soldiers, staring at him. "You have no idea how happy the Grandmaster will be when I tell him I finally got rid of you," he said.

Prajapati gave the order and the two spearmen pushed Radhagupta towards the path leading into the trees.

"You do not have to kill me, Brother," Radhagupta said.

"Do not call me Brother!" Prajapati's voice was stern. "We looked to you as a Brother, but you killed old Dasharath and escaped. That is punishable only by death."

"It was self-defense," Radhagupta stated. As they walked along the narrow path, shrubs gazed his bare legs.

"It does not matter now," Prajapati said.

Radhagupta felt the sharp, cold edge of a knife at the back back of his neck. "Where is that damn Buddhist girl? Devi of Vidisha. Where have you hidden her?"

"I will not tell you, even with my last breath."

"We will find her, never fear." Prajapati pressed the blade harder. "Nikumbh and his men are looking for her in the city. It is only a matter of time."

"What will you do with her?" Radhagupta asked, trying to hide his fear. She knew nothing of what was happening. What if they caught her in the markets or in the streets?

"We will do the same that we will do with you, scum." Prajapati replied, his voice harsh. "We have already fabricated a story about your death. You have caused enough trouble."

"How did you find me?" Radhagupta asked as they moved further along the path. He had to buy time to find some way to escape.

"I was tasked by the Order to kill the Buddhist candidate in the Kalinga elections," Prajapati narrated as they walked. "We could not allow a non-believer to gain power in the State we wished to conquer."

"And then you found me," Radhagupta murmured, "atop the terrace."

"You beat me that day and I fled to Patliputra," Prajapati nodded. 'But you will not defeat me now."

Radhagupta wondered how he was going to get out of this situation. They had broken out of the path and were now standing in a clearing. Beyond it, as far as the eye could see, there was nothing but trees.

"Halt!" Prajapati ordered. "This is a good place."

The two men pulled Radhagupta against a tree and held him as Prajapati drew a small blade. The rough bark scratched against Radhagupta's back.

Prajapati faced him. "You know how they bleed goats with one slash across the neck in the slaughterhouses? We are going to do the same to you."

Radhagupta kept calm. If this was it, he would face death bravely. He would not let Chanakya hear that he had begged and grovelled at his death. "So be it," he said.

"You do not understand," Prajapati said, rubbing his knife across a rock to sharpen it. "This way you will bleed, but slowly. And you will stay alive through all the pain. We are going to make sure you feel every bit of the pain, Brahmin."

"You will pay for your crimes one day," Radhagupta said, closing his eyes. "Of that you can be sure."

"Soon these lands will be under our control." Prajapati stopped sharpening his blade and stood up. "We will rule the entire subcontinent. If that is how we are going to pay for crimes, I would like to commit some more."

Radhagupta closed his eyes, waiting for the impending strike. The two men beside him held both his arms. He prayed, hoping for a clean death. He could hear Prajapati grunt as he raised his blade. Suddenly, he felt a gush of air whizz past him, followed by Prajapati's muffled groan. The guard beside him tightened his grip but it was followed by a shout and he heard the whizzing sound of two arrows. The grip on his arms loosened and fell away.

Radhagupta opened his eyes. Prajapati's limp body lay on the ground, an arrow having pierced him through the neck. A gurgling sound came from his half open mouth as he gasped for breath and a puddle of blood formed under him. The two spearmen had fallen as well, with arrows through their chests. Radhagupta took a step away from the tree and looked for his saviours, just as a voice called to him. Radhagupta turned to see Karuvaki emerge through the trees with five soldiers, two wielding bows.

"Are you alright?" she asked.

Radhagupta nodded. "You saved my life. I thank you."

"These men did," Karuvaki said, pointing to her archers. "Thank them."

"I thank you, my friends," Radhagupta looked at the archers. They said nothing, standing in silence. "How did you find me?" he asked Karuvaki.

"I grew suspicious when I saw the General's men form lines behind your carriage. I gathered my men and we followed you. When they took you out of the city, we knew you were being kidnapped. But with so many men, we did not dare confront them."

"And then you got your chance after the General left me in the jungle with just three men."

"Indeed." Karuvaki nodded.

"You deserve more than my thanks, Lady Karuvaki. I am indebted to you. You put your own life in danger to save mine, even after what happened in the speech." Radhagupta bowed before her.

Karuvaki sighed. "I was angry at you for the speech," she agreed. "I still am. But as they say in the Kalinga elections, 'let the better man win'."

"Or the better woman."

"If General Bheema was kidnapping you, it was against the rules," she said. "He had to be stopped. And I am glad I followed the carriage or you would be dead right now."

"General Bheema did not just kidnap me," I told her, "he spoke of taking his army to Devdatta's mansion and killing him as well."

"But that would be high treason." Karuvaki looked shocked. "If he does that, he will be drawn and quartered."

"Not if he joins the enemy first," I said. "The Mauryans are marching towards us. Soon, they will invade our lands and he plans to join them."

"What in the name of..." Karuvaki gasped. "How do you know this?"

"Look around you. These men who were trying to kill me are Mauryan spies."

"Then we need to warn Devdatta."

"No, I need to warn Devdatta." I walked towards Prajapati's body and stopped for a moment.

"I can lend you my horse," Karuvaki said. 'Come, the mounts are a few miles away. We left them at the crossroads when we entered the forests.

"Lady Karuvaki," I said in a low voice as we walked back through the narrow pathway. "Can these men be trusted?"

She nodded. "They are my personal bodyguards."

"The man who was about to kill me," I told her, "is a member of a secret Mauryan Order. He was here on a mission. His partner is still alive and in the city."

"In the city!" Karuvaki's eyes widened. "What does he want there?"

"I am going to tell you something I have never told anyone," Radhagupta said. "He is looking for my wife."

"For Devi? What does he want with her?"

"To kill her. Devi is not my wife but someone else's. I was merely protecting her."

Karuvaki stopped in her tracks. "Who is she then?"

Radhagupta took a deep breath. "She is the mother of Chandasoka's children."

Her eyes widened in disbelief. "It cannot be!" she whispered.

Radhagupta urged her forward for he knew they had no time to lose. "She is a Buddhist. The Prime Minister wanted her dead. He wanted me dead as well. I rescued her and brought her here."

"Then she is in grave danger," Karuvaki murmured.

"She is indeed," Radhagupta said. They had now reached the crossroads where the horses stood, grazing. "If anyone learns her true identity, with the coming Mauryan invasion, we cannot know what they would do with her. I would not even trust Devdatta with this news. He could use her as a hostage."

Karuvaki looked at him. "But you would trust me?"

"Aye," Radhagupta nodded. "You have met her. Besides, you are a woman, like her. You can understand her position. She was pregnant; she came here to save her children."

"Where are the children now?" Karuvaki asked, untying her horse.

"The children are safe, but she is not. I cannot warn Devdatta and save her at the same time."

"Do not fear for Devi." Karuvaki handed him the reins. "Go and warn your Master. I will take Devi with me and keep her in my protection till I hear from you again."

Radhagupta sighed deeply in relief. "And what if you do not hear from me again?"

"Then I will keep her with me as my sister and hold her secret safe."

"I thank you, My Lady." Radhagupta climbed onto the horse. "I do not know how I shall ever repay you."

Karuvaki patted her horse, "Ride like the wind and stop General Bheema."

Radhagupta nodded. He dug his heel into the horse and the animal moved into a canter, and then a gallop.

**

When Devdatta's mansion appeared on the horizon, Radhagupta urged his horse on faster. He scanned the walls and surroundings, but there was no sign of the General's men. As he rode in, he caught sight of Devdatta on the battlements, with his Chamberlain. The guards at the gates saw him from afar and flung the gates open. Radhagupta shot through the gates like a man on fire. He pulled the horse to a halt in the middle of the main square and jumped down.

Devdatta watched his urgent arrival from above. "What is the matter, my friend?" he called down. 'Are you in a hurry to take a shit?"

"Close the gates!" Radhagupta shouted, running for the stairs. "Close the gates at once!"

The guards looked at Devdatta in confusion. His grin had turned into sudden composure and he nodded. The guards ran for the wheel room to close the gates.

"What is wrong, my friend?" Devdatta asked as Radhagupta arrived at the top of the stairs, gasping for breath.

"Where is Anirbandha?"

"In the stables," Devdatta replied, surprised. "What in Gods's name is the matter?"

"Take him into custody!" Radhagupta urged. "He has betrayed you. And call for horses. We must get out now!"

"But why?" Devdatta handed the papers in his hand to the Chamberlain.

"My Lord, there is a plot. The General seeks to capture you here."

"But this is my home, my citadel."

Radhagupta looked down from the battlements. "I do not have time to exp…"

Before he could finish, the blaring of a trumpet filled the air. The soldiers around them began pointing. Radhagupta and Devdatta turned. Along the path that led to the mansion from the forest, a long column of soldiers was marching. At the front, atop a high warhorse, there was no mistaking the figure of General Bheema himself.

"What in the name of…" Devdatta cursed.

Radhagupta sighed. He had been too late. All was lost.

15
CHANAKYA:
CALM BEFORE THE STORM

———〜———

"Shiva's army has left Chitrakoot," Asoka said, excitement coursing through his veins as he pushed the doors of the audience chamber open with both arms. "He writes that they are camped near the River Narmada, and that he rides with a posse of horsemen to meet me. He should have reached the city gates by now." His face was illuminated in the light that filled the vast chamber.

Chanakya wheeled his chair in, a deep frown upon his face. "Your Senapati wastes precious time coming to see you, my Samrat," he said. "At this moment, he could have been crossing the border into Kalinga."

"Which he will do, with me," Asoka smiled. "That is why he is coming, is he not? To take me with him?"

Chanakya shook his head. "The Senapati understands the logic for not risking your life. He will do no such thing."

"Well, he is here, is he not?" Asoka took his seat on the throne. "Let us ask him."

A sentry arrived to announce General Shiva. Asoka's face filled with joy. "Send him in at once," he ordered.

"Let me at least talk to him before he sees you," Chanakya urged, "see what is in your dear friend's head."

Asoka did not reply, but sat anxiously. As Chanakya hurriedly wheeled his chair out of the doors, he saw Shiva's tall figure walking towards him. He was in full armour. A sword hung at his side and on his head was the Mauryan pointed helmet. When he caught sight of the Prime Minister, Shiva bowed to touch the old man's feet.

"Is it done?" Chanakya asked in a whisper as Shiva bent down in front of him.

"The city was empty by the time we reached it," Shiva whispered back as he rose. "They left Vidishanagri a few days before we arrived. We found an empty city."

Chanakya banged his fist angrily on the armrest of his chair. "Curse it!" he growled. "There can be only one place they could have gone to."

"Kalinga," Shiva said. "My scouts followed their trail for a bit and there is little doubt that is where they went." He hesitated for a moment and then said, "Kanakdatta led them. He turned five hundred of his blood riders who were in the North to his cause and marched South, first to Vidishanagri. There, he rendezvoused with the other Buddhists of the city and marched South."

Chanakya looked him in the eye. "Those blood riders were controlled by you."

"I told him their location." Shiva looked down at the man in the chair. "He came to me before I heard of his betrayal."

"Is that so? Or did you tell him because of your deep ties of friendship?" Chanakya hissed angrily.

"I swear on my honour," Shiva said, "if I see them in Kalinga, siding with our enemies, I will not think twice before slaughtering them. I never did like the Guild Master much, but it is Kanakdatta's betrayal that hurts me."

"You have been a loyal man of the Order," Chanakya nodded. "You have preserved your father's legacy. I admit I had my doubts when we decided to induct you in his place, after his death, but you have proved your dedication. Let's go in." Chanakya wheeled his chair around. "The Samrat eagerly awaits."

"I know I must keep the news of a march on Vidishanagri a secret from him." Shiva said quietly. "Do not concern yourself, no word will escape my mouth."

"Oh, throw all that secrecy to the crows now," Chanakya growled. "The Samrat shall hear of this treachery today, and from your mouth."

They watched Asoka hurry down the steps, both arms extended. Shiva walked up to him but did not respond to the embrace. Instead, he bowed and said, "I carry grave news. Kanakdatta has marched to Kalinga and joined forces. He has also taken the Maharaja of Vidishanagri with him."

"What! Guild Master Hardeo too?" Asoka's mouth opened in surprise. "How did you find out?"

"The Prime Minister had his suspicions." Shiva looked towards Chanakya. "He asked me to check Vidishanagri as I marched South. The city was empty, my Samrat. Not a soul left inside."

"What about their army?" Asoka asked.

"It went with them." Shiva sighed.

"How in God's name can they take an army with them?" Asoka turned away. "Do the common folk of Vidisha have no honour?"

Chanakya spoke from the side. "It is Maharaja Hardeo's betrayal which hurts me the most. After all, we made a man of his beliefs, Maharaja. How can he do this to us?"

Asoka did not respond, gazing at the high ceiling above.

"Perhaps it was all pre-planned," Chanakya continued. "Maybe, telling his merchants to smuggle goods into Kalinga was the beginning of this planned defection. I should have seen through him. I gave the Order to kill the smuggling merchants, but I never suspected him."

"It is not your fault, Prime Minister." Asoka returned to the world. "He was Devi's father. Even I would not have suspected him."

"What is done is done," Shiva shrugged. "When I find them in Kalinga, I shall offer them terms of surrender. If they choose to fight, I will slaughter them like dogs."

"When *we* find them in Kalinga," Asoka corrected him. "That's why you are here, my friend, are you not? To take me with you?"

Shiva looked sideways at Chanakya. "I cannot protect you on the battlefield," he said cautiously.

"By the Gods, Shiva! You of all people know I do not need to be protected."

"And you know that once the battle horns sound, I will not be able to stop you marching on the enemy flanks, on Ashwa, your sword upraised."

"But Shiva…"

"No, Asoka," Shiva said, speaking the Samrat's name. "The Prime Minister is right. You must stay here."

"While you risk your neck out there for me?" Asoka folded his arms across his chest, irate.

"Not for you." Shiva looked him in the eye. "For our Samrajya. There will be turmoil if you fall on the battlefield without an heir."

Asoka breathed in deeply. "So be it." His shoulders drooped as he retreated back to the throne. Once seated, he looked up. "Why are you here then, Senapati?" he asked.

Shiva noted the Samrat's formality and knew he had distanced himself. "I am here to ask you something, My Samrat," he replied, bowing.

"And what is that?"

"What should I do if I find Kanakdatta standing against me in Kalinga?"

Asoka looked down, not wishing to meet Shiva's eyes.

"There is no question," Chanakya rasped from the side. "You show no mercy to the enemy, whoever he is."

"It is the Samrat's decision to make." Shiva looked up at the throne.

Asoka looked down at them. "If you find Kanakdatta in the ranks of the enemy," he said clearly, "you shall treat him as you would any foe."

Shiva took a deep breath, "When Samrat Bindusar ordered you to fight me," he said, "Kanakdatta helped me, against you. And now you ask me to fight him."

"It was a different time," Asoka said coldly. "A different Samrat."

Shiva nodded. "So be it. I march immediately."

Asoka rose and walked down the steps. "Make me proud, my friend." He patted Shiva's shoulder. He was about to embrace him but Shiva stepped back, breaking the moment. He said nothing, merely bowing.

As Shiva turned and left the audience chamber, Asoka looked at Chanakya. "And so it begins," he said.

Chanakya smiled briefly. "No, now it ends." *Just like it had all those years ago.*

50 YEARS AGO.

It had ended with a visitor. When he was announced, I was sitting with Chandragupta in his royal chambers. The conversations between us were barely civil in these troubled times.

"They are coming, Guru!" Chandragupta was not telling me, he was shouting at me in anger. "Malayketu left with his army from Paurava a week ago. He now camps somewhere along the Beas River. The Greek army rides by his side, and is camped somewhere near him. Soon, they will cross the river and invade our lands."

"I know all this, Vrishala." I waved my hand at him. 'There is no point telling me things I already know."

"Then why are we still here, Guru?" Chandragupta burst forth. "Why are we not marching against them?"

"Because we cannot defeat them at this time. With the Greeks by their side, their army is as big as ours."

"I can defeat them." Chandragupta looked at me like an eager child yearning to set off on an adventure, being restrained by his parents. "I shall march and find the higher ground and defeat them in battle."

"And what if you do not find higher ground?" I threw his own words back at him. "What if you attack and fail?"

"Then I will retreat and fight again."

"No, Chandragupta," I said, "you are no longer a mere rebel in some Taxilan forest. You are now the ruler of these lands. You cannot be irresponsible or rash."

"Then what should we do, Guru?"

"We will wait. And we will only attack when we are sure of victory. Have faith in me."

But it appeared that the Gods did not wish for us to wait any longer, for the visitor announced by the sentry at that moment was exactly the man I had been waiting for. I walked back to my chambers to see him. When I entered, Dasharath was already at my desk, helping himself to my wine. He smiled when he saw me for it had been many days since he had been gone. With his unkempt beard and long brown hair I hardly recognized him.

"Talk to me, Dasharath," I said as soon as I saw him, but the smile on his face had already told me what I wanted to know."

"We have won, Guru," he said, beaming. "Now there is only one last thing left to do."

"Do not get ahead of yourself," I told him sternly. "Tell me all the details." I could not rely on the mere declaration of victory. I had to know all was as it should have been.

"That night I left your chamber," he narrated. "We busted Saktadasa out of his prison cell. I told him I had been sent by his dear friend Chandandasa, to get him out of the city. When he asked where, I told him we would go to Paurava, to join Amatya Rakshasa. The man's eyes gleamed with joy when I told him this and further, handed over the signet ring to him, telling him it had been sent by Chandandasa as a gesture of good faith."

I nodded in appreciation. "What happened next?"

"We rode in the dead of night, hiding during the day, for weeks, before we reached Paurava. When we finally did, Prime Minister Rakshasa was delighted to have his old clerk back, as well as his signet ring. He threw a bag of gold coins at me for my help and took me into his service."

"Wonderful!" I commented. It had happened exactly as per plan, "What job did Rakshasa offer you?"

"Since he thought I had been sent by his friend Chandandasa, Saktadasa decided to trust me and gave me the job of delivering his official as well as secret letters to their recipients." Dasharath smiled grimly. "He sealed them with the signet seal of course."

I chuckled gleefully. "So this was how you were able to send me word of his movements." Dasharath had done well, sending me coded messages of everything that was happening in our enemy Rajya. He had also notified me when the Greek army finally reached Paurava.

"What I had to do next was simple." Dasharath nodded at me. "One night, as the city slept, I stood outside Prince Malayketu's chambers and asked for audience. I told the guards I had something important to show him."

"And did Malayketu see you?"

"Malayketu knew I was Rakshasa's new messenger. He thought that it was a message from Rakshasa, so I was ushered in."

"And what did you do, my dear man, once you were in his presence?"

"What dramatic antics I undertook!" Dasharath sighed. *"Raja, I could not believe he was plotting against you! I had to see you immediately once I knew."*

Dasharath's imitation of his own act was humourous and made me laugh. "Did he believe you?"

"Certainly he did." Dasharath smiled. "I did not go to him with mere words. I went with proof."

I knew Dasharath referred to the letter we had prepared before he left the city.

"Malayketu was aghast on seeing it." Dasharath recalled. "At first, he could not believe his eyes, but Rakshasa's seal was all too evident."

"What happened next?"

"Malayketu wished to confirm if the letter really came from Rakshasa," Dasharath said. "I told him it had been dictated by Rakshasa and written by his clerk, Saktadasa. He wanted Saktadasa brought to him."

"By the Gods!" I said, my voice trembling a little. "If Saktadasa had seen that letter, he would have known when he had written it. That would have been perilous."

Dasharath bowed. "I did not let it come to that, Master. I told Malayketu that, as a loyalist, Saktadasa would never speak against his master. To prove it, I offered to summon Saktadasa and have him write another dummy letter, to compare the handwriting."

"Clever thinking, Dasharath," I said in appreciation.

"Malayketu did exactly that. He summoned Saktadasa to his chambers and had him write a dummy letter to the Greeks. When he was gone, Malayketu placed both letters side by side. There could be no doubt they were by the same hand."

"And Rakshasa?" Knowing Malayketu was famous for his towering rages, I worried if he had done something untoward. Our plan needed Rakshasa alive.

"Malayketu confronted Rakshasa," Dasharath related. "I had requested Malayketu to keep my role secret, and he had agreed. Rakshasa denied everything, but Malayketu did not believe him. He asked if the handwriting was indeed that of

Rakshasa's clerk and the seal his signet. Rakshasa had no words left to defend himself."

"So Rakshasa did not see through our plan?"

Dasharath shook his head. "As Malayketu did not want to carry the sin of *Brahmahatya,* killing a Brahmin, he ordered Rakshasa to be banished from his Rajya. However, he ordered the killing of Saktdasa immediately."

"So where is Rakshasa now?" I asked, looking out of the window at the sky.

"Somewhere in Mauryan lands, Master. If we search for him, we will find him."

"Rakshasa is powerless now without a position," I pointed out. "We will not waste our resources on him. I will make sure he comes to us in the end. Tell me what you did next, for ousting Rakshasa was a work half done."

"Aye, Master," Dasharath nodded. "After Rakshasa's ouster, I went to the Greek camp and met the man who advises their Commander, Seleucus Nicator."

"What did you tell him?" I asked with bated breath.

"How I had arranged for Rakshasa to be ousted. It shocked him, for it was Rakshasa who had enlisted their support in the first place. Rakshasa had told them we were weak and could be easily destroyed if they rode with Malayketu. They had joined him in return for the promise of the Patliputra treasury, filled with gold."

"And what did the Greek say?" I asked curiously.

"Having heard my story, the Greek realized we were not, in fact, weak." Dasharath smiled. "That it would not be easy to subdue us, for we fought with both weapons as well as guile. The Greeks did not want a prolonged fight."

I raised my hand to stop him. "Yes, I know the reasons of the Greeks. So did the man agree to your offer?"

"No..." Dasharath murmured. "He said he would only negotiate with the man in charge."

"What does that mean?"

"Master, the man will only talk to you."

I got to my feet. "You have done exceptionally well, Dasharath," I told him. "Now leave the rest to me. All you have to do now is take me to this Greek immediately."

"That will not be necessary, Master," Dasharath replied, helping himself to more of my wine, "for I have brought the Greek to you."

***

The Greek Ambassador was waiting for us in a tavern in the city. Dasharath took me to see him. We met in a dark dilapidated room above the tavern. The man's head was covered, his face in shadows, to hide his skin colour. When he saw Dasharath, he removed the hood, exposing his fair skin and blue eyes.

"I am called Megasthenes," he told me. "Advisor to the great Seleucus Nicator."

"The Prime Minister of this Samrajya welcomes you to Patliputra, Ambassador."

"Yes, I agreed to accompany your man here as I wished to see this great city of which I have heard so much." Megasthenes leaned forward. "Years ago, we tried to come here, but alas, we could not. I have always wanted to see it, and I must say it is majestic."

"You speak our tongue well," I said admiringly. "Almost as good as a local."

"I learnt it when I accompanied the Great God Alexander on his campaign in your lands." He eyed me intently. "I have seen you before, have I not?"

"Aye," I nodded. "I am the Brahmin who once warned your God Alexander in his own tent that he would never capture this subcontinent."

Megasthenes's eyes twinkled with recognition. "Aye, I remember," he said. "You were merely a learned Brahmin then. And now, less than a decade later, you stand before me as Prime Minister of this Empire. I must say I have made the right choice in coming to you, Arya Chanakya."

I folded my arms. "My man here has already told you what we offer. What interests your Master, Seleucus Nicator, is not the same as what drove Alexander. Seleucus does not wish to capture Bharat, not when his own home is not his."

Megasthenes looked me in the eye for a moment and then nodded. "I once sat to the right side of the great Alexander, as his translator. A great man he was. Alas, after his death in Babylon, the empire he built has crumbled. His Generals fought amongst themselves, dividing his lands, styling themselves *Diadochi*. I chose to follow Seleucus because he is the best man amongst them. Yet, Diadochi Ptolemy marches on Seleucus' homeland right now as we speak."

"I know you agreed to take part in Malayketu's campaign because Rakshasa said he would divide half the treasury of Patliputra with you upon capture." I stressed every word. "Your Master came here for gold, not conquest, so he could use that gold to defeat his enemies back home."

"But we now see that defeating you is not as easy as Rakshasa claimed," Megasthenes agreed. "He is himself ousted from the court of Paurava, and is nowhere to be seen, because of your actions."

"Perhaps we can help each other," I suggested.

"Would you offer us the same gold Rakshasa promised?" Megasthenes looked me in the eye.

"No." I returned his gaze without smiling. "But I offer you something you would like to buy with it. When Alexander first came to these lands, he was surprised to see big black beasts bigger than any animal he had ever seen, marching against his army. I offer you five hundred trained war elephants, along with their riders, to unleash hell upon your enemies back home."

Megasthenes looked at me. "Your man told me as much up North," he said. "The fact that I did not say yes to him means we want something more."

"You did not say yes to him because you wanted a guarantee we would not turn our backs on you once the war was over," I told him. "Knowing of your troubles, you want assurance that we will also not invade your lands after we have defeated Malayketu, like your God Alexander once invaded ours."

"The Prime Minister is wise."

I took a deep breath. "Our Samrat, Chandragupta, is a young man about the same age Alexander was when he died. I hear Seleucus' young daughter is famed to be one of the most beautiful ladies west of the Hydapses."

Megasthenes smiled. "I like what the Prime Minister proposes. I daresay Lord Seleucus will have no objection."

"Then let your Lord's daughter marry my Samrat," I said. "And let us be bound in blood as well as friendship. That is, if you agree to part from Malayketu immediately."

"It will not be difficult," Megasthenes smiled. "Only say there there are troubles back home and withdraw our army.

Yet you offer far more in return."

I smiled. "I prefer to make offers that cannot be refused."

"So be it then." Megasthenes sat back in his chair while Dasharath poured wine for us both. We raised the goblets over our heads to seal the deal in the Greek manner.

"What of Rakshasa?" Dasharath asked once we were out of the tavern.

Capturing Rakshasa was still something we needed to do before the final push towards victory, I knew. "Let us do what we must to capture him," I instructed as we walked back towards the palace. "Before you leave with Megasthenes, do one last thing for me. Take a couple of the city guards and go to that traitor Chandandasa's house and arrest him for his treachery."

"And what should the punishment for his treachery be, Master?" Dasharath asked, smiling slyly.

"There is only one punishment for treachery since time immemorial," I said as the sun rose up above our heads. "Put him in a cell to await the executioner's blade."

~

KALINGA, 262 BC

They observed the surrounding siege from atop the battlements. General Bheema had set up a small camp beside the bridge that crossed the rivulet and led to the mansion. His soldiers were busy foraging along the river banks, looking for reeds to construct ladders. The General's men rested between patrols, ready to strike as soon as possible.

"It will be hard to break this siege," Devdatta noted calmly, though despair filled his heart.

Radhagupta could tell that he maintained his composure with effort, for the others looked to him. The news Radhagupta had brought had changed everything. The Mauryans were attacking, and General Bheema was hands-in-glove with them. It threatened to destroy all they had worked for.

"The General did not plan on a siege," Radhagupta reminded him.

They had managed to overpower the traitor Anirbandha, and his body now lay in the mansion courtyard, as lifeless as the stones on which it lay. Devdatta had ordered his men to cut off his head and hoist it on a spear, possibly in intimidation of their opponent. But General Bheema had not even looked at it.

"He was counting on Anirbandha to open the gates," Radhagupta said. "Now as he waits, we have valuable time. Karuvaki carries the news to the city. When everyone learns that the General has openly broken the election vows, they will all turn against him."

"That will take time, my friend," Devdatta sighed, pointing. "Look at the river bank. They are fashioning their ladders quickly."

"We will fight them," Radhagupta said. "One of our men can take down two of those climbing the ladders."

"That we will," Devdatta nodded. "But he has many more men than twice our number. It is almost over."

"Karuvaki can bring us an army," Radhagupta pointed out. "All we have to do is hold out."

"You are too hopeful, my friend." Devdatta retreated from the battlements and walked down the steps to the courtyard. "I like that about you, but I can see the end as clear as day now."

They spent the evening in the courtyard while Devdatta's men manned the walls, looking for any action in the General's camp. Night had fallen when one of the men atop the battlements delivered the portentious news. "Their ladders are ready, My Lord," he called.

Devdatta rose to his feet and went to the armory. Radhagupta watched him rustle through the contents and draw out a pair of swords for himself. "What would you prefer?" he asked.

"A long spear," Radhagupta said, getting to his feet, suddenly recalling other battles he had fought in. Devdatta tossed a long spear to him and Radhagupta caught it in mid-air. "This is it, brother," he said.

Devdatta nodded and pulled him into a hug. "Let us kill that bastard General if we get the chance."

Radhagupta nodded. They climbed to join the other men on the battlements, who cheered when they saw Devdatta join their ranks. Radhagupta watched the files of the General's men, carrying ladders, marching towards their walls. In the meagre light, he caught sight of the General and the rest of his force, waiting at the camp. As soon as the ladders were up, he would send his forces in.

"Archers!" Devdatta commanded and a dozen archers raised their bows. "Fire!"

On his command, they let loose their arrows, but few found their mark.

"Again!" Devdatta commanded. The archers repeated their motions in unison. "Fire!"

Radhagupta raised his spear, ready to strike as soon as the first line of enemy soldiers reached the walls. As they neared, the last light in the sky disappeared, like a portent of their future. By the time the first lines reached the wall, the sky looked dark, merging with the ground.

"Attack!" Devdatta commanded and Radhagupta thrust his spear with force at the enemy below, raising their ladders. It hit one of them, knocking off his helmet. Radhagupta quickly pulled it back and attacked again. This time, its tip pierced a shoulder. The man screamed in pain as Radhagupta pulled the long spear out forcefully.

"They are too many, My Lord," one of the men to his right shouted to Devdatta.

Radhagupta noticed that two of the ladders had already been set up against the wall. He clenched his teeth and struck again. This time, his opponent was ready. He dodged the attack and two of his companions held onto the long spear. Radhagupta pulled with all his strength but could not dislodge it from their grasp. He let the weapon go to prevent himself falling with it. He unsheathed his sword and watched as another ladder was set against the wall firmly.

To the extreme right, Devdatta was not having much success either in keeping the attackers at bay. The enemy soldiers had climbed up and two or three of them were now atop the mansion walls. To his horror, Radhagupta watched a man appear on the ladder before him. He struck out with his sword but the man parried the blow with his shield. Radhagupta raised his sword again but the attacker quickly jumped onto the battlements and the man below took his place upon the ladder. Radhagupta hesitated, deliberating on which man to attack first. The first man used his momentary indecision to swing his sword. Radhagupta jumped back. The second soldier launched himself too at the same moment, separating Radhagupta from Devdatta's other soldiers upon the wall.

As the two men advanced towards him, Radhagupta retreated, his sword held above his head, alert. The first man swung his sword again but Radhagupta managed to parry. Iron hit iron with a clang as the attacker pressed on. Radhagupta let his blade slide down before pushing him back. He used the chance to lunge and kick the attacker off the wall. The man's body fell, disappearing into the darkness below. But another attacker had already taken his place. Radhagupta could feel himself moving further and further from the others as more enemy soldiers appeared. *Does it end like this?* he wondered as he raised his sword to parry another blow. *In an obscure place, at the hands of a common soldier?*

The enemies pushed forward as he fell back. Their attack became swifter, missing him by a finger's breadth but tearing his doublet. Radhagupta retreated, determined to fight until his last breath.

"Retreat!" There were sudden shouts from the ground. The soldiers fighting on the battlements looked down, confused. Radhagupta used that moment to plunge his sword into an enemy's stomach. The soldier withered with pain as hot blood spluttered over Radhagupta's feet.

"Retreat!" The cries were becoming more urgent. "The camp is being attacked! The General is being attacked!"

Radhagupta saw the men in front of him move back towards the ladders. He swung his sword but they did not counter attack. One by one, they moved down, just as they had come. Radhagupta watched them descend and wiped the sweat from his eyes with a bloodied hand. He gazed at the General's camp in the darkness. It was ablaze. Something had happened while he had been fighting for his life.

As the last of the visible enemies descended, he caught sight of Devdatta, standing across from him, still alive but smeared with blood. He smiled, brandishing his sword. "What in God's name just happened" he called.

"Look!" Radhagupta pointed. "Someone is attacking the General's camp."

Devdatta squinted into the darkness and nodded. "Sure looks like it."

As their own men tended to the wounded and flung the bodies of dead enemy soldiers over the wall, Radhagupta wondered who their mysterious saviour could be.

"It has to be Karuvaki," Devdatta said, having ordered his men to keep vigil.

"But she could not have reached the city, informed everyone of the General's treachery, gathered an army and come here in such a short time," Radhagupta said.

"If she did, I will replace you with her," Devdatta joked. "But who else could it be?"

Who else indeed? Radhagupta wondered. The carnage in the General's camp had now reached a peak. They could hear the clanging of iron on iron and men screaming in pain as the flames spread to the surrounding areas, crackling in the dark like some malevolent beast. "We'll soon find out," he muttered.

***

The burning of the General's camp continued for quite some time as Radhagupta and the others maintained their watch upon the battlements in case the enemy returned. None did however, for whatever was occurring at the camp kept them occupied.

When the sounds began to die down, Devdatta warned the men on the walls to be extra vigilant. "Whatever has happened at the enemy camp seems to be over," he told them. "Whoever won will now come to us."

They waited with quickened hearts for someone to emerge from the darkness. Radhagupta heard it first and called to the others, "Hooves! There are horsemen coming."

There were indeed horsemen, for the sound of hooves now became louder as they neared the mansion walls. "Stay sharp, men!" Devdatta called loudly to deter whoever it was in the darkness. "We do not know whether they be friend or foe."

One of the horsemen came to the front and held up the torch he carried. The flamelight fell upon him. "Stay your weapons!" he called. "We come in peace."

The voice seemed strangely familiar to Radhagupta, like a ghost from the past.

"How are we to trust you?" Devdatta called down.

In response, another horseman trotted forward and stopped by the first. "You can trust me, son!" he called. The light from the torches fell upon his face more clearly.

At his side, Radhagupta could see Devdatta shaking. "It can't be!" he shouted. "It is impossible!"

"Open the gates, son," the figure below said. "Open the gates and see for yourself."

"Open the gates," Devdatta ordered his men. "They are our friends."

"How can you be so sure?" Radhagupta asked, still watching intently. As the first horseman moved forward it all became crystal clear to him. There was no mistaking the huge figure upon the horse. But how could it be?

As the gates opened, Devdatta walked out with Radhagupta by his side. As they reached the two horsemen, joy overcame Devdatta. "Guild Master!" he cried. "You chose the perfect time to make your appearance."

The old man sitting on the horse smiled. "Are you not going to give us food and mead?" he asked with a laugh. "We saved your lives, after all."

Radhagupta stared at the corpulent man at the Guild Master's side. "Kanakdatta the Buddhist!" he said in greeting. "I never thought I would see you again in this lifetime."

"They call me Kanakdatta the Serpent these days, but I like my old name better." The fat man smiled, pulling on the reins of his horse.

Behind them, Radhagupta noticed horsemen standing in long columns. So these were the men who had rained havoc on the General's camp.

"What of General Bheema?" Devdatta asked.

"Dead," another voice said, this time that of a woman.

Two female figures rode ahead of the columns of men. Karuvaki was the first to come into sight. "He died fighting. He was a brave man, but he deserved what he received for breaking the election laws. It is good to see you safe."

The other woman was Devi. She halted by the Guild Master and smiled at Radhagupta.

"And it is good to see you safe as well," Radhagupta said. "For the men who took me were after you as well."

"It is all Lady Karuvaki's doing." Devi smiled at her companion. "She saved me from those bastards."

"Not that you cannot handle a sword," Karuvaki chuckled. "She was fighting them in your house when I managed to reach the spot." "And the children?" Radhagupta asked, staring at Hardeo. "My nephew?"

"They are all safe," Hardeo assured him. "I sent them to Junagarh for safety. They are with my people. No one will find them there."

Devdatta smiled at Karuvaki. "So you led them here. I must thank you for doing so, even after what I did to you in the speeches."

Karuvaki gave a sigh. "All that is behind us now, for an external danger approaches."

"But how are *you* here?" Radhagupta asked Kanakdatta. "Have the Mauryans attacked already? Are you their vanguard?"

"One thing at a time, friend," Kanakdatta replied, holding up his hand. "Let us rest our men and set up camp. We have much to discuss."

"And much to do," Hardeo said, his face serious.

***

The war council was held in the courtyard of Devdatta's mansion as Kanakdatta's horsemen established camp outside the city. Devdatta opened his cellar for them and his servants brought out barrels of pickled meat and wine. Having won the skirmish, the men enjoyed themselves with vigour. There were no ranks as servants and soldiers shared the food and water.

Radhagupta and the others settled near a flowering tree, around a large wooden table they had dragged out. Each related their story. Hardeo was the last. He sat at Devi's side, his eyes filled with tears of joy at seeing the daughter he had long thought dead.

"You have come far," he said to Devdatta when he had finished narrating how he had joined Kanakdatta at Vidishanagri and ridden to Dantapura, where they had met Karuvaki and Devi. Karuvaki had implored them to aid her to save Radhagupta and Devdatta. To her surprise, both names were close to their hearts, so they had departed quickly on their rescue mission. "Looks like not being in Mauryan lands has worked out well for you. I hope you have given up your old ways."

Devdatta flushed at the old man's words as Karuvaki glared at him. "Old habits die hard," he said, scratching his head. "But I channel my talents for a greater cause now, not just for myself."

"We have important business to discuss," Kanakdatta reminded them, drawing all attention to himself. "The

Mauryan army is on the march. I saw them with my own eyes when I rode with my blood riders to the South. They set out from their camp in Chitrakoot the same day we passed them."

"Their first target is Vidishanagri, my city," Hardeo said bitterly. "However, when they reach it, they will find it deserted. What time they lose in their useless excursion to Vidishanagri, is what we gain here, to prepare."

"We have the matter of the election," Radhagupta pointed out. "At this moment, Kalinga has no Governor. If there is no Governor, the country cannot stand united against an upcoming invasion."

"We must declare the elections immediately," Karuvaki agreed. "Kalinga will need to raise its army to fight the invaders. Our army is composed of common peasants who rally to the banner of their local noble, who in turn rally to the call of the Governor."

"Then we need to raise and assemble the Kalinga army in Dantapura," said Kanakdatta. "The elections must be held at the same time. Those who answer their noble's call, will also be able to elect their future leader in the capital before taking up arms."

"Good thinking," Karuvaki said approvingly. "With the General dead, there are just two contenders left. Maybe it is time to do what we earlier agreed upon. We have already declared our support for Devdatta, even though it was extracted by deceit. It is now time to stand him."

Radhagupta nodded. "Devdatta's popularity is high. The peasants and nobles alike will band behind him for the elections. When he wins, it will raise the army's morale as it prepares to face the enemy."

"There is, however, one problem," Devdatta said. "We just killed Kalinga's General, a veteran and the only man with enough experience to lead an army to face this overwhelming foe."

"The General was hands-in-glove with the Mauryans," Radhagupta said. "His stand in the elections was a hoax. If he had lived, he would have turned against the Kalingans at the time of the invasion."

"We still do not have a military leader who the people can band behind," Devdatta said to the others. "They may all love me but I have no experience fighting battles."

"I will lead the Kalingans," Kanakdatta said quietly.

Devdatta looked at him in surprise. "Why would they follow a foreigner?" he asked.

"Because he is not a foreigner," Karuvaki replied. "He is Governor Navin's son."

"What!" Radhagupta sprang to his feet in surprise.

"It is not common knowledge," Kanakdatta said, "but it is true."

"We played together as children." Karuvaki told them. "I was the Governor's ward and he Navin's son. People often ask me why Navin did not train his son Navin Kumar to take up his mantle. The fact is Navin trained his elder son to do that. But that son betrayed him and ran away from doing his duty."

Kanakdatta looked at her, his eyes steady. "I did not run away, Karuvaki," he stated. "I was banished."

"Because of your actions."

"The two of you can fight your sibling battles later," Hardeo said authoratatively. "What matters is that the men in Kalinga's military know of Kanakdatta."

"They do," Kanakdatta nodded. "I was famous for my prowess with the bow and arrow when I was a child. My skills as a *Shabda Bhedi* go way back, Guild Master. The men of the army loved me as my father's child, and they will remember me again when I walk before them,"

"Why were you banished?" Radhagupta asked curiously.

"For a strange reason." Kanakdatta looked down. "When I was fifteen, I met a Buddhist *Bhikku*, travelling through Dantapura. His ideologies inspired me so much that I took *diksha* almost immediately."

"Navin did not believe it until Kanakdatta told him with his own mouth," Karuvaki sighed. "He asked him to break his diksha, but Kanakdatta held his ground."

"My father decided he could not have a Buddhist child." Kanakdatta looking at Hardeo. "So he banished me from Kalinga, ordering me never to return until I had seen the error of my ways."

"But you never gave up on your beliefs." Hardeo looked at him affectionately. 'I am proud of you, son."

"We do not take up new beliefs on a whim, Guild Master," Kanakdatta replied reflectively. "I was a headstrong lad, determined to prove my father wrong. So I adventured into Mauryan lands and joined the war camp preparing soldiers for the upcoming Southern Wars."

"And whenever someone would ask you about your lineage, you would tell them you were a Shudra," Radhagupta said, remembering an old conversation.

"Yes, I loved to mock everything," Kanakdatta laughed. "Especially myself."

"So you will lead the army." Devdatta sat back in his chair thoughtfully. "What next?"

"We shall fight the Mauryan army," Karuvaki stressed her point. "We have to push them back."

Hardeo looked at her, pity in his eyes. "You will never be able to defeat the Mauryans. Their armies are huge and their soldiers numerous. You push one army back, another will appear on the horizon."

"Fighting is not an option." Devdatta banged his fist on the table. "I have been saying this from the very start. We must surrender, become part of their Empire, and end the blockade they have placed on Kalinga once and for all."

"The Mauryan Prime Minister is a strange man," Kanakdatta observed. "Radhagupta here will agree."

"The Mauryan Prime Minister will destroy us all if we surrender," Radhagupta agreed. "But he has a personal vendetta against the three of us sitting on this side of the table, let me assure you."

"He will make Kalingans slaves, pillage their wealth and settle his own citizens on their soil." Hardeo sighed. "We have to understand that *he* is the true enemy we are fighting."

"And the key to defeating him is sitting here with us." Radhagupta looked at Devi. "We show the Samrat she is still alive, and he will understand the evil ways of his own Prime Minister."

Devi stared back at him. "That man left me for dead," she said. "He never even searched for me. I will not return to him."

"He still loves you, Devi," Kanakdatta told her. "He has been deceived. When you see him, you will know it from his eyes."

"Even if that be true, I cannot go to Patliputra when an army approaches. I would not even reach the city before the army will be upon you."

"And Chanakya controls the city." Hardeo folded his arms across his chest. "I will not send my daughter anywhere near that city until that bastard is dead."

"I can look after him myself, father." Devi flashed him an angry glance. "I think I have proved that time and again."

Hardeo opened his mouth to speak but Karuvaki silenced him, saying as she stood up, "Then we fight. We stop the Mauryan invasion and then declare our surrender."

"We will insist the Samrat come to Kalinga," Radhagupta added. "The Prime Minister is very old and would not survive the journey. He would never dare leave the city in his enfeebled state."

"And when the Samrat arrives here, he will see Devi and own his error," Karuvaki finished.

"Then we have a plan," Hardeo said, looking around the table."

"Which has one flaw," Devdatta said. "You told us the Mauryan army is enormous. What if our army is unable to stop them?"

"We count on not having to fight," Kanakdatta said. "The man who leads the Mauryan army is a friend of mine, as well as of the Samrat. We go back to the days of the Southern Wars, when we fought as brothers."

"I have stood witness to your friendship on one occasion," Hardeo nodded.

"I shall face Shiva with the Kalinga army when he approaches," Kanakdatta said. "I will block his path. When he arrives for a pre-battle parley, I will take Devi with me."

Devi nodded. "I have not ridden free for years, feeling the wind in my face."

"When Shiva sees Devi, he will believe I speak the truth," Kanakdatta averred. "We will try to avoid a battle and send a summons to the Samrat to come to the battlefield to accept our surrender."

"It is decided then," Radhagupta said. "I finally feel hopeful that the path to victory lies in front of us."

"Though it will be hard and it will need meticulous planning to prepare the army and have elections." Kanakdatta raised his goblet of water. "But I will not stamp my foot on your joy and hope with these frightening challenges."

"Then let us get on with it. We do not have time to lose." Devdatta raised his goblet. "For Kalinga!" he said.

'For Kalinga!' they all replied together.

17
KANAKDATTA:
HOPE OF VICTORY

~

KALINGA, 262 BC

The people of Kalinga stormed into the city of Dantapura in their thousands as the call for war and elections was answered simultaneously. Devdatta and Karuvaki had worked tirelessly over the last week to send messengers to as many villages as possible. The messengers had done well in rousing the populace as most returned with all the able bodied members of the villages they had been sent to.

"We Kalingans have always been proud people." Karuvaki explained taking a break during the busy day to eat with Kanakdatta. "The stories of yore always tell how the people united when external enemies attacked."

"And unite they will once more." Kanakdatta nodded sadly. Where Karuvaki saw unity and strength, he saw the bloodbath that would soon take place if he could not stop the battle that loomed. When Karuvaki pointed to the numerous young men who were thronging the city, Kanakdatta worried that the entire youth of Kalinga would be wiped out if he could not do what he had pledged to.

He sighed as Karuvaki nudged him. "You look awfully glum, dear brother. Where is that famous mischievous grin of yours?"

"I feel like a changed man, sister," Kanakdatta sighed. "I had hoped it would not come to this; that I could stop it from happening."

"Alas, here we are," Karuvaki murmured, drinking her buttermilk.

"I wish to apologize to you for running away all those years ago," Kanakdatta said to her. "I have missed you."

"That is all long gone now." Karuvaki patted him on the shoulder. "We are together now; that is what matters."

For now, Kanakdatta thought. He feared the warmth of reunion would soon be lost. "How long will it take for people to cast their votes?" he asked, starting on his plate of rice and curd.

"The system of voting is archaic," Karuvaki replied. "The people are divided into groups based upon the village they come from. Men are sent into the forest to gather the leaves of the *Bela* tree, which are traditionally used to cast their votes. Individual earthen pots are made ready for each village. The people draw the mark of the candidate they wish to elect upon Bela leaves and drop them into the village pot."

"And then each pot is opened and the votes counted?" Kanakdatta enquired. "How long does it take?"

"People are still coming into the city through all the gates. It will be another two or three days, Kanaka."

"We do not have time, sister."

"I know," Karuvaki murmured. "That is why, due to the threat of war, we will be using a different method."

"And what will that be?"

"Devdatta is a clear winner here," Karuvaki said. "So we shall ask each group to shout the name of the candidate they wish to be their Governor. The name with the most shouts shall win."

"And how will you factor in the greater number of votes which each noble family commands?" Kanakdatta asked her, finishing his meal and washing his hands in the bowl a servent held for him.

"We will group the nobles separately. A clerk from the palace shall make the multiplications and derive the final result. This is the only way we can complete the voting in a day. Each group who had shouted their selection will be sent to the army camp being constructed along the northern perimeter of the city."

"Aye, we need all the time we can get."

"What about you? Have the men of the army accepted your leadership?" she asked.

Kanakdatta nodded. "Yes, I have been to the barracks. Some of the older men remembered and welcomed me. Those who came after my time, I silenced with a display of my skill with the bow. The common men of Kalinga will follow their army Commanders, and the Commanders shall follow me."

"That is good. How many men do you think we will be able to muster?"

Kanakdatta counted on his fingers. "I have the five hundred blood riders that I brought with me from the North, the Kalinga stables have about the same number of standing riders. Judging by the number of able bodied men thronging the city, we should be able to recruit ten thousand foot soldiers. I only wish we had war elephants."

"Oh, but we do," Karuvaki smiled. "Most of our elephant trainers and *mahouts* reside near the coastal villages of the delta region. I have sent riders, and they will soon be here."

"Then I daresay we can field a formidable force against the attackers."

"And how numerous are the enemy?"

Kanakdatta sighed. "About three times our size."

"By the Gods!" Karuvaki swore.

"Fear not, sister, battles are not always about numbers. Usually they depend on who has the higher ground and better position. I daresay we, as the defenders, will be able to grasp that advantage."

"We will do everything to increase the number of men," Karuvaki said in her characteristically firm voice.

"Aye," Kanakdatta agreed, "more men would help. Our army must appear to be a formidable force to my friend, Shiva of Avanti. If he thinks we are weak, he will launch a direct frontal assault and we will have no choice but to fight. But, if we can intimidate him, he will call for a parley. I can then show him Devi is still alive and implore him to avoid the battle."

"Too much responsibility rides on your shoulders, brother," Karuvaki said, concerned for him and the outcome. "Let me take some of it upon myself. Let me ride with you into battle."

Kanakdatta looked into her eyes. "You have always been headstrong, even as a little girl," he said. "But it is not my place to stop you. After all, this land is yours more than it is mine. The Commanders will have more faith in me when they see you by my side."

"It is agreed then," Karuvaki said, tilting her chin in the manner he remembered from their childhood. "I shall ride by your side."

"I must see the Guild Master," Kanakdatta said, getting to his feet.

"And I must return to oversee preparations." They walked out together.

Outside, Kanakdatta was instantly enveloped in the thronging thousands. People huddled in groups and it was difficult to make his way between them. He found Hardeo and Devi in the small wooden house in the city centre, which Radhagupta had said was his quarters. As he walked in, he could hear their voices raised in dispute.

"It will happen just as I have said, father," Devi said, her voice tinged with sorrow.

Hardeo looked up anxiously as Kanakdatta walked in. "Try to put some sense into her," he said exasperated. "I insist she remain in the city with me, but she refuses."

"Guild Master," Kanakdatta said, "her presence with the army is of vital importance to our plan."

Hardeo sat back with a sigh. "I understand that, but I do not want her to be in any danger. She has just returned to me from the dead!"

"Father," Devi said firmly, "you just heard what Kanakdatta said. The plan cannot work if I do not ride with him to face the Mauryan army."

"What if something happens to you, Devi?" Hardeo cried, his old face lined with worry, his eyes moist with tears. "How will I live with myself?"

Devi glared at him. "Just as you did the last five years. As if I was dead."

Hardeo looked distraught as he got to his feet. "I will take a walk," he told them and went out through the wooden door into the street.

"That was a mean thing to say to your own father," Kanakdatta said when Hardeo had left. "I would go and apologize if I were you."

"I am sorry, Kanaka, I really am." Devi looked down at the floor. "All of this is overwhelming for me. For years he believed I was dead, and now that he has found me again, he thinks he has the right to order me around."

"It is not like that." Kanakdatta folded his arms and leaned against a wall. "He lost you once. He is afraid of losing you again."

"Was it so believable, what that evil Chanakya did?" she asked.

"It was," Kanakdatta nodded. "He went to great lengths to make everyone believe you had perished in the fire. I do not know which poor woman he sacrificed to appear as your burnt body, but she had on your clothes, your ornaments."

"He would have killed me, you know." Devi looked up. "If Radhagupta had not saved me, his minions would have really burnt me alive. It brings a chill to my spine sometimes and disturbs my sleep."

"I swear, Devi, if I had known you were there in that dank brothel that day, I would have ridden out and got you out of there."

"There was no way you could have known." Devi looked away. "It is all in the past now," she said.

"You always reminded me of my sister, Karuvaki, whom I had left behind," he told her. "That was why I always looked out for you like my own. I am sorry I could not help you, Devi."

Devi reached out to take his hand. "You are helping me now, Kanaka. Let us not talk about the past for that brings only sadness and despair."

"Let us talk about the future then." Kanakdatta tried to look cheerful. "Asoka will be delirious with joy when he sees you."

"Will he?" Devi said wistfully, withdrawing her hand. "I hear he has a new wife now."

"We all thought you were dead, Devi. It pained us all; him most of all."

"He promised I would be the only woman in his life," Devi said, not meeting Kanakdatta's eyes. "He broke that promise."

'Devi..." Kanakdatta pleaded, "He is the Samrat. He had to marry again. You know that."

"No Kanaka, I do not." Devi looked at him, her eyes glittering angrily. "I do *not* know how it is. I never took another man, Kanaka. It has been five years. It is his children I have cared for. Not that I was ever tempted. Radhagupta was kind and caring, but I held to my vow." She looked away. "He, on the other hand, did not."

"Oh Devi..."

"It is not going to end the way you think, Kanaka," she said sadly. "I am not going back to him. That is not how all this ends. There is no happily ever after. I will go with you to him, to end this war, the threat of bloodshed and suffering, but after that, I will leave."

"It will break his heart." Kanakdatta said thoughtfully. "But I will not attempt to convince you anymore. As I said, you are like my sister – headstrong. You do as you want."

"Do you think we can defeat him, Kanaka?" Devi asked seriously. "Can we ever right the wrong Chanakya has done us?"

"We are trying, are we not?" He tried to comfort her with his words but he felt the same fear burning in him.

"I do not know what is wrong with me, Kanaka." Devi closed her eyes sadly. "I should be happy. I just met my father. I met all of you. For the first time in years I have a chance at something I have longed for since the day Chanakya separated me from Asoka." She opened her eyes. "Finally, I have a chance at revenge. I should feel joy, jubilation, but I feel nothing at all. Not even hope. I do not believe everything will be alright." She looked at him, her eyes wet with sudden tears. "Please tell me that everything is going to be alright, Kanaka. Please tell me. I cannot be weak in front of anyone else. I must be strong. But I see you and the years of sorrow jump out of my heart."

"It is going to be alright." Kanakdatta got to his feet. "You must rest, Devi. And take my advice, find your father before you do and apologize. For all his ways, he loves you beyond measure. Few in the world ever will."

She nodded. "Will you give me your word about something, Kanaka? For old times' sake?"

Kanakdatta looked at her. "I give you my word," he said.

Her eyes looked straight into his. "If we are left with no option but to fight, promise that you will let me fight beside you."

Kanakdatta took a deep breath. "You are our only chance of defeating Chanakya."

"You have given your word."

Kanakdatta nodded. "All I have ever wanted for you is the freedom to do what makes you happy. And I will see you happy once again. You have my word."

Devi smiled. "I will go and find my father."

When she had left, Kanakdatta sat down in thought. He realized there was one other person he wished to see before going to the tents in the northern part of the city to begin drilling the men. He stood up and walked out into crowds once again.

He found Radhagupta by Devdatta's warehouses near the docks. One had been converted into a war room of sorts. Radhagupta sat with men dressed in tunics, Navin's old Councillors. They welcome Kanakdatta with a smile.

"Have you had a look at this?" Radhagupta asked, pointing to the parchments on the table. "I must say I am quite surprised by the contents of the Late Governor Navin's armoury."

"Surprised in a good or bad way?" Kanakdatta asked, sitting down beside him.

"Oh good...good..." Radhagupta nodded. "Under him, Kalinga saw five decades of peace, so I was not sure if he had hoarded enough weapons in the armouries. I was worried we would have to ask the peasants to carry their pitchforks and the fishermen their carving knives, into battle. But these records show we have enough to arm all our men."

"My father preferred to be prepared for any eventuality," Kanakdatta said, long suppressed memories flooding his mind. "Almost every able bodied man who has come to the capital has volunteered."

Radhagupta nodded. "I know, and I repeat we have adequate weapons – swords, spears, shields, bows and arrows. We can put up a good fight."

"That is what I came to talk to you about," Kanakdatta said. "Facing the Mauryan army is just the beginning. What happens after that it is more important."

"I know where you are going with this," Radhagupta said. "Do not worry. You play your role on the battlefield and I shall play mine, here in the city."

Kanakdatta nodded. "If things go wrong, you must be here in the city to turn defeat into victory."

"You are his friend, Kanakdatta, so tell me something," Radhagupta said in a low voice. "Will our plan work? Will the Samrat ride out to accept our surrender?"

"It saddens me to say I cannot answer that with any certainty, my friend," Kanakdatta replied. "The Prime Minister holds a strange power over him. He has kept the Samrat distracted with wine and women, and God knows what else."

"But you know him better than us," Radhagupta insisted. "When Devdatta appeals to him to come to Kalinga to accept our surrender, will he disobey the Prime Minister and ride out?"

"We are counting on him to do so."

"And when he comes, will what he sees affect him?"

Kanakdatta finally understood. "So that is your real question. You wish to know if Asoka's heart is his own or whether Chanakya's influence has turned him into stone."

"We are counting on him to feel remorse, Kanakdatta. If he comes, sees but feels nothing, we lose."

"He is a good man," Kanakdatta stressed. "Of that I give you my word."

"People have been talking," Radhagupta sighed. "They call him *Chandasoka* now, the Evil One. There are stories of how he killed his entire Council of Ministers, of how he sent all the women in his harem to the gallows."

"Those were Chanakya's doings. The old man manipulated Asoka into doing all that. I know my friend's heart and I know it still has place for love...and regret."

"Devi told me about the last time she ever saw him," Radhagupta related. "It was during Sushem's siege. She said he hit her, Kanaka. He hit her. It was then she made up her mind to leave him, even if Chanakya had not captured her."

Kanakdatta looked down at the floor. "He still loves her deeply," he said. "Asoka can never know this about her. Promise me he shall never know; that you will not tell this to anyone."

Radhagupta nodded in silence.

Kanakdatta got to his feet. "I must get going to the camp. It is time we start drilling those who have enlisted. I plan to move out of the city at nightfall."

"I wish you luck, Buddhist," Radhagupta said softly. "We shall meet again."

"The same thought dwells in my heart," Kanakdatta replied, looking up. The two men embraced.

When Kanakdatta left the warehouse, a muted whistle from his left caught his attention. Devdatta was standing there, smiling at him. "I never did get to thank you for saving my life," he said, bowing.

"You can thank Karuvaki. She is the one who led us to you," Kanakdatta replied.

"But you were the one who brought the army to do the deed." Devdatta hesitated. "I want you to know that back in the Mauryan lands, all of us new merchants aspired to be like you. You were our role model – Kanakdatta the Buddhist, the most dangerous man in all of Bharatvarsha."

He smiled. "I never thought our destinies would interlink in such a way."

"You are a good man, Devdatta," Kanakdatta said. "Take good care of the land of my fathers. After the surrender, even if you are not in power, promise me that you will make this your home and these people your brothers."

"I already have," Devdatta smiled. "Be victorious, my friend!"

Kanakdatta took his leave and set off. There was one last visit he had to make before he could walk on and not look back. He found Hardeo by the docks, staring intently towards the horizon where the sea met the sky. As Kanakdatta walked up to him, Hardeo did not turn. Both men stood without talking.

"Is it not beautiful?" Hardeo finally said, breaking the silence. "We have traded on land all our lives, Kanakdatta. We turned mud into gold. But I regret we never ventured to sea."

"Still thinking of business are you?" Kanakdatta laughed. "Now that I see my old Guild Master is back in spirits, I feel better already."

"Business is perpetual, after all," Hardeo reminded him. "Wars happen. Rulers change. Nations are forged and annexed. But business goes on."

Kanakdatta nodded, watching the waves hit the wooden pillions that held up the Dantapura docks in high tide.

"If we survive after all of this," Hardeo waved his hands around, "I would like to give the sea a chance. Just think of the possibilities, my lad. Think of what different lands may be beyond these waters. Think what treasures they may hold."

"Hardeo the Sea Explorer." Kanakdatta closed his eyes. "The name suits you, Guild Master."

"There are a thousand possibilities once we cross the seas," Hardeo said. "And not just for business, my lad."

Kanakdatta looked at him. "What do you mean?"

"What has happened has pained me deeply," Hardeo told him. "But I would be a bad merchant if I did not seek the root cause of it all."

"And what is that?" Kanakdatta asked.

"The faith we chose," Hardeo sighed. "Your father exiled you because of it. They tried to kill Devi because of her beliefs. For years, our people have fought to be treated as equals, most confined to monasteries in remote places. Bharatvarsha birthed our creed, but it has not been kind to us. Perhaps the lands across the sea will be more welcoming, the people more accepting."

"True." Once again Kanakdatta acknowledged the Guild Master's wisdom.

"Think of this, my lad," the Guild Master said dreamily, "imagine what we can achieve if we think beyond this subcontinent. Could we perhaps create entire nations where the majority believed in the path shown by the Buddha? Could we raise great statues in his name, made of gold and silver? Could we build great stupas in his honour, to preserve his teachings for ages to come?"

"Give me your blessings before I set off to war," Kanakdatta said, breaking into the old man's thoughts. He bent to touch the Guild Master's feet.

Hardeo placed a hand on his head. "Keep what I said in mind when you face the Mauryans, my lad. Know that you fight not just for us, or the Kalingans, for individuals like me, Devi, or to defeat Asoka and Chanakya. You fight for the wonderful future that can be created by our brethren. It is for that future that you fight. Be victorious!"

Kanakdatta raised his head, fighting tears. The path looked blurred as he turned and left with quickened steps.

18
KANAKDATTA:
THE NEMESIS OF KALINGA

KALINGA, 262 BC

Kanakdatta halted the army's march when they reached the rolling, green hills of Dhauli, drenched by the rains that had come late this year. The ground was wet but hard still. He and his men walked without having their feet sink into the mud. Across from them was the Daya River, flowing now in full spate, so fording it downstream was no longer possible. It was the perfect location for a defensive position. Kanakdatta ordered encampments to be set up in the plains while he himself took up position above, on a hill, waiting to sight the opposing army.

By the time darkness fell, he knew how his battle lines were to be deployed – in thick rows, leaving no space between them. His archers would stand behind a wall of infantrymen, flanked by spearsmen. He would keep the cavalry in the rear, ready to strike or counter the enemy's flanking force as the battle progressed. He would place himself and his horse archer regiments on the slopes of the hill, ready to launch against the enemy. Their left flank would be solidly protected by the wide body of the river and their right flank by the the hills. Kanakdatta knew it was the best possible position he could have. If he moved further, the plains of Madhya Bharat would appear. Nor could he move back and risk the Mauryan forces getting an open entry into Kalinga. He had to make his stand here. All that remained was to wait.

That night, while the soldiers roasted meat at campfires, he summoned the older Captains from all the Kalingan divisions to his tent for dinner. Though his scouts had surveyed the land around Kalinga, he knew he could never beat the knowledge of those born here. He hoped each of his guests would support his choice of position. And almost all of them did agree that they were now entrenched in the best position available.

All except Mohapatra, the oldest Captain in the Kalingan army, his long flowing white hair a testament to his experience. "We have lost, son," he said, looking Kanakdatta in the eye.

Kanakdatta cleared his throat. "Your colleagues accept this is the best position we could possibly be in."

"The best position." Mohapatra smiled, showing his yellowed teeth. "The best position is when you can beat the enemy with minimal loss of men. Look at us now, and imagine what will happen when the vast Mauryan army falls upon us."

"We will stop them." Kanakdatta folded his arms.

"Aye we will," Mohapatra said, looking at the faces of the men around him. "But what then?"

Kanakdatta knew the old man spoke the truth. This was their last stand. There was no counter-attack, no stratagem that would follow. In the ensuing silence, a sentry announced dinner was ready.

***

They caught sight of the Mauryan army on the third day, far along the eastern horizon, marching straight at them. It was almost noon, so the sun was high above and both sides could see each other well. Kanakdatta watched the marching mass of men from atop his horse on the slope of the hill. His eyes surveyed the field of battle, from the north to south, taking in all he saw.

The Mauryans had more men. Any fool could see that. Their horsemen rode out around their columns, spread down their entire length. Far in the back they could see the silhouettes of tall elephants.

From the corner of his eye Kanakdatta carefully watched the faces of the Captains beside him. To his relief he did not see fear but a sombre determination. He knew the sight of that vast marching army was one to shake the most battle hardened soldier. He was glad he was fighting alongside brave men. "Place the white flag," he ordered calmly. The fluttering white fabric called for a pre-battle parley between the leaders of both armies.

As the sky turned crimson, they met for pre-battle negotiations on top of the hill. Shiva's army had set up camp beyond the open fields. The Kalingans, however, had not left their position. They would spend the night up on the hill.

Shiva arrived at the meeting spot, riding a black warhorse and looking majestic in his armour. Two bodyguards accompanied him. Kanakdatta was already there, astride his horse. To his left was Karuvaki, and to his right Devi. Shiva eyed all three and then fixed his gaze on Kanakdatta in the middle. Surprise clearly showed on his face. "I did not expect to see you here today, Kanaka," he said.

"The last time we met, Shiva, I told you I would show you proof of what I claimed," Kanakdatta responded.

"Instead, I see you at the head of the Kalingan army. " Shiva sighed. "Have you decided to meet your destiny as the son of the late Kalingan Governor?"

Kanakdatta shook his head. "Look at those beside me."

Shiva nodded. "Interesting company you have chosen for this parley."

"To my right is Lady Karuvaki, Foreign Minister to the Kalingan Rajya."

Shiva bowed slightly. "I regret we do not meet in more favourable times," he said.

"To my left is Devi, Guild Master Hardeo's daughter, and, as you are aware, Asoka's supposedly dead wife."

Shiva surveyed Devi from head to toe, then slowly shook his head.

"She is all the proof you need, Shiva." Kanakdatta heeled his horse closer.

If something was racing through Shiva's mind at that moment, his eyes did not betray his emotions. "All the proof you say." He spoke deliberately. "The last time we met, you told me you would find her in Kalinga and bring her to the Samrat. Yet I see you here today, at an entirely different place."

"I did not have the time, my friend," Kanakdatta declared. "After you moved your army across Kalinga's border, I had no option but to come to face you here."

"With an army," Shiva noted.

"You would have done the same in my position."

"Would I?" Shiva's horse whinnied as he turned it to face Devi. He looked at her intently for a moment. "I mean no offence to you when I say this," he said, "but this is the first time I am seeing you, if you are indeed who Kanakdatta says you are."

"I am glad to make your acquaintance," Devi bowed. "I have heard your name many times from..."

"No!" Shiva raised a hand to silence her. "You do not understand what I just said. I have never seen you before, My Lady. I have never visited Vidishanagri. The Samrat told me about you when he met me in Avanti, all that time ago, but he never described you to me. When my army joined that of Vidishanagri before the siege of Patliputra, you had already left with the Samrat."

"Shiva..." Kanakdatta said imploringly as understanding slowly dawned upon him. But the taut lines on Shiva's face silenced him.

"When we entered Patliputra in triumph, I did not see you then either, for you had left the palace to help the people in the streets. The only time I saw you was when your body was brought to the palace, burnt and unrecognisable. I can never forget Asoka's tears that day. The man loved you. He recognized you even though the body was burnt and charred."

"We do not deceive you," Kanakdatta snapped.

Shiva turned to him, furious. "And how should I believe you, Kanaka, after all you have done?" he bellowed. "How can I be sure when you face me as a foe, at the head of the very army I rode out to decimate? How can I be sure this lady is not just some strumpet from your beloved Kalinga, whom you taught a little bit of your story and brought here to pretend to be the Samrat's one true love, hoping it would cause me to turn tail and ride back?"

"Where is Asoka? He will recognize her."

"He is not here."

"Then send for him."

"And wait till he comes? Are you mad?" Shiva looked at Kanakdatta in surprise. "With an army on higher ground in front of us, you want me to tell my men to wait? You know I cannot do that."

Kanakdatta knew his friend spoke the truth. "I would not lie to you," he insisted. "You must trust me. It is the only way to peace and resolution."

"There was a day when I would have trusted you with my life," Shiva said, "but not today, Kanaka. Not anymore. You betrayed me. You betrayed our Samrat."

As a tepid breeze blew over them, Kanakdatta knew the decision had been made. A sudden calm filled his being. "Then we fight," he said.

Shiva looked at him, his gaze menacing. "I have three times as many men as you."

Kanakdatta returned the unwavering gaze. "I have the better position," he said.

Shiva did not reply. He looked down at the ground as his horse neighed and shiftd uneasily. "So this is it," he said.

Kanakdatta nodded. The dreaded possibility was at hand. "My heart grieves, my friend," he said, "that it has come to this. I hoped it would have been otherwise. But we are both left with no choice. You will not back down and there is no way in hell that I will either."

Shiva took a deep breath and looked away. "So this is how it ends. After all we have been through together."

Kanakdatta laughed mirthlessly. "You should be happy. You always said we never discovered who the better fighter between us was."

There was no hint of a smile on Shiva's face. "There was

never any question, old friend. With your antics with the bow, I never even came close."

Kanakdatta felt the wind tug at him in the silence that followed. For the first time in his life he did not know what to say. For the first time he heard his friend admit defeat.

"If it does not end well, I want you to know I was so proud to call you my friend." Shiva broke the silence.

Kanakdatta looked at the lines of their armies, like a vast mass of ants spread across the land. "Look around," he said, "there is no way this is going to end well."

Shiva did not reply, but pulled the reins of his horse slightly. The animal neighed. "We fight in the morning," he said. "May the better man win."

Kanakdatta looked into the drawn face of his friend. Tears rolled down his cheeks, surprising himself. He could not remember the last time he had cried. Shiva looked away without acknowledging the emotion. The two friends could not face each other anymore. In the deep confines of his mind, Kanakdatta knew the meeting was over. The two men turned their horses and went their separate ways.

On that fateful evening, as one descended the hill, the other climbed up. Both Kanakdatta and Shiva knew they would never see each other again, except in battle.

***

As Shiva fell onto the camp bed in his tent that night, he had trouble falling asleep. His mind roiled with thoughts. After a while his ears focused on the voices of a group of soldiers sitting by the fire outside his tent.

"It is quite cold this time of the year," one complained. "I wish the Samrat had asked us to march in summer. Wounds of battle hurt severely in winter."

"How would the Samrat know what time of year it is if he never leaves his Rang Mahal and the pleasure houses?" another offered.

"He wants us to fight his battles for him while he sleeps with the women of his harem," yet another said loudly, wine having dulled his understanding of what speech was correct and what was not. "

"Quiet!" warned one of his comrades. "If General Shiva hears you, he will have you beaten."

On a normal day Shiva would have stepped out and made an example of the soldier, but his mind was weary that night. Closing his eyes, he drifted into slumber, still listening to the soldiers talking.

*

At the break of dawn, Kanakdatta walked out of his tent, fully dressed in his armour. He could hear the Captains motivating their men. "Look sharp, men!" one shouted. "What you do today on the battlefield will be written in the books of history!"

As he walked along the far end of his lines, where the blacksmiths had set up their stations, he heard a soldier instruct sternly, "Sharpen my sword well, for I do not intend to die before killing at least ten people today." As he crossed the hastily put up fencing to the stables, he saw a cavalryman in silent prayer under a tree, with his eyes closed but his face determined. Taking a deep breath, Kanakdatta mounted his horse and rode out to the hill top, from where the downward slope began. The sun behind them would give them an advantage, blinding their enemies during the charge. Kanakdatta's eyes searched the horizon. On the plains, a small herd of deer were grazing, unmindful of what was to come. A large male was lazily slumped on the ground, digging its head into the ankle high grass. A few yards away, a doe was lovingly licking her fawn, who wanted to break free and run.

The big deer was the first to notice something amiss. All of a sudden, it left its grassy bed and rose nimbly to its feet, moving his head here and there, clearly alarmed. The doe ignored the sudden actions of its partner at first and kept licking her young one, but soon her ears were taut and up in the air as well. The big deer took a few strides, trying to get to a higher perch, its instincts alerted. At once it saw what needed to be seen. It raised its forelegs and galloped away, the other deer following immediately.

When the herd had scurried away to the left, Kanakdatta's eyes moved up and saw the lines of Shiva's vanguard marching forward in unison. The men cried their battle cries as they marched relentlessly forward. Kanakdatta took a deep breath and pulled his bow off his shoulder. Battle had begun.

He watched as Shiva's lines moved to the base of the hill and stopped. The cavalry moved to the sides, indicating they would attack first. Kanakdatta had placed himself on the right flank, watching Shiva's every move. His old comrade sat on his horse on the left flank, facing him directly. Kanakdatta looked behind to take stock of the situation. He had arranged his lines in three straight layers. At the front were the spearmen and swordsmen, most of who were from General Bheema's regular army. They would put up a good fight. Behind them were the archers, mostly country folk, armed with makeshift bows and hastily trained in archery in whatever time they had had while marching out of the city. Behind them, in the reserve, were the remaining peasants, the freemen and fishermen of Kalinga, armed with pitchforks and harpoons and whatever else they had managed to bring.

Kanakdatta turned back to look at Shiva's majestic army, professionally organized in two lines. The front line comprised the skirmishers, holding their slings eagerly, waiting for the order to fall upon the opposition. Behind them were the regulars, armed with spears, well armoured with bronze helmets and breastplates, who would follow in the second wave. He knew Shiva had gathered most of his cavalry at his left flank, facing them, while Kanakdatta had divided his equally, one group was all around him on the right flank, and one hidden behind their reserves. He knew it would be the horsemen who would decide the battle today.

The two armies stood, prepared for the onslaught, each waiting for the other to make the first move. Finally, Shiva raised his hand. There was a blast of horns and trumpets and the skirmishers began to run forward, swinging their slings in their hands.

"Brace yourself!" Kanakdatta yelled at his frontline.

They raised their shields over their heads to protect themselves from the slingshot barrage, while the men at the centre of the charge, raised theirs shoulder high. The Kalingan Captains raised their own cries. The men responded with wild cheers, filling the air with the age old sounds of battle.

Kanakdatta waited. His ears were deafened by the noise around him. It was difficult to distinguish the voices of friend from foe. To his relief, he saw that his first line, in its Testudo formation, had not moved an inch. Ahead, Shiva's skirmishers were now in range. The first stones came in a sudden hailstorm, with stones falling on their shields, but his soldiers were ready. He watched as the skirmishers moved forward again, ready to launch a second volley. His eye moved towards his left flank, where the remainder of his hidden cavalry waited, with the two women at the very front. Karuvaki saw him look their way and nodded, while Devi patted her horse, her eyes fixed on her hands.

Kanakdatta raised his hand. "Now!" he shouted. He watched as Karuvaki and Devi burst out of formation, followed by the horsemen, galloping towards the skirmishers, their swords raised. They fell upon the line of skirmishers in a flash, causing confusion and havoc as their swords cut down the enemy. Kanakdatta turned to see Shiva's reaction to this maneuver. He watched as his old friend gripped his sword in anger. Shiva's cavalry moved out in a triangular formation, with him at the very vertex. They moved towards where Karuvaki, Devi and their cavalry were routing his skirmishers.

It was time. Kanakdatta pressed his heel into the belly of his horse and rode out. On both sides, his men followed. He felt the wind tug at his face as he galloped to intercept Shiva and his cavalry. His move had worked for Shiva, realizing what was happening, had changed direction. His sword was now pointed straight at Kanakdatta and his charging men.

Kanakdatta waited till only a hundred paces separated him from Shiva, then he pulled on the reins abruptly. His men did the same. Kanakdatta saw the sudden change in Shiva's expression as he realized that the men dressed in Kalingan lungis and loose shirts facing him, were not in fact Kalingan forces, but Kanakdatta's feral riders. *Hun! Hun!* Their cries filled the sky as Kanakdatta and his horsemen suddenly turned and moved in the reverse direction. Their legs moved into the brown stirrups that were attached to their horses' sides. In unison they sheathed their swords and took hold of their bows. They were a magnificent sight. Shiva and his cavalry kept riding forward as the feral riders took aim. The arrows released together like a swarm of locusts, hitting their targets at close range. Shiva saw men fall around him as the gap between him and Kanakdatta increased.

Kanakdatta rode on away, grabbing another arrow from his quiver and placing it on the nook of his bow. With the wind chasing him like a playful child, he closed one eye and pointed the arrow at Shiva, who was chasing him, sword out. To Kanakdatta, the arrow seemed to release in slow motion, but Shiva was ready for it. In one movement his shield was up and the arrow embedded itself in it with a deadly twang, quivering like a thing possessed. A second volley of arrows fell and Kanakdatta watched Shiva's men fall from their horses. But Shiva's eyes did not move from him as he lowered his shield. Around Kanakdatta, his bowmen readied to strike again even as Shiva's remaining horsemen reached their targets.

Kanakdatta wheeled his horse in a tight circle and took aim again, this time targeting Shiva's horse. To his surprise, before he could release the arrow, he felt his horse collapsing under him. Warm blood spouted over his hands and legs from the spear lodged in the animal's belly. It slid to the ground in mortal agony and Kanakdatta fell with it, his bow dangling to one side as his face hit the dust. Quickly he pulled himself from the horse, pulling his leg from under it. Clutching his bow, he dragged himself to his feet. Shiva was nowhere to be seen. Kanakdatta gazed down at the animal, which lay on its side, whinnying in pain. There was nothing he could do.

Turning, Kanakdatta surveyed the battlefield, where the skirmishers had been ambushed by his men just a short time ago. The skirmishers were nowhere to be seen. Instead, all he saw was chaos. Shiva's main line of foot soldiers had moved forward and were about to engage the Kalingan frontline. Moving forward, he saw horsemen behind Shiva's main line, chopping at their rear in waves. So Karuvaki and Devi had managed to outflank the enemy, he thought. Now all he had to do was decimate Shiva's horsemen and count on the spirited Kalingans to hold the line.

Kanakdatta jumped back as a sword flew past him, missing him by a two finger breadths. Shiva! There was no mistaking his black armour drenched in scarlet blood. He swooped by on his horse. He pulled the back till it reared on its hind legs and then turned in one swift motion to charge at him again. This time Kanakdatta was ready. As Shiva swung his sword, Kanakdatta held up his metal bow to deflect the thrust. The tip of the sword clanged against the curve of the bow, causing the metal of both weapons to vibrate like things possessed. Kanakdatta clenched his teeth and with a twist of his hand, caught the blade in the arc of the bow before Shiva could move. Shiva struggled to free his weapon but Kanakdatta twisted his hands, making it impossible. Finally Shiva released the hilt of his sword and it fell to the ground. He moved his horse away, preparing for another charge. Kanakdatta watched his muscled arm pull the long spear attached to the harness.

Quickly glancing towards the centre, he saw that Shiva's main line was now in combat with the Testudo formation of the Kalingans. Battle raged all around. Breathing in, Kanakdatta watched Shiva turn. He placed a final arrow in his bow as he watched his old friend bend forward on his mount, pointing the spear directly at him.

As Shiva charged, Kanakdatta felt the world around him slow down. The noise of battle faded. All he could feel was his beating heart, hammering against his ribs. There was no time for thought and he let instinct take over as Shiva rode at him, his spear outstretched. Kanakdatta closed his eyes.

His hand pulled the bowstring taut, his outstretched thumb guiding the arrow. Breaking the silence, Shiva's wild roar filled his ears as he prepared to strike. Kanakdatta took a deep breath and released the bowstring held between his thumb and index finger. The arrow flew straight at the sound of his attacker. Then darkness fell upon him.

19
HARDEO:
END OF THE LINE

KALINGA, 262 BC

On the third night after the Kalingan army had left Dantapura, Kanakdatta at its head, Hardeo finally dropped into a fitful sleep, overcome by fatigue. In the darkness he dreamt of summer, of teaching the child Devi to walk, read and dance. She looked beautiful with her messy unkempt hair and joyful smile. He smiled at the bubbly energetic figure in his dream. The dreams kept him asleep for many hours, lost in happy memories of the past.

When he opened his eyes, Hardeo saw the sun was already up in the sky. He rose and dressed hurriedly for it was an important day. Outside in the streets, he saw unknown faces everywhere. Many of the men who had marched with Kanakdatta had left behind their wives and daughters in the city. Little boys, too young to wield weapons, had remained too. At every turn Hardeo could see temporary shelters erected for them to stay until the men returned. *But will they return?* Hardeo wondered.

They had received no news yet from Kanakdatta. Scouts had been sent by Devdatta to ride out and bring information. Hardeo saw that while he had slept, most of the city had remained, for there had been a heavy downpour in the darkness. The temporary shelters could not protect them from the rain so the people of Kalinga had per force stayed awake, praying for the safety of their husbands and sons.

Hardeo walked to the warehouse by the docks where the counting of votes had gone on through the night. He found Devdatta there, walking out just as he arrived. "Guild Master!" Devdatta bowed. "It appears that I am the new Governor of Kalinga."

Hardeo blessed him. "Not that the outcome was ever in doubt," he said. "Where is Radhagupta, your advisor?"

"He went with the scouts to seek news of our army." Devdatta sighed. "They have been gone three days. Radhagupta fears something terrible has happened."

"We must hope he returns with good news," Hardeo said. "What wll be your first task as Governor?"

Devdatta said looking around them. "The people need to be informed of the result first."

"So many of your people are with Kanakdatta."

"But their women and children are here," Devdatta replied. "They will not leave the city till they hear news of their men. Nor would we let them go. We must find courage together at this time."

"I suppose a speech is in order then?" Hardeo watched Devdatta's men putting up a small podium on the dock.

Devdatta nodded, his face sombre. "I must speak to the people; give them hope."

"That is a good idea," Hardeo agreed. "All of us are in this together, filled with fearful uncertainty, not knowing if the men are still alive out there. Even my daughter and Lady Karuvaki... Not knowing if their sacrifice was in vain or not."

"When Radhagupta returns, we shall know."

Devdatta's men had finished putting up the podium and were now beating a large pot of iron to summon the people. Hardeo watched as mothers with little ones upon their shoulders and clutching the hands of their daughters, hurried towards the sound.

"You have taken up a great responsibility, my son," He said, watching the growing crowd walking towards the docks. "It is one thing to become ruler of a free nation and something else to become leader of a defeated one."

"My duty is to my people either way," Devdatta replied. "Before I go up there, Guild Master, I want to ask you a question. Years ago, you banished me from the lands of the Mauryas. Today I am accepted as the leader of the lands I was exiled to. Have you forgiven me my crimes?"

"I forgave you long time ago, Devdatta," Hardeo said. "We will have a lot of rebuilding to do if we are to make our Guild what it was. The marching Mauryan army is sure to have devastated Vidishanagri on their way here."

"Aye, that we will," Devdatta nodded.

"Before coming here, I was going to step down as Guild Master," Hardeo disclosed. "Circumstances compelled me to stay on. But the time has now come to pass the mantle."

"To me?" Devdatta said, surprised. "It would be a great honour, Guild Master."

"We will have elections, by the Preferetti, of course," Hardeo said, "but I daresay you are used to that now."

The crowds had gathered at the docks by then, as they had for the election rallies, but that was all over now. They were now gathered to see their new Governor.

"It is time," Devdatta said.

"Then go and tell the people the truth," Hardeo advised him. "Remind them that the times ahead will not be easy. Tell them that their lives will change, that they will face hard times. But through grit and determination, inherent in their culture, you shall prevail together."

"I will, Guild Master."

"Then it is time I take my place in the crowds," Hardeo sighed. "While you young ones take the stage."

***

The crowd did not cheer when Devdatta walked up to the wooden platform. It was not that they did not admire him, but a subtle sorrow hung in the air, suffocating them.

"Fellow Kalingans!" Devdatta said, addressing the silent crowd. "There is no way I can lessen your dread or lift your heavy hearts, for it is indeed a troubled time for all of us. You have been dislodged from your homes. Your husbands, sons, and fathers have gone out to fight a mighty enemy. I cannot tell you that you will see them again. I cannot tell say that all of you will be safe. Nor can I tell you what the future holds for us.

What I can tell you, however, is that whatever has taken place outside our wall, and the courage shown by our fellow Kalingans to defend our way of life, will not go in vain. Even if we win the battle against the Mauryans, many will have died in the process. But their sacrifice shall not have been in vain for we will have taken charge of our own destiny. If we lose the battle, the Mauryans will sweep over us like the ocean tide, and we shall be at their mercy. But Kalingans are fierce individuals and we will find our own place inside the Mauryan order also.

But in either case, our destiny lies with the Mauryans. For years, we have lived as an independent Mahajanpada, in the shadow of our neighbours. Now we have a chance to be part of their Samrajya. We have a chance to access resources we never had before, and to rise to new heights. Whatever the future brings, there is one thing that is sure. No one can enslave the Kalingans. We are a free people even under the rule of Patliputra, we will find our freedom through our trade and our skills.

What your husbands, fathers and sons do out there today will be remembered as the stand of the Kalingans against the powerful Mauryan Empire. For thousands of years people will talk about this great battle. The memory of those who fought for our freedom will never die."

As Devdatta finished his speech, Hardeo watched the faces in the crowd. He saw in them a strange calm and a sense of hope. Hardeo smiled. His eyes fell on the figure of Radhagupta, standing there, listening to the speech. Hardeo wondered if Devdatta had seen him too.

He had. "Quick, to the warehouse!" he whispered to Radhagupta, walking away from the podium.

Hardeo followed Radhagupta, his heart beating anxiously in his chest.

"What news do you bring?" Devdatta and Hardeo asked together as they had stepped into the warehouse.

Radhagupta looked at them. "The battle is over," he said. "I saw the aftermath with my own eyes. I arrived just hours after it ended. The cowherds who lived nearby and who had witnessed it all, told us the whole tale." There was no trace of emotion on Radhagupta's face.

"So there was a battle?" Devdatta asked.

Radhagupta nodded silently.

"Who won?"

"No one."

"And Devi?" Hardeo asked. "Is she alright?"

"Your daughter is dead."

Dead silence lingered over the three men. None sought to break it. Finally, it was Hardeo who spoke. "Where is Kanakdatta? I want to look him in the eye and ask why he chose this day to fail me when he never has before."

"You cannot do that, Guild Master," Radhagupta said, his voice flat and lifeless. "Kanakdatta is dead as well."

Devdatta took both Hardeo's hands in his own. "Guild Master, I am sorry for your loss," he said quietly.

Hardeo stood silent and still. All blood seemed to have drained from his white face. Devi was dead. Why had she ever come back if only to die and shatter his heart again? Had he not wept enough? And Kanakdatta...he had been like a son... "What of Karuvaki?" he finally asked.

"She is alive, but injured. I brought her back to the city with me. She is being treated as we speak."

"Have we lost then? Is the Mauryan army marching towards the city?" Devdatta asked in despair.

"No." Radhagupta sat down. "The two armies decimated each other. Whoever survived must have fled the scene. The bank of the Daya River is littered with the bodies of men and animals alike." He looked at Devdatta. "We should send some men to count our dead and cremate them."

"What happened?" Devdatta asked, fighting to comprehend the scale of destruction. "Tell us what you heard from the cow herders."

Radhagupta told them. Hardeo and Devdatta heard him in silence, unmoving. When he was finished, Devdatta sat down, his legs shaking. "I will send men at once," he said. "We must cremate all those we can find. And there must be a burial for Kanakdatta and Devi."

"No." Hardeo's face was rigid. "This is the time to act."

Radhagupta looked at him. "Guild Master, we know you have had a great shock. Why not rest for a while?"

"Do not tell me to rest, son." Hardeo walked to a window and stared at the sky, his hands clasped behind his back. "If my daughter is dead, I cannot change it. But I *can* make sure that her death was not in vain,"

"How will we do that, Guild Master?" Devdatta asked. "We do not have another army. We have lost."

Hardeo turned and looked at Radhagupta. "Have we lost? You are a wise man, my son. You know what to do."

Radhagupta nodded. "We should send our surrender to the Samrat."

"Aye, but we must cremate our dead first," Devdatta insisted.

"No, we should not. That is the whole point." Hardeo turned towards them. "Let Asoka come here. Let him see with his own eyes what he has done; what the evil Chanakya made him to do. Let him see the bodies of his friends, Kanakdatta and Shiva, who he loved like brothers. Let him see the body of Devi, his true love, lying on the bloodstained earth. Let him see his soldiers. Only then should we send the surrender of Kalinga."

"The Guild Master is right," Devdatta nodded. "I will carry the letter to Patliputra, as leader of my people."

"No, my son." Hardeo shook his head. "Your people have suffered a massive defeat. Your place is here, with them. They need you to give them strength."

"Let me take the letter then," Radhagupta offered. "Let me ride to Patliputra as quickly as I can."

Hardeo shook his head again. "Your place is on the battlefield when Asoka arrives. It is for you to show him those he has killed. Besides, after Chanakya is gone, Asoka will need someone to take his place. That is what you were before, the Late Samrat's Prime Minister."

"So you want to be the one to go, Guild Master?" Radhagupta asked. "To ensure Chanakya is gone, once and for all? What if he does not let you meet the Samrat, like he did the last time?"

"When he knows that I speak on behalf of Kalinga, he will have to let me see him," Hardeo said. "Asoka knows me," Hardeo said thoughtfully. "I am the best person to convince him to come to the battlefield."

Radhagupta looked up. "Convincing him to visit the battlefield is not the only reason you are going to Patliputra, is it?"

Hardeo nodded, his face strangely calm. "Chanakya killed my daughter. Not once, but twice. I am not coming back from Patliputra till I have taken my revenge. The last time he attacked me in my own city. This time I shall attack him in his."

"You are going to kill him," Radhagupta said slowly as realization dawned upon him.

"I will," Hardeo said, "once and for all. The old man has overstayed his time and brought us nothing but pain and misery."

"It will not be easy," Radhagupta warned. "Look for the butcher on the East Hill. You will find him easily. He is the only butcher there. Tell him I sent you. He will help."

Devdatta broke his silence. "Then it looks like I have my first letter to write as Governor of Kalinga." He walked away, disappearing into the shadows.

Radhagupta looked at Hardeo, his face displaying neither bitterness nor anger. "When you kill the bastard," he said, his words falling like cold winter rain, "look him in the eye and ask him *why* he did this."

Hardeo nodded. It was time to go. He set off towards his chambers to prepare for the journey.

20

CHANAKYA:
DOWNFALL

~

PATLIPUTRA, 262 BC

As night fell over Patliputra that fateful day, Chanakya sat in the small space adjoining the audience chamber, quill in hand. He scribbled vigorously on the parchment before him. When he had finished filling the blank space to the very bottom, he placed the parchment upon a high stack of similarly scribbled papyrus. He drew another blank piece and placed it before him. Chanakya hesitated for a moment, breathing in deeply. His frail hand played with the light feather quill in his hand, drawing invisible circles mid-air. Then he began to scribble again.

When he had finished, he placed the latest page on the stack with the others. This time he did not draw out another blank one. His work was done. The stack beside him was complete. Chanakya looked at the leaves of papyrus with the hint of a smile on his severe mouth, just visible in the meagre lamplight. *Now my work is done*, he thought. All he had to do now was wait for one final action. He rested his head on the headrest of his chair and closed his eyes. *Adi Shakti, give me strength*, he prayed silently as he waited.

He did not have long to wait. The double doors behind him opened soon enough, as his guards escorted a man in. Chanakya glanced at his visitor. The face of Guild Master

Hardeo hung in the air above him. His black travelling cloak was soiled with dust and rain from hard travelling.

"Arya," Hardeo said as soon as they were alone, "let us do what needs to be done."

"I knew you would come," Chanakya said simply, without turning. There was a strange look upon his face. "I did wonder if it would be Radhagupta, but then it is only fair that it should be you."

Hardeo's face showed no emotion. "I come on behalf of the Kalingans," he said. "I carry a message for the Samrat."

"And you wish to deliver the message in person?"

Hardeo nodded. Chanakya clapped his hands. The two guards appeared again. "Pray take this stack of parchments to my chambers in the brothel," he told them. "Carry them with care for they are immensely valuable."

The guards obeyed. One carried the stack out while the other shut the door.

Chanakya wheeled his chair around and finally faced his quarry. "Night has fallen," he said slowly, "but I am sure sleep does not grace our Samrat in times of war such as these. I would have called upon him if I could have."

"So you will let me see him?" Hardeo said, surprised. "Now, as I am?"

"You did not hear me, my friend. I wish I could." Chanakya wheeled his chair towards the door. "It is said that the carrier of good news should not be made to wait. But in this case there is no one to give your news to."

"What do you mean?" Hardeo asked angrily.

"Anger does not become your age, Guild Master as wisdom does." Chanakya sighed. "The Samrat has left the palace. He rides to the battlefield with his bodyguards. When you stepped foot in the city, he must have set foot in Kalinga. I tried to stop him, but he insisted he go. When word was received of the devastation on the battlefield, and no one could tell him whether his friend Shiva was dead or alive, there was no way to stop him. The Samrat decided to ride to the battlefield and witness the aftermath of the battle for himself. The most I could do was convince him to take a posse of the Royal bodyguards with him."

"The battle is over," Hardeo said softly.

"Indeed, it is over," Chanakya nodded. "But what of the battle between us?"

"That too, shall soon be over." Hardeo's hand reached into his cloak and curled around the blade hidden there. But it was too risky. There were guards outside the chamber. He knew he had to get out of the palace and try again later. Fortunately, Chanakya had revealed to him his location that night when he had ordered the parchment stack to be taken to his chambers in the brothel. "If the Samrat is not here, I must take your leave," he said.

"But why?" Chanakya raised his head. "After the Samrat, I am the second person you would wish to see."

"Not under these circumstances."

"As your wish." Chanakya tapped the wooden desk. The doors opened and a guard appeared. "My guest will leave now," Chanakya announced.

Hardeo wasted no time nodding or bowing, but hurried out of the small chamber. The guard followed him out.

Alone again, Chanakya closed his eyes. This was the beginning of the end, just like it had been years ago.

50 YEARS AGO

The quill was long and sharp. It moved slowly over the long piece of yellowed parchment, leaving behind lines and shapes to seep into the texture of the fabric. The dark ink stayed on the surface for a moment, like little droplets of dark blood, before the pores in the parchment sucked it in like invisible leeches. My hand moving slowly, leaving a narrative that would last for generations to come.

The sand clock flowed in silence, a gift from the Greek General Seleucus. It emptied its bowl once every six hours. When it emptied this time, I did not turn it. I knew my time was almost up. I kept writing as I waited for my opponent to finally come to me.

This was the end game, the moment both of us had long been waiting for. For almost a year, we had played a devious game of wits, one strike after the other, from the deep chasms of our minds. It only remained to see who would have the last strike.

Crickets chirped in the darkness outside my window, declaring night had come. The time of reckoning was at hand. *The devil is in the dark,* an old Sanskrit subhashit said. The though brought a sudden chill to my spine and I felt something I had not felt in a long time – fear! I banished the feeling from my mind. This was not the moment of my judgment. It did not matter whether I faced it like a coward, or with bravado. What mattered was how my opponent would face it.

I had made my last move and now nothing remained but to wait. When the game had begun, he had been an aggressive opponent, the one to strike first, the one to break rules first. I had waited, giving him his chance. Now there was no other way. It had to end.

I kept writing. There was nothing left to do but write, to pour my heart and brain out on the parchment in front of me. I had done all I could. The future was no longer in my hands. All that was left was to discover what my opponent would do. Would he come and assassinate me? A chill spread over my body again. My work here remained incomplete. The Aryas were not yet unified. Chandragupta had not yet been made powerful. But if my opponent did indeed decide to kill me, I had decided to write down my legacy. To tell him what else needed to be done to strengthen the Samrajya. I wondered if he would take heed. Wondering was all that was left now.

Would he come and expose me? In exile, had he learnt the things I had done? I took a deep breath. *My secrets are my own*, I told myself. In any case, Dasharath stood outside my door, naked sabre in hand, ready to rush to my aid if something untoward were to take place.

A gust of air entered the chamber as the single window to my chamber opened with a creak. I had left it ajar for a purpose. It was the only way to reach me that night, and my opponent knew it. For this was his own chamber that I inhabitied. The cool air drew circles on the back of my neck, raising gooseflesh. I heard the thud of boots landing on the wooden floor. *He had come!*

"I knew you would come," I said without looking up, my hand still moving like a honeybee upon the parchment.

Prime Minister Rakshasa stared at my hunched figure for a few moments. His gaze seemed to burn into the back of my neck. I heard a soft sigh escape his mouth. "Let us do what needs to be done," he said.

I did not answer. My hand moved over the parchment, scribbling like a madman, unstoppable and unyielding, like the wind. *The moment of reckoning was upon us.*

"Arya," he said.

My hand stopped mid-air. I felt the grasp of my fingers on the quill loosen as the slender feather fell onto the desk. The ink-laden tip left a blot on the yellowed surface. "Yes," I said, turning.

"Let us do what needs to be done," he repeated, looking me in the eye.

I looked down at his feet. They were shod in leather. *An assassin would prefer to be barefoot*, I thought. My eyes slowly moved up his body. His long scabbard hung at his waist, the golden hilt of his sword shining in the yellow light. *A murderer would prefer a small knife.* I looked at his face, dreading what I would see there. I took a deep breath and looked up.

I smiled. His eyes told me everything I needed to know. It had been done. The game was over. "Let us do what needs to be done," I agreed.

"Before that..." Rakshasa sat down. "I want you to swear on the Gods that you will stay Chandandasa's execution."

"I give you my word," I told him.

"And there is one more thing. I wish to know how you beat me."

"So you acknowledge you were beaten?"

"Do I not sit before you, awaiting certain death for treason?" Rakshasa asked. "What is left to acknowledge?"

"You impress me," I told him. "I never thought you would trade your own life for that of a friend."

"I am ruined, Chanakya," Rakshasa sighed. "You have ruined me completely. If I can save one of my friends with my last breath, I will do so."

"Well said," I murmured in fleeting admiration.

"The ring," Rakshasa said. "Sending Saktadasa to me with it...that was you, was it not?"

I poured wine into two goblets and handed one to him. "When you left the city in a hurry after the siege, through the tunnels," I told him, "you did not take your signet ring with you. I saw it in the audience chamber when I entered it to slay Maharaja Dhanananda. But when I returned later, it was not there."

Rakshasa nodded. "Chandandasa retrieved it. He was the last person I saw before I left the city."

"And you requested him to keep safe your ring, and your family. I would have done the same if I were you. The ring was part of you. For people like us, who enforce their power by signing letters, a signet ring is of utmost importance."

"How did you find it?"

"My man entered Chandandasa's house and stole it." I folded my arms. "The same man gave it to Saktadasa, telling him Chandandasa had sent it, that it was indeed Chandandasa who was rescuing him from prison."

"It was you who had the letter written, did you not?" Rakshasa's finger moved over the rim of the goblet.

"Yes indeed, by Saktadasa."

"How?"

"No one can deny Saktadasa was a talented clerk," I told him. "I told him I wished to forgive him, that he should turn his loyalty from you and work for me."

"You made him your clerk."

"I made him write several letters over the course of that first week. This was one of them."

"He could not have understood what it meant when he wrote it." Rakshasa emptied his goblet. "The letter's meaning changed with the situation it was read in."

"Another of my masterstrokes," I smiled.

"And then you stole my seal and stamped the letter. You sent both Saktadasa and the letter to me, knowing I would accept the signet ring as my symbol."

I looked him in the eye. "Do you see what allowed me to play you, Rakshasa? We are alike, you and I. We think alike. I would have taken the signet too, if I were in your position. Just as rulers hold onto their seals and crowns, we have toys to which we attach our beings."

"The Greeks..." Rakshasa coughed. "How did you separate them from Malayketu?"

"With you gone, it was simple. You were the one who had sealed that alliance in the first place. After Malayketu ousted you, there was nothing to hold the alliance together. Furthermore, Seleucus had problems at home. Other Diadochis were marching on him in the far West."

"You say we think alike, but I would never have done what you did." Rakshasa put the emplty goblet down. "I have to hand it to you...the Samrat marrying a foreigner... that was unexpected."

"A necessary evil. One that won me the friendship of the Greeks. When Malayketu rebelled, no noble in the subcontinent would give their daughter to Chandragupta in marriage. They all wished to wait it out and offer the matrimonial spoils to the victor. I was angered by this behavior, but how could I punish our own vassals in time of war?"

"So it was punishment." Rakshasa nodded. "By making Chandragupta marry a foreigner, a Greek, you ensured that those who had betrayed you in your time of need, would never get a chance to establish a marital relationship with the Samrat's house."

"You read me precisely, Rakshasa," I said, lifting a hand. "It is your misfortune that you did not do so earlier. Had you married Malayketu to the Greek Princess, I would never have been able to alienate them from you. But you held to your belief that Arya blood should not be mixed with that of outsiders. The first rule of battle is to surprise your opponent, Rakshasa."

Rakshasa sat back. "Malayketu does not deserve to die." He said, "He is a good man. An honorable Maharaja."

"One who dares stand against Chandragupta, Samrat of Bharatvarsha." I stressed every word. "He has to be made an example of."

"That is what you will no doubt tell your soldiers," Rakshasa said. "But the truth is that Malayketu, if captured alive, can tell Chandragupta of your doings."

"Chandragupta is a naïve and noble fool," I replied. "That was why I did not let him march to Paurava with his army. If he had ever learnt that I promised half the subcontinent to Raja Puru, he would have made truce and divided his Samrajya with that swine, Malayketu."

"But I could have told him that as well." Rakshasa leaned forward. "Even after I had been ousted by Malayketu, I could have revealed your doings to Chandragupta by going directly to him."

"And that is why I held my ace till the very last," I smiled. "Chandandasa thought he had been very clever, that he had hidden your family right under my nose, that he could outsmart me of all people."

"When you imprisoned him after I was ousted by Malayketu," Rakshasa said, "you knew I would come to you to save him, to save my family."

"And so my deception was complete."

Rakshasa clapped his hands. "Well played, Arya. It seems the better strategist has won, after all."

I raised my goblet.

Rakshasa got to his feet. "Here I am at your mercy, so tell me Arya, how shall it be? Will you poison me? Perhaps you have already done so through this wine? Or will you have one of your minions cut me open? If you ask me my preference, I would prefer the poison. I never did like bloodshed. Whatever it is you want to do with me, do it quickly and release Chandandasa from captivity."

"Chandandasa has already been released." I smiled, enjoying his astonishment and chagrin. "I ordered the Guards to release him as soon as my men saw you sneak into the city."

Rakshasa gazed up at the ceiling ruminatively. "At least I saved an innocent man. Kill me, Chanakya. It is time."

"Stay your words, Rakshasa," I told him. "I do not wish for the sin of Bramhahatya to come upon me."

"One of your minions, then." Rakshasa looked around. "Who will it be?"

"No one." I looked up at him. "You will not be killed. You still have a role to play."

"What role, Arya?" Rakshasa asked despondently. "I have lost. I do not wish to live with this disgrace, to see the world spit on me as a loser."

"The world will do no such thing." I got to my feet. "For the world will never know that you lost."

"What do you mean, Chanakya? The war is over. Without Greek support, Malayketu will surely lose."

"But you will not be with Malayketu when he does. Malayketu will be the only one the world will remember as a loser."

"What do you mean?"

I reached out a hand and drew out a scroll with the Royal seal. I handed it to him. "I have a proposition for you. Read the Royal decree written on this parchment and then you will understand."

Rakshasa took the scroll from me, broke the seal and unrolled it. As his eyes moved over the parchment, his hands began to shake. "Is this a game?" he asked.

"As you so rightly said Rakshasa, the war is over, and so is the time for games."

"This decree bestows the title of Prime Minister upon me...Prime Minister of the Mauryans."

"This is my proposition," I said, looking him in the eye. "I will step down as Chandragupta's Prime Minister as soon as Malayketu is dead. You shall assume that office. It was your's at one time. You shall guide Chandragupta in all matters of State until your last breath. And you shall do so loyally."

"And why would you do this?"

"There are many reasons." I closed my eyes. "When we met in those tunnels, years ago, I offered you the same thing. I told you to join our side, but you refused, for you did not wish to appear to be one who had lost."

I opened my eyes and studied Rakshasa's intent face. "I had my own reasons for offering you friendship then. You are a wise man, Rakshasa, an intelligent man, just like me. Both of us possess the unique quality of prudence. Men like us are rare. Men like us should not kill each other."

Rakshasa's eyes narrowed in distrust. "Go on."

"If you had joined me then, I would have offered you the Prime Minister's post." I said to him. "You have governed many parts of this subcontinent for decades. There is no one who understands these lands, the people and the nobles who inhabit it, better than you. Not even me. I would have had to learn what you already knew. As fate would have it, I did have to learn. But what came as hard work for me, was simply old knowledge for you."

"But I refused." Rakshasa recalled his own words.

"Yes, you refused, forcing my hand," I nodded. "If I had offered you the Prime Ministership even after your refusal, you would have considered me weak. You would have attempted to oust and destroy me in your role as Prime Minister."

Rakshasa's eyes widened in understanding. "So you let me fight you."

"I let you play your little game, Rakshasa." I stressed every word. "I let you try your hand at beating me. I made you feel you had almost won, and then I did what I always do, prevail against insurmountable odds."

"And now you offer me the same position you wished to offer me then," Rakshasa murmured thoughtfully. "But this time you can be assured of my loyalty."

"For if you dare raise even one finger against us or even consider betrayal," I said, raising my brows, "the truth shall be revealed to the world and everyone from the banks of the Ganges to Greece will learn how the famed Amatya Rakshasa lost against Arya Chanakya."

Rakshasa poured himself some more wine and drank it down quickly. "I would not dare do that now," he said, breaking the taut silence. "For now I know what you can do. You are no longer an enemy I wish to have, Arya."

"That was the point of this whole exercise," I nodded.

"What will you do now?" Rakshasa asked. "What will you do when the burden of Prime Ministership is lifted from you?"

"There is much to be done, Rakshasa," I said, looking at the dark sky. Stars twinkled in the blackness like beacons of hope amid despair. "Our conquest of Bharatvarsha remains incomplete. The southern non-Arya kingdoms are still independent. To the East, Governor Navin and his Kalingans rule the seas like a great matsya." I stretched my arms. "Furthermore, for years I have wished to record my knowledge in the form of a *grantha* to guide Chandragupta and those who come after him, in the ways of *Rajyadharma*."

"I have no doubt you shall achieve all three aims," Rakshasa said, bowing.

"Time will tell, my man, only time will tell." When he looked up, I said, "There is one last thing to do."

Rakshasa nodded in understanding. He formed a fist and pressed his signet ring on the inking cloth. It glistened in the light from the lamps. He pressed it down upon the Royal decree, pressing hard. When he lifted his hand, the *mudra* was enshrined deep into the pores of the paper.

"Welcome to Patliputra, Prime Minister," I said softly. "It is time to do your duty and protect the city from its enemies. Tell us the location of Malayketu's war camp and I will end this civil war with the least possible bloodshed."

Rakshasa stared at me for a long moment, then unrolled the map that lay on my desk and placed his finger on a spot in the North. "He camps on the banks of the Beas River. He would have invaded your lands had the Greeks not betrayed him at the last moment. I need not tell you the exact spot as it is exactly where Basileus Alexander once camped, waiting to cross and conquer the world."

"It appears that particular spot is ominous for those who camp on it." I clapped and a sentry appeared. "I wish to see Captain Sunga," I told him. "Immediately."

The Captain was at the door in less than half a prahar. He stood with his arms to his sides, listening attentively. "How would you like to be the Senapati of our Samrajya?" I asked.

The man was taken aback by my question. "I would like nothing better, Guru," he replied.

"You do indeed have the skills for the position," I told him. "But you must undergo a test if you will. Fortunately, my friend here has brought just such a challenge for you. We now know the location of Malayketu's camp. You will gather your best men and ride to the Beas River. There, you will destroy his army in the dead of night. You will cut Malayketu's head off and bring it here to me. Then you shall get what you want."

"It will be done." Sunga bowed low before me.

"Be victorious!" I blessed him, placing my hand on his head. "End this civil war once and for all."

21
RADHAGUPTA:
MOMENT OF CONVERSION

~

KALINGA, 262 BC

When they reached the battlefield, the air was fetid with the stench of decomposing flesh and dried blood. High flying vultures cast their shadows on the ground as they circled and swooped, feasting on the carnage of bodies, man and animal. The river bank was littered with bodies, lying as they had fallen, where the engagements between the opposing lines had taken place. It was a ghastly sight.

Radhagupta waited in their carriage as Devdatta retched violently by the side of the road, unable to keep the bile from rising to his throat. Despite his rigid face, Radhagupta could feel the rapid beating of his heart against his ribs. He swallowed the spit in his mouth and took a shallow breath. Immediately the obnoxious vapours enterd his chest. *I am a child of East Hill*, he told himself as Devdatta returned to the carriage wiping his mouth with his uparna. *Decay should not affect me.* Though he did not feel so sure anymore for the sight before him was seen only once in a lifetime.

The driver stopped their carriage abruptly not ten paces further, jolting the two passengers. "What is it, man?" Devdatta asked, his irritation a fragile cover for the shock he felt.

"Mauryans, Governor." The driver tried to cloak his words with courage, but his fear was evident.

Devdatta fell back in his seat thoughtfully.

"How many?" Radhagupta asked cautiously. If the Mauryan reserve forces had come as reinforcements, then all was lost. They were alone, with only Karuvaki in the carriage behind them. She had insisted on returning to the battlefield to witness the Kalingan surrender. There were no soldiers with them, nor weapons.

"I cannot see clearly," the driver replied, his initial fear giving way to hapless resignation, "but I see tents and their banners flying in the wind."

"Can we turn back? Have they seen us?"

"We cannot turn back, Devdatta," Radhagupta said, his voice hard and certain. "These are no ordinary Mauryans." He was gazing at the insignia on the banners. It was one he knew only too well. "The Samrat is here."

"So soon? How could the Guild Master have reached Patliputra and brought back the Samrat before we reached the battlefield?"

"I do not think this is the Guild Master's doing," Radhagupta murmured as he watched the tents rising above the horizon. "I think the Samrat came himself."

"And why would he do that?"

And therein lies the question, Radhagupta thought as they moved towards the uncertainty in front of them. In silence they neared the Mauryan tents, hastily put up using bamboos and ropes. *We cannot tell the guards who we are or they will kill us*, Radhagupta realized, catching sight of the glinting spears.

"What should we do?" Devdatta asked.

"We will have to improvise." Radhagupta uttered the word he hated.

Catching sight of the approaching carriage, the guards straightened up, alert, sensing something was afoot. They crossed their spears, blocking the way. The carriage driver pulled on the reins, bringing the vehicle to a standstill.

"State your business," one of the guards shouted.

Radhagupta stepped out of the carriage and stood before them. "We are merely passing through," he said. Behind him, he felt the carriage shift as Devdatta too, jumped out.

The two guards looked at each other, waiting for the other to make a decision. Over their heads, Radhagupta looked at the camp, hoping to catch sight of the Samrat. He spotted Asoka soon enough, amongst the soldiers, though he recognized him only by the striking difference of his attire. He looked nothing like the hardened young soldier Radhagupta remembered seeing on multiple occasions in the capital. Asoka was obese now, his muscles slack, but there was something in his movements that reminded Radhagupta of the young warrior of yore.

"You cannot pass through here," one of the guards finally declared. "Find some other way."

"But we have travelled many kos to cross here," Devdatta protested, but in vain. The guards remained obdurate, their spears crossed.

Radhagupta glanced sideways at Karuvaki's sombre face. She too, had got down from her carriage. "You should stay inside the carriage," he said. "Your wounds need to heal."

"It is not my wounds but my mind that needs rest," she replied. "We have to do this."

They watched as the Samrat turned towards the disturbance and loud voices. From afar, Radhagupta watched the face that had changed so much. The cheeks were fuller, the hair thinner, balding on top. But the eyes appeared as sharp as before. Radhagupta remembered the last time he had seen the young Prince, when he had left Patliputra to march on the rebels of Avanti. It now appeared to him that young Prince was long dead.

The Samrat watched for a few moments and then spoke to his aide, who immediately trod towards the checkpost.

"He is coming towards us," Devdatta warned his companions.

"Do you think he will order us killed?" Karuvaki's voice was calm and unruffled. "Will coming here prove futile, after all?"

Radhagupta kept his gaze on the approaching figure. "If he indeed gives such an order, after all that has happened, then our entire lives would have been futile."

The aide stopped as he reached the guards. "The Samrat desires these men be let in," he announced.

The two guards exchanged looks before withdrawing their spears. One suddenly held up his hand as Radhagupta tried to walk through. "Weapons?" he asked. Radhagupta shook his head. The guards nevertheless checked them all before letting them pass.

Arriving before the Samrat, Radhagupta gazed at Asoka, his face expressionless.

The Samrat's eyes flitted over the others before fixing themselves on Karuvaki. "I recognize you," he said to her, looking her over from head to toe, noting her wounds. She neither bowed nor returned his gaze.

Asoka's eyes turned towards Radhagupta's tall figure. "I am surprised to see you here," he said. "You were once my father's Prime Minister, were you not?"

Radhagupta bowed. "The Samrat's memory is as sharp as his sword."

Asoka's eyes narrowed but he said nothing. He turned to Devdatta. "And who are you?" he asked.

"I am the newly elected Governor of Kalinga," Devdatta replied. "Or should I say I was?"

Asoka looked at him, his face stern. "On any other day I would have killed you for what your army has done," he said coldly. "But today, I will not. Look around. Enough blood has been spilt."

As Radhagupta looked around, he suddenly understood the importance of the spot they were standing in. The hastily erected Mauryan tents and outpost made it appear different, but it was the place he had stood to survey the battlefield after the battle. Five paces to their left, beside the bloodied corpse of a horse, lay the body of Shiva of Avanti, his mouth open, an arrow through his neck. A few strides from him lay another body – that of the mighty Kanakdatta, speared through the chest; almost unrecognizable from the blood splattered across his face. Radhagupta's eyes swung towards Asoka, knowing that if he had set up camp here, it meant he had not yet surveyed the entire battlefield.

"Many men died here," Asoka said sadly, looking at the bodies of his friends. "I do not wish any more should."

"Not just men." It was Karuvaki who spoke, her voice sounding harsh in their ears.

"What do you mean?" Asoka asked, looking at her.

"Let us show you," Radhagupta said.

***

They stood beside her body in silence, not wishing to intrude on the Samrat's grief. Devi lay at their feet, her saree soaked in blood, her person covered in mud, her eyes closed. Nevertheless, it seemed she would awaken at any moment. The Samrat was stunned by the sight, shocked into silence. Recognizing her immediately, he had fallen to his knees, holding her hand, hoping she would respond, that she would open her eyes. But she did not move.

Radhagupta began narrating their story, from the day he had escaped from Patliputra, from Kautilya's brothel, to how he had ended up in Kalinga. He told of Devi's troubled childbirth while delivering twins in an unknown land. How they had managed to survive with only the desire for revenge against Chanakya keeping them moving from one day to the next. How they had struggled to raise the two babies. How he had taken service with Devdatta, the elections, and Chanakya's attempts to murder them after they were found, finally leading to the day of battle.

Tears wet Asoka's face. He made no effort to hide them. Radhagupta felt sorrow tug at his own heart at the sight of the woman he had cared for like a sister all these years.

"I tried to save her." Karuvaki closed her eyes. "We were attacking the spearmen from the rear. She was doing hell of a good job in cutting those men down. I saw her attacker when he crept up behind her horse, spear in hand. I screamed loudly to warn her but there was too much noise around us. I watched the man pierce her through with my own eyes. I saw her fall from her horse."

"The man who killed her...who was he?"

Karuvaki pointed to a heap of bodies a few paces away. "There he lies," she told him. "Do you think I would have let her killer escape?"

"But was the man who threw the spear really the one who killed her?" Radhagupta asked.

Asoka took a deep breath, visibly shaken. When he turned around, his face was horrid. "I have been lied to! It appears that my own Prime Minister bound my eyes so I would be blind to what was happening. How will my Devi ever forgive me? How will I ever forgive myself?"

"The man who lied to you carries the weight of Devi's soul," Radhagupta said quietly. "My Samrat, I wish we could have revealed all this to you sooner, but the Prime Minister guarded you like a hawk. We do not know what reasons he had for doing this to you, to all of us. But the truth is he is the cause of the death and destruction we see around us."

"It all makes sense now," Asoka murmured, holding his head in sorrow. "Why he never let me out of the palace, why he would not allow me to go to the battlefield with Shiva. Why he hastily declared Kanakdatta a traitor. He was afraid that somehow, in the outside world, I would discover the truth. So he kept me a prisoner in a gilded cage. I feel ashamed for having remained there. I now understand, but it is too late."

"Chanakya used you," Radhagupta said. "He used us all. We were mere pawns to him to move as he wished, to discard once our use was over. Once, I respected him deeply, but I hate him with the same passion today."

Asoka sank to his knees again. "All the things he made me do bring shame to my soul. There is blood on my hands. He made me kill my own brothers."

"He made you do terrible things," Radhagupta agreed, "but there is still a ray of hope. You killed your brothers, but the youngest one lives. Prince Vittasoka. Devi is dead, but she lives on in her two sweet children, Mahindra and Sanghamitra. And a part of you lives in them as well, for they are your children, my Samrat."

Asoka remained transfixed for a moment. His children! Devi's children... "Are they safe?" he asked urgently.

"They are in a safe place," Devdatta replied. "Your brother Vittasoka is there as well. I will bring them to you safely. I swear this on my life. But only if you promise to treat my people generously in surrender."

Asoka looked up at him and nodded. "I have wronged the Kalingans, and my own people. So many homes are ruined; so many children will grow up as orphans. I look at my hands now and I cannot fathom the destruction they have caused. But it shall stop now. I give my word. I do not wish to inflict on anyone the sorrow I feel today. I will treat the Kalingans honourably."

Devdatta kneeled down before the Samrat on one knee. "I came to the battlefield with the desire to curse you for eternity. I came with the desire to show you the numerous families in Kalinga who have lost everything because of you. But now I see that you yourself have lost everything in this battle. I have nothing more to say. You are ready for the surrender of Kalinga, for only the one who truly feels their sorrow can accept their surrender."

"I should feel the joy of victory," Asoka sighed. "Yet I feel nothing but grief. I do not wish to live, yet I must, for my children. They are all that remains to me of her."

"If the children go to Patliputra, I shall too." Karuvaki declared. "Before the battle, Devi made me swear that if anything happened to her, I would take care of the children. They will need me for they are very young."

Asoka nodded sadly, agreeing to her request. Rising to his feet, he looked at Radhagupta earnestly. "You were with her all these years," he said. "Tell me Radhagupta, did she hate me in the end? Did she spit on my name? I never looked for her even once. It pains me to the core of my being to know she was alive. I accepted her death so easily. I wish I could change what I did. I promised her she would be the only woman in my life, but I broke that promise too. Did she ever forgive me for all she must have heard?"

Radhagupta looked at Asoka, his gaze unwavering. "She loved you, my Samrat," he lied, remembering his promise to Kanakdatta. "There was not one day when the love in her heart subsided. She wanted to return to you. She thought this war meant you would see her once again and she could be with you. Alas, the Gods played a different hand. She lived her life for you, and now it is your duty to ensure her death was not in vain, like before."

Asoka nodded, his eyes filled with tears. "I must right the wrongs I have done. I will ensure the Kalingans are treated with consideration. I will rebuild their nation." He looked at Karuvaki. "You were their Ambassador. Even as you accompany my children and help in their care, will you also help me rebuild their world?"

"Aye," Karuvaki nodded. "It is the least I can do."

Asoka looked at Radhagupta. "I respect the dedication you have shown. Any other man would have given up long ago. But you fought on, with the aim of making me understand the truth. I am indebted to you. Accompany me to the capital. You were once Prime Minister to my father and I will need a new Prime Minister on my return."

"You honour me, my Samrat." Radhagupta bowed. "All I did was for the lands of the Aryas."

Asoka turned to Devdatta. "You have shown yourself to be a leader who can guide your people in dire times like these. Your place is with them. Send my children to me with Karuvaki, and take your rightful place in Kalinga as their leader. Kalinga shall be part of the Mauryan Samrajya, but you shall remain their leader and help to rebuild what has been broken."

"I am grateful." Devdatta bowed, his voice wavering. What he felt was too strong to be expressed in words.

"Then it is decided," Asoka said. "We ride to Patliputra at once. The bodies of the Senapati and the Spymaster will be treated with full honours and accompany the royal carriages. I will lift Devi's body with my own hands. On our return, they shall be cremated or buried according to the beliefs they lived by and the honour they deserve. And when the last embers of their *chitas* have turned to ash, we will drag the Prime Minister from where is hiding and make him pay for his crimes."

Aye! The soldiers who had gathered around to listen to his judgement, said in one voice.

Radhagupta watched in silence as the men dismantled the tents, preparing to march on. The sky was orange by the time everything was loaded into the carts and the carriages. When they finally moved away from the field of death, it had begun to rain, as if the heavens wept. The sun had disappeared behind the rolling hills of Dhauli, causing the light to fade and plunge everything into darkness.

———————∼———————

PATLIPUTRA, 262 BC

In his chambers on the highest level of Kautilya's brothel, Chanakya sat silently, waiting for his quarry to come to him. On his desk lay the pile of papyrus which the guards had brought from the palace. Sitting there silently, Chanakya remembered when the pile of papyrus had been smaller, when he had just begun to write his version of the *Arthashastra*. He closed his eyes, recalling the time of his last defeat. As now, he had waited for it to come to him.

50 YEARS EARLIER

An old Sanskrit subhashit says that death or defeat comes to you when you are least expecting it. The irony of my life had always been that my worst defeats came at the time of my greatest success. As I felt the joy of capturing Kalinga and finally completing my hallowed dream, defeat came to me disguised in the form of Hardeo, the Guild Master. Years ago, when I had celebrated peace following the defeat of Malayketu, defeat had come in the form of someone I least expected.

There had been seven months of peace in the subcontinent. In Captain Sunga's daring raid on the enemy war camp in the middle of the night, which won him the position of Senapati, Malayketu had been killed. His head, lodged on a spear above the gates of Patliputra, was a wonderful deterrent to those who sought to carry on his legacy. All the northern kings who had joined him, surrendered, rushing to the capital to pledge allegiance to the one true Samrat.

The war with Malayketu was over, and now it was time for celebration. Chandragupta's marriage to Seleucus' daughter was conducted with pomp and show. Common people thronged Patliputra to witness the spectacle and the streets were filled with urchins and nobles alike, as Chandragupta was wedded to the Greek beauty Helena, whom I renamed Durdhara, to suit the tongue of our people. Following the marriage, for seven months, Prime Minister Rakshasa performed ably as Prime Minister. As for me, I had begun writing my rendition of the *Arthashastra*. Peace reigned until that fateful day, or should I say night, when it all ended. I still remember it vividly to this day.

It was midnight when I was woken by Chandragupta hammering on my door. If I had not pulled the door open, he would have broken it down. What I saw was a chilling sight. He stood there with the body of a woman in his arms. The fair skin of her arms, hanging limply to her sides, left me in no doubt that it was his Greek wife.

"Guru!" he said me as he saw me, "Durdhara has been poisoned."

"Poisoned?" I opened the door wide to allow him to enter. He placed the body on my bed. Her eyes were closed, and froth covered her lips. Her chest lay still, as if breathing had ceased. I instinctively placed a hand on her wrist. The pulse I felt was very low. We had almost lost her. I moved my hands over her bulging stomach to feel for any movements.

There were none, yet I felt as if the baby in her womb stared at me. "We must get the Vaidya at once," I said.

"I already did," Chandragupta replied, his eyes never leaving his wife's face.

The vaidya was soon with us and leaned over the inert body immediately. When he had examined his patient, his face was grim. "We will have to cut her open if we are to save the baby," he said.

Chandragupta looked at me, stricken. No words came from his mouth. He looked like a man stunned. I turned to the Vaidya. "Do it."

He ran out, shouting for his assistants. When he returned, two men accompanied him, carrying leather satchels with instruments. We watched as the vaidya began cutting across her stomach with his blade. Blood oozed out. He kept cutting through the layers and then putting in his hand, pulled out the head of the infant first, and then the body. His two assistants held it as the Vaidya cut the umbilical cord that bound the baby to his dead mother. I noticed the tiny *linga* of the infant, hanging between his legs. It was a boy.

I gazed at the heir of Patliputra. He did not cry so the two assistants held him up by his feet. I saw a blue spot on his stomach, where the remaining portion of the life cord lay bound to him, as if the poison had just reached him.

When it was over, the servants carried her body away. Her death would be announced to the world in the morning. They carried away the baby as well, to keep an eye on him, for he had been born prematurely. My bed was soaked with her blood.

"She was poisoned," the Vaidya said, wiping his bloodied hands on a cotton cloth.

"It was the wine in my chambers," Chandragupta said to me. "She drank it and then this happened. Someone was trying to kill me. Someone put that poison into my wine. It was intended for me, but killed her instead."

Understanding dawned upon me. "Chandragupta, it was I who put the poison in your wine," I told him.

"What!" Both men looked at me, shocked.

"But I did not put it there to kill you," I explained. "There has always been poison in your cup, Chandragupta, gradual amounts to make you immune. By now, the cup you drink is enough to make a bullock wither in pain on the ground."

"Why did you not tell me?" Chandragupta grabbed me by my robe.

"How could I Vrishala? If I had asked your permission to put poison in your cup, would you have granted it?"

Chandragupta's grip on me tightened. "Then my wife's death is on your hands."

"Is it? Your wife was pregnant, Chandragupta. Had the good Vaidya here not told you she was not to touch any wine? Why did she do so?"

Chandragupta's hands left me suddenly. "She said that in Greece, pregnant women drank wine all the time."

"Then is her death on my hands or on your own?" I asked, adjusting my dishevelled clothes.

He looked at me angrily. "I have lost the love of my life, Guru. I am in no mood to debate who caused her death."

He left my chamber hastily. I called to him but he never looked back, not once. I was unable to sleep that night, and I still have dreams of what happened to this day. Whatever fragile bond remained between him and me broke that night. Years later, the Brahmin Radhagupta would discover this incident and expose me to the weak child Bindusar, who would exile me. But even after all these years I wonder if Durdhara's death was really my fault.

***

The Greek entourage arrived in Patliputra on the second new moon after the passing of Chandragupta's wife. I met them at the city gates with an entourage, carrying gifts to welcome them. They had come to take Helena's remains back to her father. The man who led the small detachment smiled at me and I recognized the messenger we had met that night in the tavern in the city. Megasthenes looked relaxed as he accepted the garland of flowers a young courtesan placed on his neck.

"I welcome you, friend," I said in greeting. "I had not expected to see you leading the group for this task."

"In fact, I made a special request to Baselius Seleucus to be sent here again."

Seleucus was 'Basileus' now, a title he had borrowed from the late Alexander himself. He had defeated his enemies in the far west with the elephants we had provided, and had crowned himself as Alexander's successor, having captured most of the Empire.

"And how is it that you did not stay to help him govern the new Empire, as you did to forge it?" I asked.

Megasthenes looked me in the eye. "Your subcontinent has always fascinated me. At first, we Greeks thought it was inhabited by savages. But what I saw here showed you are a most civilized people, and your cities are as big as our own."

"So what do you wish to do by visiting our, ah...how do you call it...civilization?"

"I will be straight with you, Chanakya," Megasthenes said. "The others will collect the remains and leave for Persia. But I wish to remain for some time, to travel to your cities, the countryside. I will take my findings back to Persia with me."

"So you desire me to give admittance to our fortresses to our potential enemies?" I laughed.

Megasthenes laughed. "I would say the same if I were in your position. You would be a bad Prime Minister if you did not suspect my motives. But I ask you to trust me. What I seek to find here is not for such petty reasons as invasion and war."

"But I am no longer Prime Minister," I protested. "I gave up that position for a greater task."

Megasthenes' lips bent in a smile. "I have done the same, my friend. I am no longer Advisor to Seleucus, just a student of our world. I write down what I see around me so future generations may understand the world as we knew it."

"So now you wish to see *our* world."

"We are both philosophers, Chanakya," Megasthenes observed. "We play at war and conquest because it is food for our thoughts, but you know our true calling is conserving the wisdom of our cultures. My notes shall remain even after my death, and those writings will pass on the greatness of these times to future generations."

I nodded. "I have similar thoughts, and can now trust your objective. But as I said, such permission is not mine to give anymore."

"Then perhaps it is finally time to meet your Samrat," Megasthenes said.

***

Chandragupta nodded slowly as he listened to what the old Greek had to say. When Megasthenes had finished speaking, Chandragupta raised one hand. "You shall have free passage through my Samrajya, honoured guest," he decreed. "I shall even give you a detachment of guards for your protection. May you have safe journeys, and write an account of my empire that the whole world will read."

"I thank you Samrat." Megasthenes bowed humbly.

"However," Chandragupta continued, "before you go, you must pledge loyalty to me, and vow never to use your knowledge to betray me in the future, by kissing my ring."

"A man with a clear conscience needs no convincing." Megasthenes quoted as he walked forward. He climbed two of the five steps to the throne and took Chandragupta's outstretched hand. Bending, he placed his lips on Chandragupta's ring. "I pledge my loyalty to you and your dynasty," he said. "All I seek is knowledge to spread, not intelligence to use."

Chandragupta seemed satisfied. But Megasthenes kept looking at the ring on the Samrat's finger. "Strange..." he muttered. "An Indian Samrat wearing a Grecian ring, to which he draws allegiance. Did the fair Helen give this to you as a marriage gift, My Lord? Do you wear this in her beloved memory?"

Chandragupta laughed. "This ring is not from Greece."

"Not in your hands, no," Megasthenes said. "But this was certainly made by a Greek jeweller. I even know his name. He is one Anasteas, resident of Athens."

My heart hammered as if it would leap out of my chest. "Surely you are mistaken," I said.

"No one can mistake the work of Anasteas." Megasthenes

said clearly. "This ring is one of a kind. There is no other like it, for Anasteas is a magician with gems and metals."

"Only one of a kind you say?" Chandragupta placed one hand over the other. But his eyes were not on the ring or the Greek Ambassador, but staring straight at me.

"How can this be, esteemed guest?" I cleared my throat. "This ring is an heirloom of our Samrat's dynasty. It has been here for centuries."

"Has it?" Megasthenes looked at me and then at the Samrat. "Anasteas has been around for just a few decades. He is fifty years of age at the most. Honoured Samrat, my Master, the Great Seleucus Nicator, retained me as an Advisor because of a singular ability I possess." He paused and then said, "I am most observant. I see things normal people do not. My eyes do not miss the small details that regular folk do not even look at."

Chandragupta smiled politely. "And what is it your eyes see in my humble ring, Ambassador?"

"I see Anasteas' work." Megasthenes said without hesitation. "If that ring was not made by him, then I am not Greek. This ring is not as ancient as you claim. I see the signature markings on the gold far too clearly. It was made by Anasteas. And I can say so confidently because no one has been able to forge gold like he does. He has designed his smelter himself and holds the secret close."

Chandragupta watched without emotion as Megasthenes retreated. The Greek stopped beside me. "I take your leave, Arya, he said, "for I desire to leave the city at once and get on with my task."

I nodded, braving a smile. The Samrat and I watched as he walked out of the audience chamber. When he had disappeared, the smile on both our faces vanished.

"I can explain," I said hurriedly.

"There is no longer any need to explain." Chandragupta's eyes were suddenly as clear as crystal. "It all makes sense to me now. You sent a man to Greece when we set off on the campaign, if I recall correctly. It was your minion, Dasharath."

"Please allow me to explain, Vrishala."

Chandragupta leapt to his feet in anger. "I can see it clearly now. When you first met with the members of the Ancient Brahminical Order, you knew they would not accede to an outside invader. So you made it look as if I was not a foreigner but one of their own."

"*Vrishala*, that was not how it was…"

"Was it not!" Chandragupta thundered. "You fabricated the story you told in the dungeons that day, of my being a Prince, heir to a royal legacy. And with what passion you did tell it, Guru, for after listening to you, for the first time in my life, I felt I had found my home."

I knew the lie would hold no more. "I did it for you," I told him. "So you would become Samrat. I did it so we would finally have the chance of uniting these lands."

"So you lied, Guru? You used me just like you use everyone else, for your own benefit."

"For my own benefit?" I felt anger course through me.

"Yes, so you could hold power."

"Power?" I raised my hands, palms upwards in the gesture of humble submission. "What power do I have, Chandragupta?"

"Is it not the same reason that you put poison into my wine and fabricated the story about making me immune to it?" Chandragupta retorted angrily. "For then you would have had an infant on the throne, with only you to lead the Samrajya forward."

"If that were so, why would I have handed the Prime Ministership to Rakshasa?"

"Oh, when you want it back Guru, I am sure you hold some string to pull him out. Because that is what you are – a puppet master. We are all puppets to you, to do as you ask, not humans of flesh and bone, with emotions."

I opened my mouth to speak but Chandragupta silenced me with a wave. "I thought once that you loved me as your own son," he said his voice deep with sorrow, "but I am just another pawn in your game of Chausar."

"Vrishala..." I pleaded, holding out my hands.

Chandragupta turned away in distaste. "Do not call me that! I do not wish to be a Raja based on a lie." He descended from the throne and threw the golden circlet he wore onto the ground. It hit the floor with a heavy thud.

"Do not say so," I pleaded. "I beg of you, our mission is not yet complete.

"*Our* mission?" he snorted in derision. "It is *your* mission, Guru, your's alone. "

"Permit me to explain."

"No!" Chandragupta raised his hand imperiously. "Leave me alone. I need time to think." His footsteps echoed in the vast chamber and then faded away.

That night, sleep eluded me. When it did come, I dreamt of Chandragupta revealing my secret to the world. I saw Avarak's angry face as he heard the truth. I woke up panting in fear. When morning came, I hurried to his room, but Chandragupta was not there. Interrogating the maids and servant boys, I came to know he had gone. He had left the city with a group of Jain ascetics who had been visiting. Had he spoken to me, things would have been different, but his secretive action made us do what I did.

On that fateful day, as the whole court was filled with whispered confusion, I walked into Dasharath's chamber. "Pack your bags," I told him. "We have to go."

"Where to?" he asked.

"You are the one to answer that question," I replied him angrily. 'First, you let him escape the city, and now you do not know where he has gone!"

"There was no way I could have known, Master." He bowed before me sadly. "He is the Samrat. I could not question him about where he was going."

"You should have known!" I burst forth, even as, within me, I knew there was truth in his words. Fortunately, I had spoken to the Jain ascetics when they had entered Patliputra. They told me they were on their way south, on a pilgrimage to the holy place, Shravan Belgola. I did not know whether Chandragupta had gone with them forever or just to clear his head. But I did know one thing – he could not be permitted to return.

"I wish I could go back and change what happened," I said regretfully.

"What is done is done, Master." Dasharath looked me in the eye. "What do we do next?'

"Something I had hoped we would never have to do," I replied sadly. "We will wait for a few days, then go."

"To do what?"

"To right the wrong that has been done.

CHANAKYA: REMORSE OF THE WICKED

50 YEARS AGO
SHRAVAN BELGOLA, JAIN PILGRIM CAMP

"Do you really wish to do this?" Dasharath faced me. There was no trace of emotion on his face, but he must have seen something on mine. We stood in a small clearing by a river, with nothing but forests surrounding us. This was where the Jain ascetics had set up camp. The night sky was dark, without a moon. The pilgrims slept in the open, below the dark starry sky.

"Master?" Dasharath said, waiting for my decision.

I sighed. There was no hiding my hesitation from this man. "I hoped it would not come to this."

"There may be another way," Dasharath suggested.

"No." I said sternly. Chandragupta knew too much. He had promised me he would not reveal what I had done, but I did not trust promises. I did not trust anything but the closed lips of a dead man. "Do it," I said.

Dasharath nodded and ran lightly forward to the edge of the clearing. His hands fell upon the sleeping man's face like rocks on water. The handkerchief in his hand was pressed over Chandragupta's mouth. The eyes opened suddenly as Chandragupta struggled, but Dasharath's grip on him was far too strong and the aroma of the handkerchief far too potent. His struggles slowly subsided as he fell back down, unconscious. Dasharath placed one hand on his forehead and with the other, held his jaw open. I brought forth the glass vial containing the famed Kalkoot and watched his face as I silently emptied the crystal clear liquid into Chandragupta's mouth.

When Chandragupta's body went cold, Dasharath's grip loosened and he looked up at me. "What have we done! "

His words were icy shards, like Taxilan snow.

"The one who gives is the one who takes away," I quoted a Sanskrit subhashit as I watched Dasharath pull the signet ring from Chandragupta's finger.

He bowed and handed it over to me. "For Bharatvarsha," he said.

"Aye, for Bharatvarsha," I nodded as I looked at the lifeless body of my pupil. I took the ring that had been the cause of this and wrapped it in my handkerchief. "The world must think the Samrat left his throne to pursue a life of peace and enlightenment," I told him. "No one must ever think anything else."

Dasharath nodded. I gazed at Chandragupta's face one last time. It looked peaceful and strangely serene.

"We must go." Dasharath pulled my arm.

Once back in Patliputra, we would hastily declare the news that Chandragupta had abdicated his throne and joined a group of Jain monks down South. We would waste no time in placing the baby Bindusar on the throne. With great resolve and passion, I had once again managed to control a situation that was spiralling out of my hands. However, what happened that night in Shravan Belgola remained the only true regret of my eventful life.

~

PATLIPUTRA, 262 BC

The streets were deserted that night but for the file of twelve men in the darkness. The butcher's men led him expertly through the narrow dirt paths between the huts of East Hill, though Hardeo was sure he would have found his way to his quarry tonight even if left to his own devices, for the desire for revenge burned in his chest like fire, and in his head and arms he could feel its radiating heat. There was no one in Patliputra who could stop him from doing what he had come to do. His hands tightened around his walking cane, the decorative edges hurting his fingers. But the blade hidden within would hurt his victim in far greater measure.

"We are here," the butcher declared with an air of finality as they stopped beside a high wall.

Hardeo looked around, eager to catch a glimpse of their destination. "Where is the entrance?" he demanded.

"We are not at the entrance." The butcher unsheathed his sword and the men around him did the same.

Hardeo's heart skipped a beat. Had the vile Chanakya corrupted the butcher too? Had they brought him here to kill him? Suspicion had entered his breast when Chanakya had welcomed him into the city without any objection.

He had even let him go to the audience chamber to verify that Asoka had left the city. Hardeo had felt defeated, for his whole strategy revolved on his meeting the Samrat. Standing in the empty audience chamber, staring at the empty throne, he had been almost certain Chanakya would use the opportunity to seize and imprison him. But nothing like that had happened. The old snake had left him to his own devices. He had also made certain Hardeo knew where he was to be found that night.

His doubts had deepened on asking the butcher on East Hill for help. The man was a complete stranger. But Radhagupta had vouched for the man. The butcher had listened quietly to Hardeo's plea and been too quick to nod and say, "I will guide you through the alleys to Kautilya's brothel as you ask. I will help you kill him. It should have been done long ago." Hardeo had been surprised by how quickly the man had agreed to place his own life and those of his men, in mortal danger. He wondered if it had all been a plan. While he waited for events to unfold, he saw the last two men behind him come forward, a bundle of rope slung over their backs. "Going over the wall?" Hardeo asked softly.

"Aye," the butcher nodded. "We cannot risk the gates. You never know how many guards the old bastard has placed there."

Hardeo watched in silence as the two men fixed a metal hook on the rope and tightened the knot to hold it in place. They handed it to the butcher, who held it firmly in his right hand and took aim. His throw was clean and the metal clanged loudly as the hook fell into place and settled around a pole. The butcher yanked hard, testing the tautness. He handed the rope to the man by his side. Placing his foot on the wall, the man pulled himself up.

Hardeo watched them climb up, one by one. "I am grateful to you for doing this," he said to the butcher truthfully. He realized now that there was no way in heaven he could have infiltrated these high walls on his own.

The butcher shrugged. "I am not helping you. I have wanted to do this for a long time. All this trash you see around us, this entire hill, is his doing, you know."

Hardeo nodded solemnly. "Yes, I know."

"If we non-Aryas are ever to be freed from bondage, this man must die." The butcher muffled a cough. "Our creed is good at serving, not leading. I am glad you came to us tonight. It was high time somebody did. Besides, I would do anything for Radhagupta."

"And why would that be?" Hardeo wondered.

"We are untouchables, you see," the butcher sighed, "yet he, a Brahmin, felt no shame in holding our hands and hugging us, from the time he was a child till he became Prime Minister."

Hardeo nodded in silence, thinking how the virtue of kindness worked wonders in the world.

"I helped him escape, you know." The butcher spit to one side as they watched the last man go up. "It was a shame what happened. He was the Prime Minister of the Mauryas. The things he did for this hill in six months of his tenure, no Samrat did in sixty. Come, it is time."

Hardeo held onto the rope. He fought the weakness in his arms and back as his legs lifted above the ground. Gritting his teeth with determination, he pulled himself up, his legs pressing against the wall for support. Two of the men on top reached down and pulled him up. When he stood on the wall, he felt the chill night air envelop his body. Or was it fear?

They descended the wall as slowly as they had climbed it, careful not to make any sound. The butcher was the last man, and he yanked off the rope as he reached the ground.

"We do not know if we can escape at the same spot we entered by," he said, handing the rope to one of his men. "Study the lay of the land," he ordered.

As three men broke away to scout the area, the rest of them crawled through the decorative shrubs in the gardens that led to the large ornate doors. To Hardeo's surprise, they stood ajar, as if to welcome them in.

"We are lucky," the butcher muttered. "There appear to be no guards anywhere."

"Is that by chance or design?" Hardeo asked. His gut told him they were walking into a trap. But it did not matter anymore. If he could be the harbinger of death for the old man, even if it cost him his own last breath, Hardeo was prepared.

They walked into the brothel in a semicircular formation, the butcher in front. The vast hall was deserted, drenched in darkness.

"The old man resides on the uppermost floor," the butcher informed Hardeo. "Radhagupta once told me so."

"Then let us climb to the top." Hardeo pointed to the staircase leading up.

They climbed in single file. With each step Hardeo felt his heart beat louder. When they reached the topmost floor, everything was cloaked in darkness, but light emanated from one chamber at the end of the corridor. They stopped outside, unsure what to do.

Finally, Hardeo tapped with his cane. "I will go in first," he said. As he pushed on the door, his mind was whipped with conflicting feelings, from a strange sense of calm to a feeling of turbulent anxiety. But when the doors opened and his eyes adjusted to the light, he saw only one thing.

Chanakya sat on his chair, across from a lone wooden desk. Two golden goblets glimmered on the table in the light of the *mashals* on the walls. The only sounds were the crackling fire and the chirping of crickets outside. For a brief moment the two men stared at each other.

Hardeo turned to the butcher. "He is here," he said. "Guard the passageway. Make sure nobody comes."

"Nobody *will* come." Chanakya's deep nasal voice filled the chamber as Hardeo turned, shutting the door. "It seems you have not come here through the main doors tonight, Guild Master, for if you had, you would have noticed there are no guards here tonight."

Hardeo gripped his cane as he walked forward. "And why would that be?" he asked.

"Are your non-Arya friends outside the door here to witness our conversation?" Chanakya asked with amusement. "If they are, I would say it is poetic justice that the people I tried to destroy are now privy to my greatest secrets, which I shall reveal to you."

"What secrets?"

"Let us not prevaricate, Guild Master. I know why you have come here in the darkness of the midnight hour. I knew why you had come the minute you set foot inside the city."

"Then I am glad we understand each other."

"Do not misunderstand. I am truly glad we do." Chanakya smiled. "I have met many men and women in my long life, but few understood me. So few that I can perhaps count them on my fingers. For a time, I was afraid it would be Radhagupta who would come to me at the end, to stop the weak heart beating in my chest, but I am happy that it is you, for if I can be sure of anything, it is that you will understand me. The Brahmin would not have. He is too young, yet to see much of the world. Sure, he will understand me someday in the future perhaps, but I did not wish to die leaving doubts in the minds of my enemies as to what exactly I desired to do in this world."

"Are we enemies?" asked Hardeo. Only the wooden table separated them from each other.

"We are, but then, in a way we are not. Perhaps the right answer is that we *were*. Right up to the moment the last man fell on the banks of the Daya River"

Hardeo gazed into the sunken eyes. To his surprise, instead of anger and hatred, he saw wisdom.

"I hope you will understand my quest for *Akhanda Bharat*," Chanakya continued. "You, like me, have built a vast enterprise from nothing. I built an entire nation. You know that to build, something needs to be sacrificed. Unity is strength. Our people were weak and puny until I forged them together with blood and iron. "

"Yes, I know." Hardeo sat down in the chair opposite Chanakya. He gazed at the golden goblets filled to the brim with a dark red liquid.

"You, like me, know that a good future is built upon a bad present." Chanakya closed his eyes. "All my life I have been afraid of just one thing – of running out of time. I never felt I had enough time to do everything I wanted to. I was always in a hurry. All my actions were to ensure that if I failed in my endeavors, it would not be for want of time. But with it came the ingrained loneliness. Sometimes, I regret that while building this nation, I could not spend time nurturing the few closest to me."

Hardeo nodded, comprehending only too well.

"The first such was my father. When I was young, I hated my father," Chanakya rasped. "My mother died giving birth to me. He was the only family I had. The man loved me. I can see it today. I can see his little actions; he would cook for me after being out all day in the sun; he would always make sure I got the better portions of the meagre food we had. Yet I still hated him. He was a beggar, you see. He would go around the village asking for *bhiksha*. I hated him for that, and I showed it through my words and actions. But he never once laid a finger on me. I felt disgusted by the way he spent his life, dependent on others. One of the first promises I made to myself as a little boy was never to beg from anyone in my entire life."

Hardeo breathed in, knowing, understanding.

"And yet, when Chandragupta told me he would step down from his throne, I begged." Chanakya's eyes were moist when he opened them. "I begged him with all my heart not to leave the mission we were embarked upon. But he did not listen. I raised him like my son, a mere orphan boy with no past, and yet I could never make him understand what he was to me. I was not a good father to him. I was a thousand times better than my own father, yet I could not learn the one thing my father was good at. So when I killed Chandragupta that night in Shravan Belgola, and ended the relationship I could have made better, the face that appeared before my eyes was that of my father, and me shouting on him for his dependence on others."

Hardeo was shocked by the Chanakya's admission. No one had known where the Samrat had gone when he had left Patliputra, never to return.

"With Radhagupta, I had another chance." Chanakya looked down at his fingers. Despite their skeletal appearance, they retained a deceptive strength. "I saw something of myself in him. But there are some things about life which you cannot teach others, only time can. I was afraid he was too distracted with petty issues. He considered things like emancipating the non-Aryas and helping the Buddhists more important than the task at hand. Do not get me wrong. These things are important, but only after we have completed our goal of an Akhanda Bharat. I was not sure what he would do if I allowed him to stay as Prime Minister of the Mauryas. So I gave the order to have him killed. But I underestimated Kanakdatta the Buddhist's wont to show compassion."

"And what of Devi?" Hardeo asked, his mouth grim.

"She was a mere hindrance," Chanakya muttered with a tinge of sadness in his voice. "She showed great spirit. I often wondered if there was another way. She would have been a wonderful Queen. But again, I did not have time. I had to force things to happen and she was in my way. You will have to agree there was no other option."

Hardeo breathed in deeply. "I do," he said.

"With Chandragupta, there was great promise," Chanakya continued. "With Bindusar, I worried whether forcing him prematurely from his mother's belly had forever tainted the Maurya line. However, in Sushem, I saw something of his grandfather again."

"So why sacrifice him?" Hardeo asked.

"Time, my friend, time..." Chanakya sighed. "I did not have enough time. Sushem was a headstrong man whom I had no access to when he was a child, thanks to Bindusar ousting me from the court. Chandragupta was headstrong too, but he respected me until events tore us apart. Sushem did not see me in the same light. I was not sure if I could control him if he ascended the throne. And I did not wish to waste time in trying to control him."

"What of Asoka?" Hardeo asked.

"The stronger a man appears on the outside, the weaker he is on the inside," Chanakya replied. "This has always been the curse of our civilization. Asoka had no problem in breaking arms and backs on the battlefield, but when it came to executing justice, his hand wavered. He could not condemn men to death penalties easily; he considered cheating in battle a disgrace; he hated men who proposed striking the enemy in the back. I would have loved to conquer Kalinga fair and square, but we return to the same point where we started – I did not have any time. And yet, now when I sit opposite you, I feel like I have all the time in the world to tell you these things because now I am sure you understand me."

"Do you?"

Chanakya raised his head. "I only introduced Asoka to wine and women. Maybe his own inner hurt at Devi's desertion made him sink into them. But it gave me free rein to control the rajya as I wanted."

"It was venal, what you did," Hardeo said.

"It was indeed, but as you know, not the first dirty deed I took upon myself. I underestimated you, you know. When you came to me in Patliputra, I threatened you. I expected you to surrender, be afraid. I had counted on it. Instead, you defied my judgment. I realize today that it is you who was the catalyst that turned my own plans against me. Not Radhagupta, not fat Kanakdatta, but you. The moment you decided to stand against me, irrespective of all that had happened, this day was written in the books of fate."

"But you have won." Hardeo said, his voice low.

"Have I?" Chanakya wondered. "I know what happened on the battlefield of Kalinga, Guild Master. Just as I am good at planning, I am also good at predicting. I know who died and who survived. I know what Asoka will see when he reaches there, and I know who will meet him and reveal all my wrongdoings, causing that old anger to flare again."

"Why did you not stop him from going?"

"What was the point in doing so?" Chanakya's thin lips stretched in the caricature of a smile. "My task was over. Yes, I planned it to happen differently. My men were supposed to catch and kill both Radhagupta and Devi before the invasion began. The Kalingan General Bheema was supposed to hand over the country to us on a platter. But only fools stick to one plan and hope everything will go according to it."

"Shiva's army was your back-up plan," Hardeo noted. "If your men could not accomplish their task in Kalinga, as they did not, then Shiva would march and lay waste the Kalingan defense."

"Yes, but I did not count on four events happening together. First, you standing against me and leaving Vidishanagri with your army; second, my men failing to kill Radhagupta and Devi; third, the Kalingan army decimating our army; and lastly, Asoka choosing to ignore my advice and going to the battlefield. The nation now needs a benevolent ruler, a compassionate and able Prime Minister, who will rebuild. What better way to make Asoka feel benevolent than to fill him with remorse?"

"He will kill you when he knows the truth."

"But my body died many years ago. It is my mind that still lives and that can never be killed." Chanakya pointed to the stack of parchments. "When you give this to the Samrat," he said, "do not tell him they were written by Chanakya. Instead, use my other name. Tell him it was written by a great sage called Kautilya. Instruct him to hand them over to his Prime Minister, as guidance in how to hold this vast land together against all odds. "

Hardeo nodded, understanding the treasure contained within the large stack on the table.

Chanakya closed his eyes in remembrance, as if watching his whole life in the blackness behind his lids. "Chandragupta thought he understood me," he sighed wearily. "He thought it was revenge that motivated me. He was never more wrong in his life." The old man opened his eyes and leaned forward in his chair. "All I did, I did for this land of the Aryas. People may not believe me or even understand, but one thing is certain, they will remember me, Guild Master, for as long as Aryas reside in this subcontinent, my name will live."

"It is time," Hardeo said.

Chanakya raised a hand with some effort and pointed to the goblet on the table. "Share a last toast with me," he said, "for I have nothing against you at this moment. And if I am right, after all I have told you tonight, you do not have anything against me either."

Hardeo and Chankya gulped down the contents of their goblets. Hardeo set his empty cup back on the table, but Chanakya's palm froze around his, the Kalkoot in his wine taking effect. The eyelids fell over Chanakya's misted eyes as Hardeo watched the wisdom of a hundred years fade into nothingness.

Epilogue

～

On the Samrat's return to Patliputra, Radhagupta was made Prime Minister of the Mauryas. He held the title for decades, leading the Mauryans into a golden age of peace and prosperity. For thirty years, the Mauryan Samrajya flourished under Samrat Asoka.

On a full moon night, the Samrat converted to Buddhism. He ordered the construction of Buddhist *viharas* across the country to propagate the faith. He constructed rock cut edicts in every major town of his Empire to enlighten the common people about the importance of peace, and the change that had come to him after the Kalinga war. In memory of his beloved Devi, the *Samrat* commissioned a great stupa to be built in the forest of Sanchi, in Vidisha, at the spot where he had first met her.

After the war, Hardeo and the Guild shifted their focus to ship-building, focusing on crossing the seas and spreading their trade beyond the subcontinent. With Devdatta's seafaring experience to guide them, their enterprises flourished. They also spread Buddhist culture and teachings far and wide.

Under Hardeo's able guidance, Mahindra and Sanghamitra, Asoka's children, grew into educated and gifted individuals. They became famed sea explorers who were instrumental in spreading Buddhism to lands across the seas, especially the island kingdom of Sinhala or Lanka. Karuvaki accompanied Asoka to the capital as he had requested and assumed the role of Advisor in matters of State. The change in the Samrat gradually brought them together in love, and they married. Karuvaki became Asoka's third and principal Queen.

One evening, standing atop the palace at Patliputra, staring at the sky, Asoka asked Radhagupta sorrowfully, "Will people only remember me as the weak Samrat, manipulated by Chanakya into doing his bidding? Will I ever regain the respect I have lost? Can I ever repent for my sins, or will I forever be remembered as Chandasoka?"

Standing beside him like a tall pillar, Radhagupta placed a hand on Asoka's shoulder. "You are young," he said. "You still have time to change from being Chandasoka to something far more. The world will remember that."

***

History knows him as Asoka the Great, one of the most important figures of Indian history, whose symbol, the twenty-four-spoked *chakra*, sits proudly on our national flag. Mauryan rule dominated the Indian subcontinent (what is today India, Afghanistan, Pakistan, Nepal, Bangladesh and Thailand). At the time, the Mauryan Empire was the richest and most powerful in the entire world. Arya Chanakya and his works remain alive, vivid reminders of that age.

Acknowledgements

―――――∽―――――

Good books are rarely the result of efforts by a single person. It thus behoves me to highlight those without whom this book would not have been possible.

I thank my parents, Rajeev and Swati, without whose continued support I would not be a writer.

I thank my Publisher, Leadstart Publishing, for having faith in my work. I thank Malini Nair, for bringing me into the Leadstart fold, and I am indebted to my Commissioning Editor, Chandralekha Maitra, who has believed in me, inspiring me to write stories worthy of that faith. I thank her with all my heart for waving her magic wand over my story, totally transforming it into from what it was to what it deserved to be. I also thank Swarup Nanda, for being a great Publisher, and Preeti Chib, for her wonderful marketing support. And Paramita, for the impactful cover.

Finally, I thank you, my readers, for picking up a book by a new, yet unknown, author. I hope I have been able to enchant you with this story, transporting you to ancient India of two thousand years ago. If you liked this book, please rate it on Amazon & Goodreads and share the word on Social Media. If you hated it, please let me know what you did not like so I can work to improve as a writer. In anycase, email me at shre14uses@gmail.com with any questions regarding the book or visit my website at www. authorshreyas.wordpress.com

I hope that, with your support, I shall come up with many more books that speak of our country and the people who shaped its history.

THE ASOKA TRILOGY
BOOK I
PRINCE OF PATLIPUTRA

BHARATVARSHA, LAND OF THE ARYAS: 272 BC

Bindusar, second *Samrat Chakravartin* of all the Aryas, rules from his capital, Patliputra. Fifty years previously, his father, Chandragupta Maurya, had laid the foundations of this vast *Samrajya*, guided by the famed Guru, Arya Chanakya. But the pinnacle of the Empire's wealth and glory has now passed… As the *Samrat*'s health declines due to a mysterious illness, problems, in-fighting and rebellion raise their heads across his realm. There is no clear successor among his ninety-nine sons.

Bharatvarsha waits for a warrior-king to rise up and lead once again. Can young Prince Asoka, least favoured of Bindusar's sons, take on his grandfather's mantle? Can Radhagupta, a mere Councillor at Court, be the inspiration Chanakya once was to his Emperor and his people?

Book I of the epic *Asoka Trilogy* revolves around the haunting question: Who will be the next *Samrat*? The first book of this riveting narrative captures the decline of a golden age, the upsurge of greed and chaos, the dark aspirations of royal heirs, and the dramatic events in the remarkable life of a man of destiny.

THE ASOKA TRILOGY
BOOK II
STORM FROM TAXILA

BHARATVARSHA, LAND OF THE ARYAS: 270 BC

Bindusar, the *Samrat Chakravartin* of all the Aryas, ruler of the Indian sub-continent, is dead. Chaos rules as the royal succession turns upon intrigue, dark coalitions, violence and death. The realm stands divided and civil war ensues.

In Vidishanagri: Asoka kills his brother's *Ashwamedha* stallion and marches to Patliputra with his army. And Radhagupta travels to fulfill the task allotted to him by the Secret Brahminical Order. Kanakdatta, the Buddhist, stands up to stop him. *In Taxila*: The rightful heir, Sushem, raises an army to meet the challenge posed by his ambitious and gifted brother, Asoka. He prepares to march to the capital and seize the throne by force. *In Junagarh*: Guildmaster Hardeo sets out on a private mission to acquire the great salt pans of Sindh. Will he succeed in his secret enterprise?

The winds of war howl over the sub-continent, blowing every last person one way or the other. Blood will be spilled, secrets revealed and men ruined. History shall be made. In Book II of the epic *Asoka Trilogy*, the storm approaches – the harbinger of death and destruction. When the dust finally settles the great question will be answered: Who will be the next *Samrat* of the revered lands of the Aryas?

Wish To Publish With Us?

We are always keen to look at interesting content across genres. Please email your submission to: **submissions@leadstartcorp.com**

The submission should include the following:

1. Synopsis

A summary of the book in 500 – 1000 words. Please mention the word count of the manuscript.

2. Sample chapters

Two chapters, not necessarily in order; just send the two best.

3. A Note About The Author

An interesting note about yourself (about 200 words).

4. Additional Information

- Target audience,
- Unique selling points
- List of illustrative content (if any)
- Other comparative titles
- Your thoughts on marketing the book.